WISHES FOR TOMORROW

NEW YORK TIMES BESTSELLING AUTHOR

# BRENDA JACKSON

## WISHES FOR TOMORROW

*A Westmoreland Novel*

**HARLEQUIN**® KIMANI ARABESQUE®

**WISHES FOR TOMORROW**
ISBN-13: 978-0-373-09149-2

This edition published January 2014.

Copyright © 2014 by Harlequin Books S.A.

The publisher acknowledges the copyright holders of the individual works as follows:

WESTMORELAND'S WAY
Copyright © 2009 by Brenda Streater Jackson

HOT WESTMORELAND NIGHTS
Copyright © 2010 by Brenda Streater Jackson

Recycling programs for this product may not exist in your area.

**Printed in U.S.A.**

**H HARLEQUIN®**
™ www.Harlequin.com

## CONTENTS

# THE WESTMORELAND FAMILY

## Scott and Delane Westmoreland

| John (Evelyn) | | | | | | | James (Sarah) | | | | | Corey (Abbie) |
|---|---|---|---|---|---|---|---|---|---|---|---|---|

Corey (Abbie)
Madison

| ③ | ④ | ⑤ | ⑦ | ① |
|---|---|---|---|---|
| Thorn (Tara) Trace | Stone (Madison) Rock, Regan | Storm (Jayla) Shanna, Johanna, Slate | Chase (Jessica) Carlton Scott | Delaney (Jamal) Ari, Arielle |

| ② | | | | | | | |
|---|---|---|---|---|---|---|---|
| Dare (Shelly) AJ, Allison | | | | | | | |

| ⑥ | ⑪ | ⑧ | ⑨ | ⑭ | ⑮ |
|---|---|---|---|---|---|
| Jared (Dana) Jaren | Spencer (Chardonnay) Russell | Durango (Savannah) Sarah | Ian (Brooke) Pierce, Price | Quade (Cheyenne) Venus, Athena, Troy | Reggie (Olivia) Ryder |

| ⑩ |
|---|
| Casey (McKinnon) Corey Martin |

| ⑫ | ⑬ |
|---|---|
| Clint (Alyssa) Cain | Cole (Patrina) Emilie, Emery |

① Delaney's Desert Sheikh
② A Little Dare
③ Thorn's Challenge
④ Stone Cold Surrender
⑤ Riding the Storm
⑥ Jared's Counterfeit Fiancée

⑦ The Chase is On
⑧ The Durango Affair
⑨ Ian's Ultimate Gamble
⑩ Seduction, Westmoreland Style
⑪ Spencer's Forbidden Passion
⑫ Taming Clint Westmoreland

⑬ Cole's Red-Hot Pursuit
⑭ Quade's Babies
⑮ Tall, Dark…Westmoreland!
⑯ Dreams of Forever

# THE DENVER WESTMORELAND FAMILY TREE

**Raphel and Gemma Westmoreland**

**Stern Westmoreland (Paula Bailey)**

Thomas (Susan)

Adam (Clarisse) ⑯

Micah (Kalina) ㉑
Macon

Jason (Bella) ⑳
Clarisse and Caroline

Riley
(Alpha)

Canyon

Stern

Brisbane

Dillon (Pamela)
Denver
Dade

Zane

Derringer (Lucia) ⑲

Megan (Rico)

Gemma (Callum) ⑱
Callum

Adrian

Aidan

Bailey

Ramsey (Chloe) ⑰
Susan and Colton

⑯ *Westmoreland's Way*
⑰ *Hot Westmoreland Nights*
⑱ *What a Westmoreland Wants*

⑲ *A Wife for a Westmoreland*
⑳ *The Proposal*
㉑ *Feeling the Heat*

㉒ *Texas Wild*
㉓ *One Winter's Night*

Dear Reader,

It's hard to believe that I introduced the Westmorelands to my readers over ten years ago. Though at the time, little did I know that you would welcome them into your home and hearts the same way I have allowed them into mine. Originally, the Westmoreland family series was intended to be just six books, Delaney and her five brothers—Dare, Thorn, Stone, Storm and Chase. Later, I wanted my readers to meet their cousins—Jared, Spencer, Durango, Ian, Quade and Reggie. Finally, there were Uncle Corey's triplets—Clint, Cole and Casey.

The Westmorelands living in Denver were a whole new breed but they still had Westmoreland values and of course those Westmoreland good looks. I was able to show the way family connects and the bond that holds them together through the good and bad times. I wanted to display how a family can pull together and stay together as well as look out for each other.

Wishes for Tomorrow contains the first two stories in the Denver Westmorelands saga—*Westmoreland's Way* and *Hot Westmoreland Nights*. In *Westmoreland's Way*, we are introduced to Dillon, the head of the Denver clan. In search of the truth about his great-grandfather, he meets Pamela Novak, the woman who is destined to be by his side forever. Then in *Hot Westmoreland Nights*, we are introduced to Ramsey, a sheep rancher and a man who thinks he doesn't need a woman around. But Chloe Burton proves just how wrong he is from the first day that she sets foot on his property.

I was very happy when Harlequin Kimani responded to my readers' requests that the books in the entire Westmoreland series be reprinted. And I'm even happier that the reissues are in a great, two-in-one book format.

I hope you enjoy reading these special romance stories as much as I enjoyed writing them.

Happy Reading!

Brenda Jackson

To the love of my life, Gerald Jackson, Sr. You're still the one after all these years!
Apply your heart to instruction and your ears to words of knowledge.
—Proverbs 23:12

# WESTMORELAND'S WAY

# *Prologue*

"I know how much finding out everything there is about your grandfather means to you, and I wish you the best in that endeavor. If you ever need anything, you, your brothers and cousins should know that the Atlanta Westmorelands are here. Call on us at any time."

Dillon Westmoreland drained his wineglass before meeting the older man's eyes. He'd only met James Westmoreland eleven months ago. He had arrived in Denver, Colorado, with his sons and nephews, claiming to be his kin. They'd had the documentation to prove it.

"Thank you, sir," Dillon said. Their unexpected appearance at the Shady Tree Ranch had answered a lot of questions, but generated even more. After years of thinking they had no living relatives outside of Denver, it was nice to know there were others—others who hadn't hesitated to claim them as their own.

Dillon glanced around the wedding reception given for his cousin Reggie and Reggie's wife, Olivia. Dillon and the other Denver Westmorelands had officially met Reggie with a bunch of other Westmorelands from Atlanta at the family reunion a few months before. All it took was one look to know they were related. Their facial features, complexions and builds were practically the same. No surprise, given the fact their great-grandfathers, Reginald and Raphel, had been identical twins.

Dillon now knew the story of how his great-grandfather, Raphel Westmoreland, had split from the family at the age of twenty-two. He'd left Atlanta, Georgia, with the wife of the town's preacher. It had been considered a despicable act and Raphel had immediately become known as the black sheep in the Westmoreland family, never to be heard from again.

Many assumed he had died before his twenty-fifth birthday with a bounty on his head for wife-stealing. Few knew that Raphel had eventually made it to Denver, married and produced a son who had given him two grandsons, who in turn had blessed him with fifteen great-grands. Dillon was proud to say, at thirty-six, he was the oldest of Raphel's great-grandchildren. That left the Denver Westmoreland's legacy right smack on Dillon's shoulders.

It hadn't been easy, but he had done his best to lead his family. And he hadn't done too badly. All fifteen of them were successful in their own right, even the three that were still in college. But then you had to really try hard to overlook his youngest brother, Bane, whose occasional brush with the law kept Dillon down at police headquarters more than he would have liked.

"Are you still determined to find out the truth about whatever happened to your great-grandfather's other wives, or whether his previous relationships were even wives at all?" James Westmoreland asked him.

"Yes, sir. I'm taking time off from my company later this year, sometime in November, to travel to Wyoming," Dillon said.

Through James Westmoreland's genealogy research he had found Dillon's family. Now it was up to the Denver Westmorelands to find answers to the questions that still plagued them about their ancestry. That was one of the reasons why the trip to Wyoming was so important to him.

"Okay, Dillon, Uncle James has had your ear long enough."

Dillon couldn't help but chuckle when his cousin Dare Westmoreland walked up. If there had been a doubt in anyone's mind that the Atlanta and Denver Westmorelands were related, all they had to do was to compare him to Dare. Their features were so similar they could have been born brothers instead of cousins.

"I don't mind," he said truthfully. "I'm enjoying myself."

"Well, don't have too much fun," Dare responded with a huge grin. "As soon as Reggie and Olivia leave for their honeymoon, we're heading over to Chase's Place for a game of poker."

Dillon raised a brow. "The last time I played poker

with you all, I almost lost the shirt off my back," he said, unable to suppress a grin.

Dare gave him a huge pat on that back. "All I can say to that, Dillon, is welcome to the family."

# Chapter 1

"Have you totally lost your mind, Pam? No matter what you say, we can't let you do it. You've given up so much for us already. We just can't."

Pamela Novak smiled as she glanced over her shoulder and saw the three militant faces frowning at her and quickly decided it would be best to give them her full attention. Drying her hands on a towel she turned away from the sink to face them.

She wondered what it would take to make her sisters see reason and understand that she had to do what she had to do. Not just for her own benefit but mainly for theirs. Fletcher was pushing for a Christmas wedding and here it was the first week in November already. So far they hadn't set a date, but he would bring it up every time she saw him. He'd let it be known that he didn't want a long engagement and, considering everything, a long engagement wouldn't be in her best interest, either.

She nibbled on her bottom lip, trying to come up with a quick yet effective strategy. If she could convince her sister Jillian of the importance of what she had to do, then Paige and Nadia would quickly come on board. But convincing Jillian was the big challenge. Jill didn't like Fletcher.

"And what makes you think it's something I'm being forced to do, rather than something I want to do?" Pamela finally decided to ask the three of them.

Of course, it was Jillian who stepped out to speak. Jill, as she was called by most people in Gamble, Wyoming, at seventeen was a senior in high school and was a spitfire. She was also smart as a whip. It was Pam's most fervent desire for Jill to leave Gamble next fall to attend the University of Wyoming in Laramie and pursue her dream of one day becoming a neurosurgeon.

And Paige, fifteen, and Nadia, thirteen, would soon be ready to pursue their aspirations. Pam wanted to make sure that funds were available for college when that time came. She also wanted to make sure that if her sisters wanted to return to Gamble, they would still have a home here. Pam felt certain that accepting Fletcher's marriage proposal made those things possible.

"You're sacrificing your happiness, Pam. We aren't stupid. What woman in her right mind would want to marry a jerk like Fletcher Mallard?" Jill boldly said.

Pam had to fight to keep a straight face when she said, "He is not a jerk. In fact, Fletcher is a nice man."

"When he's not being obnoxious and arrogant,

which is most of the time. Already he thinks he can run things around here. We've been doing just fine without him," was Jill's bitter response.

Jill took a quick breather and then went on to say, "We don't care if we lose this house and it wouldn't bother us in the least if we don't get a college education. We refuse to let you marry the likes of *that* man to protect what you see as our bright futures. Speaking of futures, you should be back in California working on a real movie instead of spending your time teaching students at the acting school. You got a degree in drama, Pam. Being an actress has always been your dream. Your passion. You shouldn't have given it up for us."

Pam inhaled deeply. She had been through all of this before with her sisters. The problem was that they knew too much about the situation, something she wished hadn't happened. Unfortunately for her, they had been home that day when Lester Gadling, her father's attorney, had dropped by to deliver the bad news and they had overheard Lester's words.

"But I'm not in California. I'm perfectly satisfied being here in Gamble and running the acting school, giving others the same opportunity that was given to me," she countered.

She paused for a second and then said, "Listen, ladies, I've made these decisions because I love you."

"And we love you, too, Pammie," Nadia replied. "But we can't let you give up the chance to one day meet a really nice guy and—"

"Fletcher is a nice guy," she interjected. However, all she received for her effort were three pairs of rolling eyes.

"No, he's not," Paige spoke up to say. "I was in the bank one day when he went off on one of the tellers for making him wait in line for so long. He thinks he's all that, just because he owns a chain of grocery stores."

"Okay, you saw his bad side just that one time," Pam said. "Deep down he's a kind person. He's willing to help us out, isn't he?"

"Yes, but look what he'll be getting. Our home and the most beautiful single woman in Gamble," Jill pointed out.

"A single woman who isn't getting any younger and who will be turning thirty in a few months. Don't you think it's time I get married?"

"Yes, but not to him," Jill implored. "Anyone but him."

Pam glanced at the kitchen clock that hung on the wall. Fletcher was coming to dinner and would be arriving any minute, and she needed to make sure her sisters put this behind them. They had to accept that she was now an engaged woman and move on.

She of all people knew that Fletcher had his flaws and could be arrogant at times, but she could deal with that. What she refused to deal with was letting her sisters lose the only home they knew and a chance to fulfill their dreams by attending the colleges they desired.

She couldn't help but wonder what her father had been thinking to put a second mortgage on their home—a mortgage for which the full balance was due within a year of his death. There was no way she could come up with a million dollars. Fletcher, in the role of a friend, had made her an offer that she couldn't refuse. It would not be a love match, he was fully aware of that. She would, however, as agreed, perform her wifely duties. He wanted kids one day and so did she. And Pam was determined to make the most of their marriage and be a good wife to him.

"I want the three of you to make me a promise," she finally said to her sisters.

"What kind of promise?" Jill asked, lifting a suspicious brow.

"I want you to promise me that you will do everything I ask regarding my engagement to Fletcher. That, you will make me, as your oldest sister, happy by supporting my marriage to him."

"But will you be truly happy, Pammie?" Paige asked with an expression that said she really had to know.

No, she wouldn't *truly* be happy, but her sisters didn't have to know that, Pam thought. They must never know the extent of her sacrifice for them. With that resolve in mind, Pam lifted her chin, looked all three of them in the eyes and told a lie that she knew was going to be well worth it in the end.

"Yes," she said, plastering a fake smile on her lips. "I will truly be happy. I want to marry Fletcher. Now, make me that promise."

Jill, Paige and Nadia hesitated only for a moment and then said simultaneously, "We promise."

"Good."

When Pam turned back to the sink, the three girls looked at each other and smiled. Their fingers had been crossed behind their backs when they'd made their promise.

It was probably inconsiderate of him to show up without calling first, Dillon thought, as he turned into the long driveway that was marked as the Novak Homestead.

He had arrived in Gamble, Wyoming, earlier that day, with his mission on his mind. What had happened to his great-grandfather's other four wives, the ones he had before he married Dillon's great-grandmother, Gemma? According to the genealogy research James Westmoreland had done, Gamble was the first place Raphel had settled in after leaving Atlanta, and a man by the name of Jay Novak had been his business partner in a dairy business.

Dillon would have called, but he couldn't get a signal on his cell phone. Roy Davis, the man who owned the only hotel in Gamble, had explained that was because Gamble was in such a rural area, getting a good signal was almost impossible. Dillon had shaken his head. It was absurd that in this day and age there was a town in which you couldn't get a decent cell signal when you needed it.

He had finally gotten a signal earlier to contact his secretary to check on things back at the office. Not surprisingly, everything was under control, since he had hired the right people to make sure his billion-dollar real estate firm continued to be a success whether or not he was there.

Dillon parked his car behind another car in the yard and glanced up at a huge Victorian house with a shingle roof. It was very similar in design to his home in Denver and he wondered if that was a coincidence.

According to what he'd heard, four sisters occupied the house and the oldest was named Pamela Novak. He understood Ms. Novak had had an up-and-coming acting career in California but had moved back to Gamble upon her father's death. She was now operating the drama school a former teacher had recently willed to her.

When Dillon got out of the rental car he took time to stretch his legs. Like most Westmorelands he was tall, and because of his height he'd always enjoyed playing basketball. He'd been set to begin a career in the NBA when he'd gotten word of the plane crash that had claimed the lives of his parents and his aunt and uncle, leaving fourteen younger Westmorelands in his care.

It hadn't been easy and Tammi, his girlfriend from college, had claimed she would stick by his side no matter what. Less than six months into their marriage she had run back home hollering and screaming that she couldn't handle living on a ranch with a bunch of heathens.

That was after she had failed to convince him to put his youngest brother, Bane, who'd been eight at the time, his cousins—Adrian and Aiden—the twins who'd been ten, and Bailey, who'd been seven, into foster care because they were always getting into some kind of mischief.

He had understood that most of their antics had been for the attention they'd needed after losing their parents. However, Tammi had failed to see it that way and wanted out of the marriage. One good thing that had come out of his divorce was that he'd realized it was meant for him to be single and, as long as he was the head of the family, he would stay that way.

Another good thing about his divorce was that the younger Westmorelands—all of them with the exception of Bane—had felt guilty about Tammi leaving and had improved their behavior. Now the twins and Bailey were in college. Bane...was still Bane.

"You lost, mister?"

Dillon quickly turned around to look into two pairs of dark brown eyes standing a few yards away. Twins? No, but they could pass for such. Now he could see that one of the teenage girls was a head taller than the other.

"Well, are you?"

He smiled. Evidently he hadn't spoken quick enough to suit them. "No, I'm not lost if this is the Novaks' place."

The taller of the two said, "I'm a Novak. We both are."

Dillon chuckled. "Then I guess I'm at the right place."

"Who did you want to see?"

"I want to see Pamela Novak."

The shorter of the two nodded. "That's our sister. She's in the house talking to *him.*"

Dillon raised a brow. He had no idea who *him* was, and from the distasteful way it had been said, he really wasn't sure he wanted to find out. "If she's busy I can come back later," he said, moving back toward the car.

"Yeah, because he might get mad if he thought you'd come calling just to see Pammie," the taller one said.

A look of mischief shone in their eyes as the two girls looked at each other and smiled. And then, screaming to the top of their voices, they called, "Pammie, a man is here to see you!"

Dillon leaned against his car with arms across his chest, knowing he had been set up, and the two teens were having a little fun at his expense. He wasn't so sure how he liked it until the door to the house swung open. At that moment he literally forgot to breathe. A strikingly beautiful woman walked out. It didn't matter that she was frowning. The only thing that mattered was that she was definitely the living, breathing specimen of the most gorgeous woman he'd ever seen.

She couldn't have been any taller than five-eight, and was slim with just the right curves in the jeans she was wearing. She had shoulder-length black hair flowing around her shoulders and a medium brown complexion that complimented the rest of her features. Her eye color was the same dark brown as the two scamps, and she had a pixie nose that was perfect for her face. She was definitely a stunner. A raven-haired beauty that made him nearly breathless.

"Hey, you're trespassing. May I help you?"

He looked beyond her to a big hulk of a man standing directly behind her in the doorway who'd asked the question in a high-pitched and agitated tone. And he was glaring at Dillon as if his very presence annoyed the hell out of him.

Dillon quickly figured that this must be the "him" the girls had been referring to, and was about to open his mouth to speak when the taller of the two girls spoke up. "No, you can't help him because he didn't come to see you, Fletcher. He came to see Pammie."

A dark scowl covered the man's face at the same time a smile touched the teen's lips. It wasn't hard to see she was deliberately trying to get a rise out of the man.

"Paige and Nadia, shouldn't you be upstairs doing

your homework?" the gorgeous woman asked the two before turning her curious gaze on Dillon. Unlike her male friend, she smiled brightly and had a cheerful look on her face.

"Pamela Novak?" he heard himself ask, trying to force air into his lungs. He'd seen beautiful women before, but there was something about her that was doing something to everything male within him.

"Yes," she said, still smiling while stepping down the steps toward him. He pushed away from the car and began moving toward her, as well.

"Wait a minute, Pamela," the hulk of a man called out. "You don't know this man. You shouldn't be so quick to be nice to people."

"Maybe you should follow her lead, Fletcher."

A new voice Dillon hadn't heard before had spoken up, entering the fray. He glanced behind the hulk to see a young woman, probably around seventeen or eighteen, stepping out the door. Another sister, he quickly surmised, due to the similarities in their features.

Pamela Novak continued walking and when she came to a stop in front of Dillon, she offered her hand. "Yes, I'm Pamela Novak, and you are…?"

He accepted her hand and immediately felt a warmth that began to flow all through his body. Then a fluttering he felt in the pit of his stomach began to slide downward. Even the engagement ring he'd noticed her wearing couldn't stop the sensations engulfing him.

He watched her mouth move, fascinated with her lips and thinking they had a nice shape. He felt his stomach tighten when he raised his gaze from her lips to her eyes. "I'm Dillon Westmoreland."

He watched her brow lift ever so slightly, although she kept her smile in place. He could tell she was searching her memory for when, how and where she recalled the last name. He decided to help her. "I understand that my great-grandfather, Raphel Westmoreland, was once a business partner of your great-grandfather, Jay Winston Novak."

The smile on her lips transformed into a full chuckle. "Oh, yes, Raphel Westmoreland. The wife stealer."

He couldn't stop his lips from twitching in a smile. "Yes, so I've heard. In fact, that's the reason I'm here. I—"

"What does he want, Pamela?"

Dillon could tell by the stiffening of Pamela Novak's shoulders that she wished the hulk would keep quiet for once. "Is he your fiancé?" he couldn't help asking.

She met his gaze and studied it for a moment before saying, "Yes."

She then inclined her head to call back over her shoulder, "This is Dillon Westmoreland. Our great-grandfathers were once business partners so I consider him a friend of the family."

She quickly turned back to Dillon, presented him with another smile and whispered, "You know I say that loosely, don't you, considering your great-grandfather's reputation."

Now it was Dillon's time to chuckle. "The reason I'm here is to find out all I can about that reputation since I only recently discovered he had one and—"

"What does he want, Pamela?"

Before she could respond the shortest of the teen imps said, "We already told you. He wants Pammie."

The hulk's frown deepened and Dillon knew the young girl hadn't meant it the way it sounded, but basically she had spoken the truth. He *was* attracted to Pamela Novak. Encroaching into another man's territory had been Raphel Westmoreland's style, but was not his. However, at that moment Dillon didn't feel any guilt about the thoughts going through his mind, especially since it was apparent the woman was engaged to an ass. But that was her business, not his.

The man came down the steps and moved toward them and Dillon quickly sized him up. He wore a suit and an expensive pair of black leather shoes. His shirt and tie didn't look cheap, either, which meant he was probably a successful businessman of some sort.

When he stopped in front of him, Dillon offered the man his hand. "I'm Dillon Westmoreland, and like Ms. Novak said, I'm a family friend. The reason I'm here," he decided to add, "is because I'm doing research on my family's history."

The man shook his hand. "And I'm Fletcher Mallard, Pamela's fiancé," he said, as if he needed to stake a claim by speaking his position out loud.

Dillon took it in stride and thought that you could tell a lot about a man from his handshake, and this man had all the telltale signs. He was using the squeezing handshake, often used to exert strength and power. A confident man didn't need such a tactic. This man was insecure.

Mallard looked at Dillon skeptically. "And just what is it you want to know?"

The smile dropped from Pamela Novak's lips and she actually glared at her fiancé. "There's no reason for you to ask all these questions, Fletcher. Mr. West-moreland is a family friend and that's all that matters right now."

As if her words settled it, she turned to Dillon with her smile back in place. "Mr. Westmoreland, please join us for dinner, then you can tell me how we can help in your quest to learn more of your family's history."

It would have been so easy and less complicated to decline her offer, but there was something about Fletcher Mallard that outright irritated Dillon and pushed him to accept her invitation.

"Thank you, Ms. Novak, and I'd love to stay for dinner."

# Chapter 2

Pam knew she had made a mistake inviting Dillon Westmoreland to dinner the moment he was seated at the table. She wished she could say Fletcher was in rare form, but she'd seen him behave this way before, when another man had shown interest in her.

But what was strange was that Dillon hadn't actually shown any interest in her, so she couldn't understand why Fletcher was being so territorial. Unless… he had picked up on her interest in Dillon.

She pushed such utter nonsense from her mind. She was *not* interested in Dillon. She was merely curious. What woman wouldn't be interested in a man like Dillon Westmoreland. He was at least six foot four with coffee-colored features. He had an angular face that boasted a firm jaw, a pair of cute dimples, full lips and the darkest eyes she'd ever seen on a man. She was engaged to be married, but not blind. And when he had sat down at the table to join them for dinner, his presence was powerfully masculine in a distracting way. She glanced around the table and couldn't help noticing her sisters' fascination with him, as well.

"So just where are you from, Westmoreland?"

Her spine stiffened with Fletcher's question. She hadn't invited Dillon to dinner to be interrogated, but she knew Fletcher wouldn't be satisfied until he got some answers. She also knew once he got them he still wouldn't be contented.

"I'm from Denver," Dillon answered.

Fletcher was about to ask another question when Dillon beat him to the punch. "And where are you from, Mallard?"

The question had clearly caught Fletcher off guard. He had a way of trying to intimidate people, but she had a feeling that Dillon Westmoreland was a man who couldn't be intimidated.

"I'm from Laramie," Fletcher said gruffly. "I moved to town about five years ago to open a grocery store here. That was my first. Since then I've opened over twenty more in other cities in Wyoming and Montana. It's my goal to have a Mallard Super Store in every state in the union over the next five years."

Pam couldn't help but inwardly smile. If Fletcher thought that announcement would get a reaction from Dillon, then he was sadly mistaken. Dillon didn't show any sign that he was the least impressed.

"Where are you staying while you're in town?" Fletcher asked, helping himself to the mashed potatoes.

"At the River's Edge Hotel."

"Nice place if you can do without cable television," Jill said, smiling.

Pam watched how easily Dillon returned Jill's smile. "I can do without it. I don't watch much television."

"And what is it that you do?" Fletcher asked in a voice that Pam felt was as cold as the iced tea she was drinking.

Dillon, she saw, gave Fletcher a smile that didn't quite reach his eyes when he said, "I'm into real estate."

"Oh, you sell homes," Fletcher said as if the occupation was beneath him.

"Not quite," Dillon said pleasantly. "I own a real estate firm. You might have heard of it, Blue Ridge Land Management."

Pam saw the surprise that lit Fletcher's eyes before he said, "Yes, I've heard of it."

She had to force back a chuckle because she was sure that he had heard of it. Who hadn't? The Blue Ridge Land Management Company was a billion-dollar corporation, well known in the Mountain States, that had a higher place on the Fortune 500 list than Mallard Super Stores.

Seeing that Fletcher was momentarily speechless, she stepped in to say, "Mr. Westmoreland, you said that—"

"I'm Dillon."

He had raised his gaze to meet hers and she saw a friendly smile lurking in the dark depths of his eyes. Her heart rate began accelerating in her chest. "Yes, of course," she said quickly. "And I'm Pam."

After taking a sip of her tea, she continued. "Dillon, you said that you were here to research your family's history?"

"Yes," he said, his gaze still on her. "For years I was told by my parents and grandparents that my brothers, cousins and I didn't have any living relatives, and that my great-grandfather, Raphel Westmoreland, had been an only child. So you could imagine my surprise when one day, out of the clear blue sky, a man, his two sons and three nephews showed up at my ranch to proclaim they were my kin."

Intrigued by the story, Pam placed her fork next to her plate and gave him her full attention. "How did they find you?"

"Through a genealogy search. The older man, James Westmoreland, knew that his grandfather, Reginald Westmoreland, had an identical-twin brother. It was discovered that that twin brother was my great-grandfather, Raphel, who had left home at twenty-two and had never been heard from again. In fact, the family assumed he'd died. They had no idea that he had eventually settled in Denver, married and had a son, who gave him two grandsons and then a slew of great-grands—fifteen, in fact. I am the oldest of the fifteen great-grands."

"Wow, that must have been a shocker for you to discover you had other relatives when you assumed there weren't any," Jill, who was practically hanging on to Dillon's every word, said. "What does your wife think about all of this?"

Pam watched Dillon smile and knew he hadn't been fooled by the way the question had been asked. Jill wanted to know if he was a married man. Pam hated to admit that she was just as curious. He wasn't wearing a ring, but that didn't necessarily mean a thing.

"She didn't have anything to say because I'm not married," Dillon replied smoothly. "At least not anymore. I've been divorced for close to ten years."

Pam glanced over at Jill and prayed her sister had the decency not to inquire as to what had happened to end his marriage.

Fletcher, disliking the fact he wasn't the center of attention, spoke up in an authoritative negative voice. "Sounds pretty crazy to me. Why would you care about a bunch of people who show up at your place claiming they were your relatives, or better yet, why would you want to find out your family history? You should live in the present and not in the past."

Pam could tell Dillon was fighting hard to hold his temper in check, and his tone was remarkably restrained when he finally responded. "Do you have a family, Fletcher?"

Again, by Fletcher's expression it was obvious he didn't appreciate being the one receiving the questions. "No, I was an only child. My parents are deceased, but they didn't have any siblings, either. I'm the only Mallard around for now." He glanced over at Pam and smiled. "Of course, that will change once Pamela and I marry."

Dillon nodded slowly. "But until that changes, I wouldn't expect you to understand the significance of what a family means. I already do. Westmorelands are big into family and, after meeting my other relatives, my only regret is not having known them sooner."

He glanced over at her and, for a second, she held

his steady gaze. And she felt it. There was a connection between them that they were trying to ignore. She looked down at her plate as she continued eating.

Nadia asked him a question about his siblings and just as comfortably and easily as a man who was confident with himself and who he was, he began telling her everything she wanted to know. Without even trying, Dillon was captivating everyone at the dinner table… with the exception of Fletcher.

"How long do you plan to stay in town?" Fletcher rudely cut into the conversation between Dillon and the sisters.

Dillon glanced over at Fletcher. "Until I get all the questions I have about Raphel Westmoreland answered."

"That may take a while," Fletcher said.

Dillon smiled, but Pam knew it was just for Fletcher's benefit and it wasn't sincere. "I got time."

She saw Fletcher open his mouth to make another statement and she cut him off. "Dillon, I should be able to help you with that. My great-grandfather's old business records, as well as his personal journal, are in the attic. If you want to drop by tomorrow and go up there and look around, you're welcome to do so."

"Thanks," he said, smiling. "I'll be happy to take you up on your offer."

"I don't want you meeting with that man alone, Pamela. Inviting him here tomorrow while your sisters are away at school wasn't a good idea. And tomorrow I'll be out of town visiting my stores in Laramie."

Pam glanced over at Fletcher as she walked him to

the door. He was upset and she knew it. In fact, there was no doubt in her mind that everyone at the dinner table had known it since he wasn't a person who hid his emotions well.

"So," he continued, "I'll get word to him tomorrow that you've withdrawn the invitation."

Fletcher's words stopped her dead in her tracks just a few feet from her living room door. She stared at him, certain she had missed something, like a vital piece of their conversation, somewhere along the way. "Excuse me?"

"I said that since you agree that you shouldn't be alone with Westmoreland, I'll get word to him that you've withdrawn your invitation for tomorrow."

She frowned. "I don't agree to any such nonsense. The invitation I gave to Dillon Westmoreland still stands, Fletcher. You're acting controlling and terri-torial and there's no reason for it."

She saw the muscle that ticked in his jaw, indicating he was angry. "You're an attractive woman, Pamela. Westmoreland isn't blind. He noticed," he said.

"And what is that supposed to mean? I agreed to marry you but that doesn't mean you own me. If you're having seconds thoughts about this engagement, then—"

"Of course I'm not having second thoughts. I'm just trying to look out for you, that's all. You're too trust-ing with people."

His gaze then flicked over her before returning to her face. "And I think that you're the one having sec-ond thoughts," he said.

She lifted her chin. "Of course I'm having second

thoughts. I agreed to marry you as a way to save my ranch. I appreciate you coming to my rescue but you deserve better than that. And that's why I plan to pay Lester Gadling another visit this week. I want him to go back over those papers. It's hard to believe Dad did not make arrangements for the balance on that mortgage to be paid off if anything happened to him."

Fletcher waited for a moment, then said, "If you feel that strongly about it then I agree that you should go back to Gadling, since he was your father's attorney, and ask him about it. But don't worry about what I deserve. I'll have you as my wife and that will make me a happy man."

Pamela didn't say anything. She and Fletcher weren't entering into their marriage under false assumptions. He knew she was not in love with him.

She took a moment to reflect on a few things. She had left home upon graduating from high school with a full scholarship to attend the University of Southern California Drama School. It was during her sophomore year that Alma, her stepmother, had died. Her father had married Alma when Pam was ten, and Alma had been wonderful in filling the void after losing her mother.

She had thought about dropping out of college and returning home, but her father wouldn't hear of it. He was adamant about her staying in school and insisted that he would be able to care for her sisters, although Nadia had been only three at the time, the same age she'd been when she'd lost her own mother.

"Pamela?"

Pam blinked upon realizing Fletcher had called her

name. "I'm sorry, Fletcher. I was just thinking about happier times, when Dad and Alma were both alive."

"And you will have even happier times once we're married, Pamela," he said, reaching out and taking her hand in his. "I know you don't love me now, but I'm convinced you will grow to love me. Just think of all the things I can give you."

She lifted her chin. "I'm not asking for you to give me all those things, Fletcher. The only things I've asked for, and that you've promised, are to make sure my sisters retain ownership of our home and to put my sisters through college."

"I promise all of that. And I'll promise to give you more if you would just let me," he said in a low, frustrated tone.

She didn't say anything for a long moment and knew her silence was probably grating on his nerves, but she couldn't help it. "I don't want anything more, Fletcher, so please let's just leave it at that."

Pam had met Fletcher four years ago on one of her trips back to Gamble to visit her family. After that, whenever she came to town, he would make it a point to ask her if she would go out with him.

After her father died and she'd moved back home, he had come calling on a regular basis, although she had explained to him that friendship was all there could ever be between them. At the time, he had seemed satisfied with that.

Then Lester Gadling had come visiting and dropped the bombshell that had changed her life forever. Fletcher had stopped by that evening and she had found herself telling him what had happened. He had listened attentively before presenting what he saw as an easy solution. She could marry him and her financial problems would be over.

At first, she'd thought he'd fallen off the deep end, certain he had taken leave of his senses. But the more she'd thought about it, the more his suggestion had taken shape in her mind. All she had to do was marry him and he would see to it that her ranch was saved and would establish a trust fund for her sisters, so when the time came for their college, everything would be set.

She didn't accept his offer at first, determined to handle things without Fletcher's help. She had gone to bank after bank trying to secure a loan but time and time again had been turned down. She had only accepted Fletcher's proposal when she'd seen she had no other choice.

Glancing down at her watch, she said, "It's getting late."

"All right. Don't forget to be careful around Westmoreland. There is something about him that I don't trust."

"Like I said, Fletcher, I'll be fine."

He nodded before leaning in closer to brush a kiss across her lips. As always she waited for blood to rush fast and furious through her veins, fire to suffuse her insides, but as usual, nothing happened. No stirring sensations. Not a single spark.

For months she had ignored the fact that she was not physically attracted to the man she was going to marry. It hadn't bothered her until tonight when she discovered she was *very* physically attracted to another man. And that man's name was Dillon Westmoreland.

\* \* \*

Dillon eased his body into a huge bathtub filled with warm water. Whatever amenities the little hotel lacked, he would have to say a soak in this tub definitely made up for them. There weren't too many bathtubs around that could accommodate his height comfortably.

He closed his eyes and stretched out, thinking he'd never been able to relax in a tub before. It had been a while since he'd been able to sit in a tub and not worry about being disturbed by some family member needing his help or advice.

*Family.*

Damn, but he missed them already. He wasn't worried about the family he'd left in Denver since he'd left Ramsey in charge. He and Ramsey were only separated in age by seven months and were more like brothers than they were cousins. If truth be told, Ramsey was his best friend. Always had been and always would be.

He couldn't wait until he began digging into information about Raphel. He could have hired an agency to do it for him, but this was something he wanted to do himself. Something he felt he owed his family. If there was something in his great-grandfather's past, then he felt he should be the one to uncover it. Good or bad.

Dillon shifted his body. He kept his eyes closed while thinking that tonight he'd met the most beautiful woman he'd ever seen in his life. A woman who looked totally out of place in Gamble, Wyoming. A woman whose voice alone could stir something deep inside of him.

*A woman who was already taken.*

There was no denying he was attracted to her, but

wanting her was taboo. So why was he thinking about her even now? And why in the hell was he so eager to see her again tomorrow?

He inhaled deeply, wondering how Fletcher Mallard could get so lucky. It was easy to see the man was a jerk, a pompous pain in the ass. But Fletcher was no concern of his, and neither was the man's engagement to Pamela Novak. Dillon was in Gamble for one thing and for one thing only. He was there to find out everything he could about Raphel, and not to encroach on another man's property.

He would do well to remember that.

# Chapter 3

Glancing out the window Pam saw Dillon's car the moment it pulled up in front of the house. She took a sip of her coffee while watching him, grateful that the window was designed in a way that gave her a view of anyone arriving. From what she'd been told, her great-grandfather had deliberately built the house that way to have an advantage over anyone who came calling without their knowledge.

Today she was making full use of that advantage.

After he brought the car to a stop, she watched as he opened the car and got out. He stood for a moment to study her home, which gave her an opportunity to study him.

He was tall—she'd noticed that last night. But last night she hadn't had time to fully check him out. She couldn't help but appreciate what she saw now. Nice shoulders. Firm abdomen. Muscled chest. Taut thighs. He was wearing jeans and a blue Western shirt that revealed strong arms, and a black Stetson was on his head.

She sighed deeply, thinking that inviting him to come back today might not have been a good idea after all, just as Fletcher had claimed. She glanced down at her hand holding the coffee cup and couldn't miss the diamond ring on her finger, the one Fletcher had put there a week ago.

Okay, so she was an engaged woman, one who would be marrying a nice guy in a few months. But being engaged, or married for that matter, didn't mean she couldn't appreciate a fine specimen of a man when she saw one. Besides, her best friend from college, Iris Michaels, would give her hell if she didn't check him out and then call to give her all the hot-tamale details.

She blinked as she nearly burnt her tongue on a sip of coffee when Dillon looked straight at her through what she'd always considered her secret window. How had he known about the side view? To anyone else it would appear to be a flat wall in the shadow of a huge oak tree.

There was only one way to find out. She pushed her chair away from the table and stood. As she made her way out of the kitchen toward the living room, she decided maybe it would be better for him not to know she'd been sitting here watching him since he'd arrived.

She slowly opened the door and was afforded an opportunity to watch him unseen some more when his attention was diverted by a flock of geese in the sky. While he studied the geese, she again studied him, taking in the angle of his face while his head was tilted slightly backward. He was standing with his legs braced apart and with his hands in his pockets. There was something about that stance, that particular pose—especially on him—that made her just want to stand there and stare.

While living in Los Angeles for five years she'd been surrounded by jaw-droppingly, stomach-stirringly handsome men, many from some of the world's most elite modeling agencies. But none could hold a light to the man presently standing in her yard. His features were distinct—sharp facial bones, firm jaw and full lips. His hair beneath his Stetson was close cut and trimmed neatly around his head.

A moment passed. Possibly two. When suddenly he turned his head and looked over in her direction.

She had been caught.

And she was immediately enveloped in his intense gaze. She was unable to do anything but return his stare while wondering why she was doing so. Why were her senses, her entire being, homed in on everything about him? This wasn't good, she thought.

At least that was what her mind was telling her, but her common sense hadn't gotten there yet. It was being held captive within the scope of the darkest pair of eyes she'd ever seen.

Somewhere in the not-too-faraway distance she heard the sound of a car backfiring and the sound ripped right into the moment. It was only then that she was able to slide her gaze away from his to look over across the wide expanse of yard.

After taking a deep breath she returned her gaze

to his, wrestled with those same senses she had lost control of earlier, placed a smile on her face and said, "Good morning, Dillon."

She wasn't just off the boat, and knew that during the brief moment when their gazes had held, something had happened. Just as it had last night. She wasn't sure of what, but she knew that it had. She also knew she would pretend that it hadn't. "It's a beautiful day, isn't it?" she added.

"Yes, it is," he said, turning to walk over toward her. Holy cow! she thought, swallowing deeply. The man's strides were sure, confident and deliberately masculine. He had one hell of a sexy walk, and what was so disturbing about it was that it seemed as natural as the sun rising in the morning.

He came to a stop in front of her and met her gaze fleetingly before glancing up at the sun. His gaze then returned to her. "It might rain later, though."

She nodded. "Yes, it might." She knew they were trying to get back in sync and to lessen the intensity of what had passed between them.

"I hope I'm not too early," he said in a deep, husky voice, breaking into her thoughts.

"No, you're fine. I was just having my morning coffee. Would you like to join me?"

With an ultrasexy shrug of his massive shoulders, he smiled as he removed his hat. "Umm, I don't know. I feel I'm taking a lot of your time already."

"No problem. Besides, you want to know about Raphel, right?"

"Yes. Is there something you can tell me other than

he was your great-grandfather's partner and that he ran off with your great-grandmother, Portia Novak?"

Pam chuckled as she led him through the house and headed toward the kitchen. "Portia wasn't my great-grandmother," she corrected. "A few years after she'd run off, he met my great-grandmother and they married."

When he sat down at the table, she said, "I'm sure you've heard some stories about Raphel and Portia." She proceeded to pour him a cup of coffee.

"No, in actuality, I hadn't. I'd always assumed my great-grandmother Gemma was my great-grandfather's only wife. It was only after my Atlanta Westmoreland relatives showed up and explained how we were related that I found out about Portia Novak and the others."

Pam lifted a brow. "There were others?"

He nodded. "Yes, Gemma was his fifth wife."

Dillon was more than curious about what had happened to a preacher's wife, a woman by the name of Lila Elms. Although she was already legally married to the preacher, had she and Raphel pretended to be married for a spell before he dumped her for Portia, the wife of Jay Novak?

And then what happened to Clarice, wife number three? And Isabelle, wife four? All four women's names were rumored to be connected to Raphel in some say. If what they'd discovered so far was true, Raphel had taken up with the four women before his thirty-second birthday, and all had been married to another man or engaged to marry someone else. It seemed Raphel's reputation as a wife stealer was legendary.

Dillon took a sip of coffee, deciding for the moment not to inform her that the others, like Portia, were women who belonged to other men, legally or otherwise. But he would throw out the name of one she might have heard about already. "My goal is to find out what happened to Lila Elms."

"The preacher's wife?"

So, she had heard about Lila. "Yes." He took another sip and then asked, "How do you know so much about this stuff?"

She chuckled as she sat down at the table with him after refilling her own cup of coffee. "My grandmother. As a little girl we would spend hours and hours on the porch outside shelling peas, and she would fill my ears about all the family history. But the one subject she didn't shed a lot of light on was Portia. For some reason, any conversation about her was taboo. Jay wanted it that way and my great-grandmother respected his wishes."

Dillon nodded, trying to concentrate on what she was saying and not on how smoothly her lips would part each time she took a sip of her coffee. How the bottom lip would hang open a little and how the top one would fit perfectly around the rim of the cup.

He felt his gut tightening and took a sip of his coffee. When he had been standing out in her yard and he'd turned and seen her staring at him, he had tried not to speculate just what was going on in her mind. He didn't want to even consider the possibility that it had been close to what had been going on in his.

Her gaze had touched him deeply, in a way he doubted she even realized. Something about Pamela Novak was calling out to him in the most elemental way, and that wasn't good. Since his divorce, he had dated on occasion. But if the truth be told, he'd made it a point to date only women who, like him, weren't interested in anything long term. All of those women had been unattached.

"Are you ready to go up to the attic?"

Her question reined his thoughts back and he glanced over at her and immediately wished he hadn't. Every muscle in his body immediately seemed to weaken yet at the same time fill him with an intensity that made him draw in a long breath. It was time to acknowledge it for what it was. Sexual chemistry.

He had heard about it but had never actually experienced it for himself. He'd been attracted to women before, but it never went further than an attraction. What he was beginning to feel was an element of something greater than a mere attraction. There were these primitive vibes he was not only emitting but was also receiving. That meant Pamela Novak was in tune to what was going on between them, although she might choose to pretend otherwise. Of course, he understood her reluctance to acknowledge such a thing. After all, she was an engaged woman. And she didn't come across as one who would deliberately be unfaithful to her fiancé.

But still…

"Yes, I'm ready," he finally said. "But first I want to clear the air about something." He watched her lips quiver nervously before she set her cup down and met his gaze. He tensed, trying to ignore the sensations rolling through him every time their eyes met.

"Clear the air about what?"

He'd been too busy watching her lips to pay any attention to the words flowing out of them. He fought back the urge to lift the tip of his finger and run it across those lips.

He cleared his throat. "About last night. My showing up here without calling first. I think I may have rattled your fiancé a little, and I regret doing that. It was not my intent to cause any problems between the two of you."

He watched as her shoulders gave a feminine shrug. "You didn't cause any problems. Don't worry about it."

She then stood. "I think we should go up to the attic and see what's there. There's a trunk that contains a lot of my great-grandfather's business records."

Dillon nodded. She had responded to his question and in the same breath, had effectively switched topics, which let him know the subject of her relationship with Fletcher Mallard was not up for discussion.

He pushed his chair back and then got on his feet. "I'm ready, just lead the way."

She did and he couldn't help but appreciate the backside that strolled in front of him as he followed.

With his long legs, it didn't take Dillon long to catch up with her, Pamela thought. Not that she was trying to leave him behind. But for a few moments she'd needed to get her bearings. The man had a way of making her not think straight.

He was silent as she led him up the stairs and she couldn't help looking sideways to gaze at his profile. What was it about him that affected her in a way Fletcher didn't? Her heart rate accelerated when she noticed he even climbed the stairs with an ingrained sexiness that made her senses reel.

When they reached the top landing he moved slightly ahead of her, as if he knew where he was going. "If I didn't know better I'd swear you've been here before," she said as they continued to walk toward the end of the hall that led to the attic stairs.

He glanced down at her and smiled. "This might sound crazy but this house is very similar to mine back in Denver. Was it built by your great-grandfather?"

"Yes."

"Then that might explain things, since the house I live in was built by Raphel. I'm thinking he liked the design, and when he decided to build his home he did so from his memory of this one."

"That would explain how you knew about our secret window." She regretted the words the moment they left her lips. She had just admitted to spying on him out the window when he'd arrived.

"Yes, that's how I know about it. I have one of my own just like it and in the same place."

"I see." But, in a way, she didn't see, which made her as eager to find out about Raphel as Dillon was.

She then walked on and he joined her. When they reached the door that led to the attic she opened it. Judging from the expression on his face, it was as if he'd seen the view before, and that made her determined to know why his home was a replica of hers.

Unlike the other stairs in her home, the attic steps were narrow and Dillon moved aside for her to go up ahead of him. She could feel the heat of his gaze on her back. She was tempted to glance over her shoulder but knew that wouldn't be the appropriate thing to do. So she did the next best thing and engaged him in conversation.

She broke into the silence by saying, "At dinner you mentioned that you were the oldest of Raphel's fifteen great-grands." She glanced briefly over her shoulder.

"Yes, and for a number of years I was the legal guardian for ten of them."

Pamela swung around so quickly, had she been standing on a stair she probably would have lost her balance. "Guardian to ten of them?"

At his nod, she blinked in amazement. "How did that come about?" She stepped aside when he reached her, noting there still wasn't a lot of room between them, but she was so eager to hear his answer she didn't make a move to step back any further.

"My parents and my aunt and uncle decided to go away for the weekend together, to visit one of my mother's friends in Louisiana. On their way back to Denver, their plane developed engine trouble and went down, killing everyone on board."

"Oh, how awful."

"Yes, it was. My parents had seven kids and my aunt and uncle had eight. I was the oldest at twenty-one. My brother Micah was nineteen and Jason was eighteen. My other brothers, Riley, Stern, Canyon and Brisbane, were all under sixteen."

He braced a hip against the stair railing and continued. "My cousin Ramsey was twenty, and his brother Zane was nineteen and Derringer was eighteen. The remaining cousins, Megan, Gemma, the twins Adrian and Aiden, and the youngest, Bailey, were also all under sixteen."

She also leaned against the rail to face him, still full of questions. "And family services didn't have a problem with you being responsible for so many little ones?"

"No, everyone knew the Westmorelands would want to stay together. Besides," he said, chuckling, "no one around our parts wanted to be responsible for Bane."

"Bane?"

"Yes. It's short for Brisbane. He's my youngest brother who likes his share of mischief. He was only eight when my parents were killed and he took their deaths pretty hard."

"How old is he now?"

"Twenty-two and still hot under the collar in more ways than one. I wish there was something holding his interest these days other than a certain female in Denver."

Pam nodded. She couldn't help but wonder if there was a certain female in Denver holding Dillon's interest, as well.

"Do all of you still live close to one another?" she asked.

"Yes, Great-Grandpa Raphel purchased a lot of land back in the thirties. When each Westmoreland reaches the age of twenty-five they are given a hundred-acre tract of land, which is why we all live in close proximity to each other. As the oldest cousin, I inherited the family home where everyone seems to congregate most of the time."

He then asked her, "How old were you when your great-grandfather passed?"

"He died before I was born, but I heard a lot about him. What about Raphel? How old were you when he passed?"

"He died before I was born, too. My great-grandmother lived until I was two, so I don't rightly remember much of her, either. But I do remember my grandparents, Grampa Stern and Gramma Paula. It was Grampa Stern who used to tell us stories about Raphel, but never did he mention anything about past wives or other siblings. In fact, he claimed Raphel had been an only child. That makes me wonder how much he truly knew about his own father."

Pam paused for a moment and then said, "I guess there are secrets in most families."

"Yes, like Raphel running off with the preacher's wife," he said.

"And you think Raphel eventually married her?"

"Not sure of that, either," Dillon replied. "Since she was legally married to the preacher, I don't see how a marriage between them could take place, which is why I'm curious as to what happened to her once they fled Georgia."

"But her name, as well as Portia's, are shown as former wives on documents you've found?" she asked, trying to get a greater understanding of just what kind of life his great-grandfather may have led.

"Two of my Atlanta cousins, Quade and Cole, own a security firm and they did a background check, going as far back as the early nineteen-hundreds. Old land deeds were discovered for Raphel and they list four separate women as his wives. So far we know two of them—the preacher's wife and Portia Novak—were already legally married. We can only assume Raphel lived with them pretending to be married."

He paused a moment and then glanced around and asked, "Do you come up here often?"

His question made her realize they had been standing still long enough and were awfully close, so she shifted toward the attic door. "Not as often as I used to. I just moved back to Gamble last year when my father passed. Like you, I'm the oldest and I wanted to care for my sisters. I am their legal guardian."

Dillon nodded and stepped back when she opened the attic door. He had noticed the way she had interacted with her sisters last night at dinner. It was obvious they were close.

"That's my great-grandfather's trunk over there. It's my understanding that he and your great-grandfather were partners in a dairy business, which was very profitable at the time. I know there are a lot of business records in there, as well as some of Raphel's belongings. It seems he made a quick getaway when he left Gamble."

Dillon shot her a glance. "You have some of Raphel's belongings?"

"Yes," she said, moving toward the trunk. "I didn't mention it at dinner last night."

He understood the reason she hadn't done so. Her fiancé probably would have had something to say about it. It was quite obvious the man could make an argument out of just about any subject.

Instead of immediately following her over to the

trunk, Dillon stood back for a moment and watched her go. His gaze was focused on her. The possibility that some of his great-grandfather's belongings might be inside that trunk intrigued him. But she intrigued him more.

She was wearing jeans and a pretty pink blouse that added an ultrafeminine touch. He couldn't help but notice the seductive curves outlined in those jeans. Walking behind her up the stairs to the attic had been hell. He was certain sweat had popped out on his brow with every step she'd taken.

When she saw he hadn't followed her, she turned and slanted him a glance. "Are you all right?"

No, he wasn't all right. One part of his brain was trying to convince him that, although she was an engaged woman, she wasn't married yet, so she was still available. But another part of him, the one looking at the ring on her finger, knew to make a pass in any way would be crossing a line. But hell, he was tempted.

She held his gaze, and he realized at that moment he hadn't given her an answer. "Yes, I'm fine. Just overwhelmed." If only she knew how much and the reason why.

"I understand how you feel. What you said last night at dinner is true for me, as well. I consider family important. Although you never knew him, you want to know as much about your great-grandfather as you can learn. I think it is admirable that you want to do so."

She glanced down at the trunk and then back at him. "I just hope you don't think you're going to find out everything there is to know about your great-grandfather in one day, Dillon. Even after I open that trunk it might spur you to ask more questions, seek more answers."

"And if I need to come back here?" he asked, knowing she knew where he was going with the question.

"You're welcome to come back for as long as it takes."

His gaze held hers intensely as he asked, "Will Fletcher be okay with it? Like I said earlier, I don't want to cause any problems between the two of you."

"There won't be any problems. Now, aren't you going to open this trunk? I've been dying to do so for years, but growing up we were always told it was off limits." Her lips curved at the corners. "But I will admit to defying orders once and poking around in there. At that time, I didn't see anything that held my interest."

Dillon smiled as he crossed the floor toward her. Like his at home, the attic here was huge. As a boy, the attic had been one of his favorite places to hide when he wanted some alone time. This room was full of boxes and trunks, but they had been arranged in a neat order, nothing like the way his attic looked back home. And there was that lone, small rectangular window that allowed just enough sunlight to shine through.

Kneeling, he pulled off a key that was taped on the side of the trunk and began working at the lock. Moments later he lifted open the lid. There were a lot of papers, business books, a couple of work shirts that had aged with time, a bottle of wine, a compass and a tattered looking journal.

He glanced up at Pam. "Mind if I take a look at this?"

"No, I don't mind. In fact, there's a letter inside."

He lifted a brow as he opened the journal and, sure enough, a letter whose envelope had turned yellow, lay on the front page. The name on the envelope was still legible. It simply said *Westmoreland.* He glanced back over at her.

"Like I said, although the trunk was off limits, I couldn't help but snoop that one time. That's how I knew about that letter."

Dillon couldn't hide his smile as he opened the sealed letter. It read, *"Whomever comes to get Raphel's belongings just needs to know that he was a good and decent man and I don't blame him for leaving and taking Portia with him."*

It had been signed by Pam's great-grandfather Jay. Dillon put the letter back in the envelope and glanced up at Pam. "This is all very confusing. Think you can shed some light on it?"

She shook her head. "No, sorry. For a man not to hold any animosity against the man that took his wife is strange. Perhaps Raphel did Jay a favor if he didn't want to be married to her anyway. But that theory is really stretching it a bit. A man's wife is a man's wife, and Portia had been Jay's wife."

"And what about Lila Elms?"

She shrugged. "I can't tell you anything about her, other than they must have parted ways between Atlanta and here, because from all I've heard when Raphel arrived in Gamble he was a single man."

She glanced at her watch. "There are a few phone calls that I need to make, so I'm going to leave you for a while. Take as much time as you like up here, and if you need me for any reason, I'll be downstairs in the kitchen."

"All right."

She moved toward the attic door.

"Pamela?"

She glanced back around. "Yes?"

He smiled. "Thanks."

She smiled back. "Don't mention it."


Dillon released a deep breath the moment Pam left, closing the attic door behind her. Pamela Novak was a temptation he had best leave alone. All the while she had been in this room, he had tried keeping the conversation going, anything to suppress the desires that had run rampant through him.

What was there about her that ruffled his senses every time she was within ten feet of him? What was there about her that made a number of unnamed and undefined sensations run through him? It had been hard as hell to maintain his composure and control around her.

Perhaps his dilemma had to do with her understanding of his need to delve into his family's history, his desire to know as much about Raphel Westmoreland as he could find out. Even some of his siblings and cousins didn't understand what was driving him, although they did support him. He appreciated them for it, but support and understanding were two different things.

However, he had a gut feeling Pamela did understand. She not only understood but was willing to help him any way she could...even if it meant stirring her fiancé's ire.

Deciding he needed to do what he'd come to Gamble to do, he pulled a chair out of a corner and placed it in front of the trunk. Picking up Jay Novak's journal, he began reading.

# Chapter 4

Pam glanced at the clock on the kitchen wall. Dillon had been up in the attic for over an hour, and she couldn't help but wonder how things were going. More than once she'd thought about going up to find out but had talked herself out of it. Instead she got busy looking over scripts for new plays her students had submitted.

The ringing of her phone interrupted her thoughts and she had a feeling who the caller was without bothering to look at caller ID. Sighing deeply, she picked up the phone. "Hello?"

"How are you, Pamela? This is Fletcher."

"I'm fine, Fletcher. How are things in Laramie?"

"They are fine, but I received a call and I'm going to have to leave here and go to Montana and check on a store there. A massive snowstorm caused a power failure that lasted a couple of days, and a lot of our refrigerated items were destroyed."

"I'm sorry to hear that."

"So am I. That means I'll be flying to Montana to meet with the insurance company representative. It may take a few days and I might not be back until the end of the week."

She could lie and say she was sorry to hear that, but she really wasn't. She had felt the two of them needed space and this was a way she could get it. Since agreeing to marry him, he'd made it a point to see her practically every day.

"You can make me happy and come spend some time with me here." His words intruded into her thoughts. The two of them hadn't slept together. Although he had brought up the idea several times, she had avoided the issue with him.

"Thanks for the invite, but I have a lot to do here. Besides, I need to be here for my sisters."

She didn't have to see him to know his jaw was probably tight from anger right now. This was not the first time he had tried to talk her into going out of town with him since they'd become engaged.

He didn't say anything for a moment and when he did speak again, she was not surprised by his change in subject. "And where is Westmoreland? Did he show up today?"

She had no reason to lie. "Yes, he showed up. In fact, he's still here, upstairs in the attic going through some things."

"Why couldn't he take the stuff with him and go through it back at the hotel?"

Fletcher's tone, as well as his words, annoyed her. "I saw no reason for him to take anything back to the hotel. I regret you evidently have a problem with it."

"I'm just looking out for you, Pamela," he said after a brief pause. "I still feel you don't know the man well enough to be there alone with him."

"Then I guess you just need to chalk it up as bad judgment on my part. Goodbye, Fletcher."

Without waiting for him to say anything else, she hung up the phone. He would fume for a few hours and then he would call her back later and apologize once he realized just how controlling he'd acted.

Pam eased back to the table and picked up the papers once again, determined to tuck Fletcher and his attitude away until later. She had agreed to marry him and she *would* marry him, since her sisters' futures and not losing her family home meant everything to her.

Dillon closed the journal and stood to stretch his legs. He was used to being dressed in a business suit every day, instead of casual jeans and a shirt. That morning he had checked in with Ted Boston, his business manager, to see how things were going at his real estate firm and, not surprisingly, Ted had everything under control. He had made his firm into a billion-dollar company with hard work and by hiring the right people to work for him.

He glanced at his watch, finding it hard to believe that two hours had passed already. He looked down at the journal. At least part of his curiosity had been satisfied as to what had happened to Lila, the wife of the preacher from Georgia.

According to what Raphel had shared with Jay, the old preacher had been abusing his young wife. Church members had turned their heads with the mind-set that what went on behind a married couple's closed doors was their business, especially when it involved a preacher.

Evidently, Raphel hadn't seen it that way. He had come up with a plan to rescue Lila from the clutches of the abusive preacher—a plan his family had not supported. After taking Lila as far away as Texas, Raphel had helped her get established in the small Texas town of Copperhead, on the outskirts of Austin. Raphel had been her protector, never her lover, and before moving on he had purchased a small tract of land and given it to her to make a new beginning for herself.

Dillon smiled, thinking, at least in the case of Lila, Raphel had been a wife saver and not a wife stealer. Given the woman's situation, Dillon figured he would have done the same thing. He'd discovered that when it came to the opposite sex, Westmoreland men had this ingrained sense of protection. He just regretted that Raphel had severed ties with his family.

At that moment Dillon's stomach started to growl, reminding him that he hadn't eaten anything since early that morning and it was afternoon already. It was time for him to head back over to the hotel.

Pam had been intensely involved in reading one of her students' scripts when suddenly she felt sensations curl inside her stomach at the same time chill bumps began to form on her arms.

She glanced up and met Dillon's gaze as he stepped

into the kitchen. She wondered how her body had known of his presence before her mind. And why even now the sensations curling her stomach had intensified. She decided to speak before he had a chance to do so, not sure what havoc the sensations combined with his deep, disturbingly sexy voice would play on her senses.

"How did things go? Did you discover anything about your great-grandfather that you didn't know before?" she asked, hoping he didn't hear the strain in her voice.

He smiled, and the effect of that smile was just as bad as if he'd spoken. He had a dimpled smile that showed beautiful white teeth. "Yes. At least, thanks to your great-grandfather's journal, I was able to solve the mystery of Lila, woman number one."

"Did they eventually marry?" she asked, curiously.

"No, from what I read, Lila's preacher husband was an abusive man and Lila sought out Raphel's help to escape the situation. He took her as far as Copperhead, Texas, hung around while she got on her feet, established her with a new identity and then moved on."

Pam nodded. "That explains why he wasn't married when he arrived here in Gamble."

"Yes, but it doesn't explain why he would run off with your great-grandfather's wife. And so far nothing I've read explains it, but then I didn't get through the entire journal. Not even halfway. Jay would digress and talk about the dairy business and how it was doing. But from what I've read so far, it seemed that he and Raphel were close, which doesn't explain how my great-grandfather could betray him the way he did."

Pam didn't say anything for a moment and then

she asked, "So, are you taking a break before reading some more?"

"No, it's getting late and I think it won't be a good idea to be here when your fiancé arrives this evening. I've outstayed my welcome today anyway, and I appreciate you giving me a chance to read the journal."

"You're welcome." And before she could think better of her actions, she said, "And I'd like to invite you to stay for dinner. I'm sure my sisters would love hearing what you've discovered today. I think you piqued their interest at dinner yesterday and they see this as some sort of family mystery needing to be solved. At some time or another everyone has heard about Raphel Westmoreland and how he ran off with my great-grandfather's first wife."

Dillon leaned against the kitchen cabinet. "I'm surprised no one in your family has been curious enough to find out what really happened."

Pam shrugged. "I guess you have to understand how some women think, namely my great-grandmother. I'm sure she could have cared less why her predecessor ran off with another man, and the less the family talked about Portia, the better."

She tilted her head and looked up at him. "So will you take me up on my invitation and stay for dinner?"

Pam's words intruded into his thoughts and he looked up and over at her, holding her gaze a moment. "And what about Fletcher? How is he going to handle me sitting at your dinner table two evenings in a row?"

He watched as she nervously bit her bottom lip and then lifted her chin. "There's nothing wrong with me inviting someone I consider a family friend to dinner. Besides, Fletcher is out of town for a few days."

He nodded, considered her words and decided not to read anything into them. It was an invitation to dinner, nothing more. As long as he remembered she was an engaged woman, everything would be all right.

Only problem with that was that the more he saw her, and the more he was around her, the more he was attracted to her. And the more he was attracted to her, the more he could admit, whether it was honorable or not, that he wanted her.

He swallowed and intentionally glanced out the window, needing to break eye contact with Pam. What he'd just inwardly admitted wasn't good, but he was being honest with himself. That meant as soon as he could find out all the answers he wanted about Raphel, he hoped in the next couple of days, he would return home.

He glanced back at her, met her gaze, felt the pull, the attraction, and although she might never admit it to anyone, not even to herself, he knew it was mutual. He knew he should ask if he could take the journal back to the hotel and spend the next several days reading it, out of such close proximity to her and this unusual sexual chemistry he felt whenever they were near each other.

But for some reason he couldn't. "If you're sure it will be okay then, yes, I'd love to join you and your sisters for dinner."

"And you're sure he's coming back for dinner, Pammie?" Nadia asked with excitement in her voice as she helped her oldest sister set the table.

Pam lifted a brow. She couldn't remember the last time Nadia or Paige had gotten excited about someone coming for dinner, least of all a man. The first time she had invited Fletcher, they had almost boycotted dinner until she'd had a good, hard talk about being courteous and displaying Novak manners.

"Yes, he said he was going back to the hotel to change clothes and would be coming back."

"And don't you think he's very handsome, Pam?" Paige chimed in to ask.

Pam turned after placing the last plate on the table and faced her three sisters. Although Jill hadn't voiced her excitement, Pam knew it was there—she could clearly see it on her face. The one thing she didn't want her sisters to think was that Dillon's presence at dinner had anything to do with her engagement to Fletcher. She knew what they were trying to do, and it was time she made sure they understood that it wasn't working.

"Yes, he is handsome, Paige, but so is Fletcher. But I'm not marrying a man because of his looks. I'm not that vain and I hope the three of you aren't, either. To set the record straight, so the three of you fully know that what you're doing isn't working, I *will* be marrying Fletcher."

Jill smiled. "We have no idea what you're talking about, Pam."

Pam rolled her eyes and was about to give them a good talking-to when the sound of the doorbell stopped her. "Okay, that's our guest and I want you on your best behavior, and please keep in mind that I am engaged to marry Fletcher."

Jill made a face and then said, "Please, don't remind us."

* * *

"We're glad you found out something about your great-grandfather today, Dillon," Nadia said, smiling.

Dillon couldn't help but return her smile, thinking she reminded him a lot of his cousin Bailey when she'd been Nadia's age. There was an innocence about her, while at the same time if you looked into her eyes long enough, there was mischief there, as well. The same thing could be said about Paige, but Jill was a different story.

There was something about her and her antics tonight that reminded him of Bane. The thought of a female Bane made him cringe more than a little. Her eyes twinkled when she encouraged him to talk about his family. He couldn't help but wonder if she was truly interested, or if her inquisition was a ploy. And he was smart enough to figure out it all came back to the same thing as last night. For some reason Pam's sisters were not happy with the man she had chosen to marry. It didn't take a rocket scientist to see that.

"Would you like something more to eat, Dillon?"

He glanced over at Pam. Their gazes met across the table and he smiled while at the same time fought down the tightening of his gut. He'd never been a man easily distracted by a beautiful face, but in the last forty-eight hours he'd known the real experience of feeling weak in the knees and having his heart thud mercilessly in his chest.

"No, and I appreciate your invitation to dinner."

"Tell us some more about Bane. He sounds like someone I'd like to meet one day," Jill said.

"No, he's not," both Dillon and Pam said simultaneously, and then they couldn't help but glance across the table at each other and laugh. They agreed with each other on that point.

Pam excused herself to go get dessert, a chocolate cake she had baked earlier. Dillon smiled at the three females staring at him and, as soon as Pam left the room, he was surprised when they lit into him with questions they dared not ask while their older sister was still in the room.

Nadia went first. Her dark eyes, as beautiful as her older sister's, stared him down. "Do you think Pammie is pretty?"

He smiled. That was easy enough for him to answer and do so truthfully. "Yes, she's pretty."

"Do you have a girlfriend?" Paige quickly asked.

He chuckled. "No, I don't have a girlfriend."

"Would you be interested in Pam if she wasn't engaged?"

Jill's question would have shocked the hell out of him if he hadn't gotten used to her tactics by now. She shot straight from the hip and he intended to answer her the same way.

"The key point to remember is that your sister *is* engaged, so whether I would be interested is a moot point, now, isn't it? But to answer your question, my answer would be yes, I would be interested."

"Interested in what?" Pam asked, returning and toting a plate with a huge chocolate cake.

"Nothing," three voices said at once.

Pam lifted a brow as she glanced at her sisters. She then looked over at Dillon and he couldn't help but smile and shrug his shoulders. Joining Pam and her sisters for dinner made him feel right at home and he wasn't sure that was a good thing.

"I think I need to apologize for anything my sisters might have said that could have grated on your nerves tonight," Pam said, walking Dillon out to his car. She had convinced herself this would be the only way she could get a few private words in without her sisters' ears perking at each and every word.

He chuckled. "Hey, it wasn't bad. I enjoyed their company. Yours, too. And dinner was wonderful."

"Thanks."

They didn't say anything for a few moments and then she asked, "Will you be coming back tomorrow? To continue reading Jay's journal?"

When they came to his car he leaned against it to face her. "Only if you say it's okay. I don't want to wear out my welcome."

She chuckled. "You won't be. Besides, finding out more about Raphel and Portia is like a puzzle waiting to be pieced together."

Pam knew she probably should suggest that he take the journal with him—that way he wouldn't have to bother coming back tomorrow—but for some reason she couldn't do that.

"Well, I guess I'd better let you go now. See you tomorrow," she said, backing up, putting proper distance between them.

"Good night," he said.

Dillon opened the door and got into the car but sat there until Pam had raced up the stairs, let herself inside and closed the door behind her. He saw three pairs of curtains automatically fall back into place in upstairs windows, and couldn't help but chuckle at the notion that he and Pam had been spied on. To be honest, he wasn't surprised.

As he drove off, he could only shake his head when he remembered his siblings' and cousins' reaction to Tammi when he'd brought her home, a year before they'd married. Although his parents and aunt and uncle had tried making the Westmoreland clan behave, it had been pretty obvious that Tammi hadn't been too well received. But that hadn't stopped him for marrying her the following year and bringing her home as his wife. Now he wished that it had.

He shifted in his seat to pull his cell phone out of his jeans pocket, hoping tonight he could pick up a signal. He smiled when he did and immediately placed a call home.

Ramsey answered on the second ring. "The Westmorelands."

"Hey, Ram, it's Dillon. How are things going?"

"As well as can be expected. Bane's been behaving, so that's good."

Yes, that was good, Dillon thought.

"I went up to the big house and got all your mail," Ramsey was saying.

"Thanks."

"You find out anything on Raphel yet?" Ramsey asked.

"Yes." Dillon then spent the next half hour bringing his cousin up to date on what he'd uncovered that day from Jay's journal.

"And Jay Novak's great-granddaughter is actually

nice to you? After Raphel ran off with her great-grand-father's wife?"

Dillon chuckled. "Yes, she's operating on the premise of good riddance. If Portia hadn't left then Jay would never have met and married her great-grand-mother. Needless to say, Pam has no problem with Raphel running off with the woman."

"Pam?"

Dillon heard the curiosity in Ramsey's voice and knew why. Ramsey of all people knew how hard it had been in making the real estate firm he had inherited from his father and uncle into the billion-dollar company it was today, taking care of the Westmoreland stronghold and being responsible for all those Westmorelands who were still dependent while they were away at college.

"Yes, Pam is her name, and before you ask, the answer again is yes, she is beautiful. The most beautiful woman I've ever set eyes on."

And before Ramsey could say anything, he quickly added, "And she's engaged."

"Umm, have you met her fiancé?" Ramsey wanted to know.

"Yes, and he's an ass."

Ramsey chuckled. "How did a beautiful woman get engaged to an ass?"

"Beats me and it's none of my business."

"That's the difference between me and you, cuz. I would make it my business, especially if she was the most beautiful woman I'd ever seen. You know what they say about it not being over until the fat lady sings?

Well, in this case, she's not off limits until the wedding is over."

"That's not my style, Ram."

"Typically, it's not mine, either, being the loner that I am, but I've learned that with some things you need to know when and how to adjust your thinking, be flexible and restructure your thought process. Especially if it's a woman you want."

Dillon blinked, taken aback by Ramsey's statement. "What makes you think she's a woman I want?"

"I can hear it in your voice. Do you deny it?"

Dillon opened his mouth to do that very thing and then closed his mouth shut. No, he couldn't deny it, because his cousin who knew him so well had just spoken the truth. And the question of the hour was whether or not he intended to do anything about it.

## Chapter 5

Pam was trying, desperately so, to convince herself that the only reason she was sitting at the kitchen table and staring out the window was to study all the Indian paintbrushes that were still blooming this late in the year.

It wasn't working.

Just like it wasn't working to try and convince herself the only reason she'd gone to bed with thoughts of Dillon on her mind instead of the man she was engaged to marry was because Dillon had been to dinner the last couple of nights. The reason that argument wouldn't hold up was because, although Fletcher had been dropping in for dinner quite often, she had yet to take visions of him to her bed. She had yet to remember, in vivid detail, what he'd been wearing the last time she'd seen him, and yet to hear the sound of his voice in her head in the wee hours of the morning.

So why was Dillon Westmoreland causing so much havoc in her life when she should be concentrating on setting the best date to marry Fletcher? The main thing that had been nagging at her since meeting Dillon was the fact that he could arouse feelings and sensations within her that Fletcher didn't. Was that something she should be concerned about, she wondered.

She quickly decided that it didn't really matter if she should be concerned, since Fletcher was the only one capable of getting her out of such a dismal situation. Their marriage would not be one of love and, the way things were looking, it wouldn't be one of passion either. But she would make do. She really didn't have a choice.

The ringing of the phone intruded her thoughts. Getting up from the table she quickly crossed the room to pick it up, but turned to make sure she still had a good view out the window. "Hello."

"I called to see if you've come to your senses and called off your engagement."

Pam couldn't do anything, but shake her head and smile. She wasn't sure who was worse, her sisters or her best friend from college, Iris Michaels. From Iris's initial meeting with Fletcher, he had rubbed her the wrong way and she hadn't gotten over it yet. "No, sorry, the wedding is still on, so I hope you haven't forgotten your promise to be my maid of honor."

Pam could picture Iris sitting behind the desk of the PR company she owned in Los Angeles with a beautiful view of the Pacific. Iris would be tapping a pen either on her desk or to the side of her face, trying to think of a way to get out of the promise she'd made their second year in college together over a peanut butter and jelly sandwich. Their days in college had been hard. Money had been tight, so they had made do, shared practically everything and had become best friends for life.

Right out of college, Iris had met, fallen in love with and married Garlan Knight. Garlan, a stuntman, had been killed while working on a major film less than a year into their marriage. That was four years ago and, although Iris dated on occasion, she had long ago proclaimed that she would never give her heart to another man because the pain of losing the person she loved wasn't worth it.

"I'm trying to forget I made that promise. So what's been going on with you lately?"

At first Pam couldn't decide whether she should mention anything about Dillon and then thought, why not? Chances were, when Iris came to visit, her sisters would tell her about him anyway, and then Iris would accuse her of holding secrets. "Well, there is something I need to tell you about. I had a visitor this week."

While periodically glancing out the window, Pam told Iris how Dillon had shown up two nights ago. Surprisingly, Iris didn't ask a lot of questions; she listened attentively, giving Pam the chance to finish. "So, there you have it," Pam finally said, glad it was over and done with. She made an attempt to move to another subject—about how things were going at the drama school—when Iris stopped her.

"Hey, not so fast, Pam. What aren't you telling me?"

Pam rolled her eyes. "I've told you everything."

"Then why did you deliberately leave out any details about how this guy looks? You know I'm a visual person."

Pam breathed in deeply. "He's good-looking."

"How good-looking?"

"Very good-looking, Iris," she said, hoping that would be the end of it.

"On a scale of one to ten with ten being the sexiest, how would you rate him?" Iris asked.

"Why do you want to know?"

"Just answer the question, please," Iris demanded.

When Pam didn't say anything for a moment, deciding to keep her lips sealed, Iris said, "I'm waiting."

Pam rolled her eyes again and then said, "Okay, he's a ten."

"A ten?"

"Yes, Iris, a ten. He is so darn pleasing to the eyes it's a shame," she said, inwardly blaming Iris for making her tell all.

"What about his personality?"

Pam thought about how dinner had gone yesterday and how pleasant it had been for her sisters to feel included in the dinner discussions. Dillon had held their focus because he had paid attention to them, as if what they had to say was important, not trivial like Fletcher would often do. Yes, she would have to say he had a nice personality.

"He's nice, Iris, and his personality goes right along with it."

"Would he be someone that would interest you if you weren't engaged to Fletcher?"

Pam frowned. "Why would you ask me something like that when I *am* engaged to Fletcher?"

"Cut all the drama, Pam, and answer the question."

Pam's frown deepened because she knew the answer to Iris's question without thinking much about it. "Yes, he would be. In a heartbeat." And then because she had to tell someone and Iris, being her best friend, was the likely candidate, she said, "I'm attracted to him. Isn't that awful?"

"Why is it awful? You and I both know why you're marrying Fletcher, which I still think is a mistake. I refuse to believe there is not a bank anywhere that will loan you the money you need to pay off that second mortgage."

"We're talking about a million dollars, Iris. You know how much hassle you got from the banks when you wanted to borrow half that much to start your PR business. I have very little in savings and what I do have Jill will need for college next year. And Paige and Nadia need a home. I can't expect them to move away from the only home they've known. A home that's been in the Novak family for over a hundred years." Pam sighed in frustration. "I still can't believe Dad didn't take all that into consideration when he took out that second mortgage."

"If Fletcher was really a nice guy, he would co-sign for you to get that money without any strings attached," Iris said. "For him to put stipulations on his help by asking you to marry him is just downright underhanded, if you ask me."

Pam didn't say anything since she had heard it all from Iris before, several times. When Iris finally ended her spiel, Pam said, "Marrying Fletcher won't be so bad, Iris."

"It will be if you're sentencing yourself to a life without love and passion, and we both know that you are. I loved Garlan and the passion we shared was wonderful. I can't imagine being married to a man I didn't love or who didn't do anything for me sexually."

Pam was silent for a moment and then said quietly, "Well, I can. I don't have a choice, Iris."

For a short while Iris didn't say anything, either. "Then maybe now is the time to enjoy passion while you can."

Pam blinked. "Just what are you suggesting?"

"You've admitted you're attracted to Dillon Westmoreland, so take advantage of that attraction and think about yourself for a change, not the house or the land or your sisters. Think about Pamela."

"I can't do that," Pam said.

"Sure you can. Are you going to deny you haven't been thinking about Dillon Westmoreland in the wee hours of the night?"

Pam almost dropped the phone. "How did you know?"

Iris laughed. "Hey, you said the man is a ten. Men who are tens can't help but find their way into a woman's nightly dreams, regardless of whether she's single, engaged or married. It happens. My advice to you is to bring him out of your dreams into your reality. You will be married to Fletcher until death do you part. Do you want to go through the next fifty, sixty or seventy years without feeling any passion again?"

"I told you about my past experiences with passion, Iris," she said, remembering the couple of times she had slept with guys and the disappointment she'd felt afterward. She hadn't heard the bells and whistles, nor had she felt any earthquakes like Iris had claimed she would.

"That's why you owe it to yourself to try things out one more time. I bet Mr. Ten will deliver."

At that moment Pam saw Dillon's car pull into her yard. Moments later she watched him get out. Today he was wearing a pair of khakis and a dark green shirt. And just like yesterday and the day before, he looked handsome and utterly sexy.

Her gaze scanned over his body and, as if he knew she was staring out the window, he turned and looked directly toward her. She immediately felt heat suffuse her body at the same time blood gushed through her veins. Yes, there was no doubt in her mind that if given the chance he could deliver.

"Pam?"

"Yes?"

"When will you be seeing him again?"

Pam licked her lips as she continued to stare. Dillon hadn't moved. He was still standing in that same spot gazing through the window. He couldn't see her, although she could see him. Yet it was as if he knew she was there, knew he was holding her attention. She wondered if he had any clue about the thoughts flowing through her mind at that particular moment. If he did, he would probably jump back into the car and hightail it off her property.

"Pam?"

"I see him now, Iris. Through the kitchen window. He just drove up and has gotten out the car."

"Then the ball is now in your court, Pam. And you owe it to yourself to play it."


Dillon leaned back against his car as he stared into what he knew was Pam's secret window. Somehow he knew she was there, looking at him, with the same intensity with which he was looking at her.

Ramsey's words of last night rang in his ears, and the thought of wanting her made his breathing quicken and his guts clench. If she knew what he was thinking she probably wouldn't let him within a foot of her, and definitely not inside her house.

He had soaked in the bathtub in his hotel room last night with his eyes closed and thought about her. He had gone to bed thinking about her. And he had awakened that morning thinking about her. A woman who belonged to another man.

Not yet though, as Ramsey had pointed out to him last night.

He would be out of line to make a pass at her, so he wouldn't. But he intended to do everything to incite her to make a pass at him…if she was interested. If she wasn't, then he knew he would have to control his urges. But if she *was* interested, then those urges would be set free.

There was a chance that he was reading too much into the looks they had exchanged across the dinner table last night, or the heat that he'd felt. But there was only one way to find out. If she decided to indulge in this thing he felt between them, then that meant her relationship with Fletcher wasn't as tight as it needed to be.

Deciding he couldn't stay outside and stare into the window for the rest of the day, he drew in a deep breath before shifting his eyes away to move toward her front door. He took his time walking up the steps and by the time he lifted his hand to knock, the door had opened and she stood there.

His guts clenched harder as he lowered his hand to his side. She looked as beautiful as usual, but today she was wearing her hair differently. It appeared fluffed up and it billowed around her shoulders like she had used one of those curling irons on it.

His gaze moved from her head to her eyes and saw her watching him as intently as he was watching her. He then moved his gaze lower to her lips. They were the same lips he had dreamed about last night. Many times.

Then his eyes followed the hand that she nervously ran down her throat to the V of her knit top. He couldn't help but notice how her breasts swelled in perfect formation against the blouse.

"I've been waiting for you," she said, snagging his attention as his gaze shifted back to her face. Captured her eyes.

"I know," he said in a voice that sounded husky to his own ears.

He didn't think he needed to explain. For some reason he sensed that she fully understood. "Am I allowed in today?" he asked as a smile touched his lips. She had yet to move from in front of the door.

She blinked as if she'd just realized that fact. "Oops.

Sorry about that. Yes, please come in," she said before stepping aside.

He strolled past her, took a whiff of her scent and felt his entire body respond. Instantly. Why was the sexual chemistry between them stronger today than yesterday? More potent. Today, they seemed to be on instinct, with little or no control.

When she closed the door behind her and leaned back against it, she eyed him warily. He didn't say anything for a while. "And how are you doing today, Pam?"

"I'm doing fine," she said, in what sounded like a strained voice. "What about you?"

"I'm doing okay," he said. No need to tell her about his restless night, in which he had dreamed endlessly of her and all the things he wouldn't mind doing to her.

"I guess you're eager to get back to reading that journal."

He chuckled. He was eager all right, but that journal wasn't what was driving his eagerness. "Sort of."

Again he wasn't entirely sure just what was going on between them. What had happened since yesterday to make them so sexually charged that the very air they were breathing sizzled. He pulled in a deep breath, both feeling it and fighting it.

"I'm going up to the attic now," he said in a low voice, just loud enough for her to hear. "You probably have a lot to do, so forget that I'm here."

She smiled in a way that sent blood rushing all through him. "I doubt I'll be able to do that."

"Do what?" he asked.

She held his gaze. "Forget that you're here."

He wanted to ask why, but decided not to do so. She

was the one who was engaged. If any boundaries were going to be crossed, she would have to be the one to take the first step over. "You can try," he suggested.

"And if I can't?" she asked in a somewhat shaky tone.

Holding her gaze, he breathed in and pulled more sexually charged air into his lungs. He felt it stirring in his chest and flowing in his extremities, causing the lower part of him to harden. Throb. He even felt a sheen of sweat form on his brow, which compelled him to say, "Then you know where I am."

Without saying anything else, he turned and headed slowly up the stairs to the attic.

Pam leaned against the door and watched as Dillon disappeared up the stairs before releasing the breath she'd been holding. She was too shaken to think straight, and too tempted to follow him up those stairs to move away from the door.

She glanced down at the ring on her finger, the ring Fletcher had placed there. Instead of feeling guilt, she felt desperation as Iris's words rang loud in her ears. *"Then the ball is now in your court, Pam. And you owe it to yourself to play it."*

If only Iris knew just how much she wanted to play it. Maybe her best friend did know, which was why she'd said what she had. Iris did know love and she understood passion. She had been happy with Garlan and when Garlan had been taken away from her so suddenly and unexpectedly, Iris's life had nearly fallen apart.

She had been there for Iris, to encourage her to go

on with life, and now Iris was there for her, encouraging her to do something for herself before it was too late. Before she legally became Mrs. Fletcher Mallard.

But still, she needed to pull herself together and wondered why she would even consider following her impulses with a man she'd met only three days ago. What was there about Dillon that drew her to him, made her feel things she'd never felt before? Made her desire things she'd never before wanted?

*Something you'd tried twice and left you disappointed.*

Why did she think with him it would be different? Why did a part deep inside of her know that it would? It might be the way he looked at her, the heated intensity she felt from his gaze, the desire she saw even without him speaking a single word.

Those were the things that were urging her to move away from the door and propelling her to walk up the stairs, one step at a time.

Dillon stared at the words written in the journal, his eyes feeling the strain of seeing the words but not comprehending them. He had read the same sentence three times, but his mind was not on what Jay Novak had written close to a century ago. Instead his mind was on the woman he had left downstairs.

Why did some things have to be so complicated? Why had the Novaks' homestead been the first place on his list in his quest to find the key to his heritage as the eldest son of the Denver Westmorelands? And why was he lusting after a woman who another man had already claimed?

Dillon closed the journal and rubbed his hand down his face. Fletcher Mallard was a successful business-man and probably a prime catch for any woman in these parts. Evidently there was something about the man Pam had found to her liking.

*And there was evidently something about him that she'd also found lacking.*

No matter how things appeared, and regardless of the fact he'd only known her for three days, he refused to believe, or even consider the possibility that Pamela Novak was the type of woman who could love one man and mess around with another. So he could only come to the conclusion that she was not in love with Fletcher. Then why was she marrying him, Dillon wondered.

*Wealth? Prestige? Security?*

It hadn't been hard to figure out that Tammi had only been interested in him because he had made the pros, and the thought of being the wife of a profes-sional basketball player had stroked her fancy. When he had given it all up, had walked away to handle his family's business, he'd known she assumed it was only short term, although he'd always told her differently. When she couldn't get him to walk away from family obligations, she had left.

Dillon's thoughts were interrupted by the soft sound of footsteps approaching. He felt a quick tightness in his stomach. His entire being tensed in anticipation, knowing it could be only one person. He could no lon-ger sit, so he stood and had placed the journal aside by the time Pam crossed the threshold.

His heart began beating wildly in his chest and his body automatically hardened at the sight of her standing there. She had come to him. He hadn't been certain that she would, but she had.

His gaze scanned her body. He had meant to tell her earlier that he thought the outfit she was wearing, a white blouse and a dark blue skirt, looked good on her. It had been the first time he'd seen her legs and they were definitely a beautiful pair.

"Looks like it might rain later," she said. She strolled over to the window to glance out. While she looked out the window, he was looking at her. The sun was still shining so he wondered how she figured it might rain later. If anything, he figured it might snow. Like Denver, Gamble had its sunny days and cold nights, especially this time of the year. But at the moment he didn't care about either. The only thing on his mind right now was Pam.

She glanced over at him and he realized he hadn't responded to her earlier comment about the weather. "Yes, it just might rain," he said quietly.

She nodded and turned back to the window. His throat had started to go dry, while at the same time liquid fire raced through his veins. At that moment he decided she had made the first move and now it was time to make his.

Helplessly and with an urgency he felt all the way to the bottom of his feet, he slowly crossed the room, knowing each step was taking him closer to the woman he wanted. When he came to a stop behind her, she turned and looked up at him.

He gazed down into her face thinking she looked uncertain and indecisive. "You give. I take. No regrets," he said in a thick voice.

Dillon hoped she understood because he meant every word. She glanced down at the engagement ring on her hand and his gaze followed hers. And while he watched, she twisted the ring off her finger and then placed it on the windowsill.

Then she looked up, met his gaze and said in a soft, barely audible voice the exact same words he'd spoken to her. "You give. I take. No regrets."

Her words touched an inner coil within him, made desire drum through his entire body at a pace that had him breathing in deeply.

He took another step toward her and heard himself groan low in his throat at the same moment he reached out and pulled her into his arms. And with a hunger that he felt all the way to his toes, he lowered his mouth as she parted her lips. The connection was explosive, and sensations rocked through him as his mouth greedily took hers, desire flooding him from all corners and settling in his body part right below his belt.

His hands tightened around her waist when she began to tremble in his arms, and she kissed him back in a way that made everything within him, every single molecule, feel new, revitalized and energized. He couldn't recall the last time he had feasted on a woman's mouth the way he was feasting on hers.

He didn't want to take the time to pause to pull air into his lungs. He just wanted to keep kissing her, continue pressing against her middle to let her feel the hard, solid evidence of just what she was doing to him, how she was making him respond.

The kiss went on, seemed unending until the cell phone in his pants pocket sounded. Of all the times to get a damn signal, he thought, and for a moment he refused to release her mouth, needing to ply it over and over again with strokes of his tongue, although each flick inside her mouth was causing his muscles to contract in a way they had never contracted before.

He hoped the phone would stop ringing but when it didn't, he reluctantly pulled his mouth away from hers, after he'd swept his tongue against her already moist lips.

The ringing had ceased by the time he snatched the phone from his pocket and saw the missed call was a text from Ramsey. He checked the message and it said one word. Bane. Dillon gritted his teeth, wondering what the hell his baby brother had gotten into now.

He glanced over at Pam and thought at that moment he really didn't care, since Ramsey's message had interrupted the most passionate kiss of his entire life. Never had a kiss left him with his senses spiraling out of control and his entire body feeling like it had been torched into flames.

He knew Pam had been as affected by the kiss as he had. She seemed to be trying to pull herself together. They had done more than just grasped the moment, they had taken total control of it in a way that had them both still scraping for breath.

He watched as she slowly moved away from him to return to the window. She gazed out and he couldn't help wondering if she had reneged and now had regrets. He tensed, refusing to let her off his hook that easily. "Come to my hotel room tonight, Pam."

She swirled around and met his gaze but before she could open her mouth to say a single word, he reached out, pulled her back into his arms and took control of her mouth all over again.

The last time, he had kissed her with a need. This time it was with desperation. He refused to let her incriminate herself in any way, and if kissing her was the way to keep it from happening, then so be it. He would stand here and ply her mouth with his kisses forever if that's what he had to do.

A short while later, when he finally released her mouth, she looked somewhat dazed and her lips appeared slightly swollen. He lifted his hand and pushed her hair from her face, tempted beyond reason to sink his mouth onto hers again. Just the thought of doing so made his hand tremble. He hoped she knew this wasn't the end. Just the beginning.

And to make sure of it, he repeated the words he'd said earlier. "Come to my hotel room tonight, Pam."

Again she looked up and met his gaze. Her lashes fluttered just seconds before she replied, "No."

But before his heart could drop to the floor, she added, "Mr. Davis, the owner of the hotel, knows me, so that won't be a good idea. However, my drama school is only a few blocks away on Durand Street. Will you come there?"

He nodded quickly. "What time?"

"Eight," she said almost in a whisper. "I have a class tonight and everyone should be gone by then."

A moment of silence purred between them and then she searched his eyes. "So, will you come?"

A smile touched his lips and he reached out and stroked her cheek with the back of his hand, leaned closer to her and responded in a low, husky voice, "Sweetheart, nothing short of death is going to keep me away from you tonight."

# Chapter 6

Pam glanced around at the excited faces of her students. Practice had gone perfectly, with all of them knowing their lines. There was no doubt in her mind that nine-year-old Shauna Barnes had an acting career in her future. Everyone was gearing up for the play Dream Makers Drama Academy would be presenting next month, Charles Dickens's classic *A Christmas Carol*.

"Do you need me to stay behind and help you straighten things up?" Cindy Ruffin asked a short while later, after all the students had been dismissed and were rushing out the door. It hadn't rained as Pam had predicted, but a light layer of snow flurries were coming down.

"No, I'm fine," she said smiling.

Cindy had been a godsend. Her husband, Todd, had

been a classmate of Pam's and, like her, Todd had left Gamble for college. He'd played pro football until an injury ended his career. A few years ago, after Hurricane Katrina, Todd had decided to move his family from New Orleans and back to his hometown. Everyone in town was glad for Todd's return and within a year had talked him into running for mayor.

"I think the kids did an awesome job at practice tonight, don't you?" Cindy asked as a bright, cheery smile touched her lips.

"Yes, and I have to thank you and Marsha for it. You're the ones who have been working tirelessly with them while I've been dealing with paperwork," she said.

"Yes, but having you here is such an inspiration to them since it shows how successful you can be with hard work. You graduated from high school and went off to California to pursue your dream of acting. Do you miss it? All the glitz and glamour of Hollywood?"

Pam thought about Cindy's question. A part of her did miss it, but since she hadn't yet become a part of the "Hollywood crowd" there wasn't a lot she'd had to give up. She had gotten parts in a few low-budget movies, and her dates were mostly those planned by her agent for publicity purposes. She'd spent most of her free time studying her lines for auditions.

"No, I really don't miss it," she said honestly. "At least not as much as I thought I would. I have so much going on for me here."

"Yes, I can see that," Cindy said, glancing down at Pam's engagement ring. "You didn't make an official announcement about your engagement, but I gather a wedding is coming soon. Have you set a date yet?"

Pam swallowed deeply as she looked down at her hand. She had put the ring back on after Dillon had left. Whenever she thought about the kiss they had shared, she could feel her eyes glaze over and her cheeks burn. She had never been kissed that way before. Never.

Clearing her throat she said, "No, not yet."

After a few minutes more of conversation, Cindy left, leaving Pam all alone in the spacious residence that now housed the acting school. Several of the bedrooms downstairs had been converted into office space and classrooms, and the walls had been removed from the entire upstairs area to transform it into one vast studio.

The huge basement had been transformed into a mini-movie-set where scenes could be filmed. It was here at Dream Makers that she had starred in her first low-budget movie for the Gamble theater group. She would always appreciate her very humble beginnings here.

She glanced at her watch. It was a little past seven. She would have a chance to be by herself for a while before Dillon arrived, she thought.

*Dillon.*

She couldn't think about him without remembering the kiss they had shared earlier that day. And every time she did sensations too numerous to count would invade her body, sending a thrill through her. She'd heard of a man pushing a woman's buttons but, in Dillon's case, he not only pushed them, he had leaned right on them and pretty heavily at that. He had pressed them into another zone. She still felt wired up.

He had left her home shortly thereafter, saying he thought it would be best if he did so, fearing if he were to stay he might not be able to control himself. So she had watched him leave, Jay's journal tucked under his arm, while flutters of desire had overtaken her stomach.

Fletcher had called before she'd left home to tell her he had arrived in Montana safely but wouldn't be returning to Gamble at the end of the week as he'd planned. The insurance company was being difficult, so it would be the first of next week before he got back.

He had asked about Dillon, wanting to know if he was still hanging around town, and she had been up-front with him. Pam had informed him that Dillon had been invited back to dinner and had come to the house to finish going through the items in the attic. She could tell from the tone of Fletcher's voice he hadn't been pleased.

She had dropped by Lester Gadling's office before arriving at the academy and asked him to recheck her father's papers to make sure he hadn't missed something the first time. The attorney had seemed agitated by her visit, and had told her that he would do as she requested, but was confident that nothing would change. She had been hoping that somehow he had made a mistake.

After phoning in and checking on her sisters to make sure everything was okay and all their home-work was done, she began walking through all the rooms, tidying up as she went along. As it got closer to eight o'clock, she began to feel a nervousness tugging at her insides. And that same outlandish bout of desire that had overtaken her earlier that day was working its way upward from her toes to her midsection.

There was no doubt in her mind that tonight she and Dillon would do more than just kiss. She knew they would be sharing passion of the most intense kind. They would both give, they would both take and she was truly counting on neither of them having any regrets. Now that she'd thought everything through and was comfortable in her decision, she would admit that she needed him tonight. She wanted him. And she intended to have him.

After pulling into the empty parking lot, Dillon switched off the ignition and checked his watch. Noting it wasn't quite eight o'clock, he decided to stay put for a while.

Adjusting the car seat to accommodate his long legs, he stretched them out in front of him as he released a deep sigh. It seemed as if time had done nothing but drag by since he had seen Pam earlier. He'd nearly gone crazy waiting so he had tried reading more of the journal. So far all Jay Novak had written was information about the dairy business and how well he and Raphel worked together. Apparently, Jay hadn't been suspicious of the relationship between Raphel and Portia.

Dillon's thoughts shifted back to Pam. On the drive over from the hotel he had given himself a pep talk. Getting hyped up over a woman wasn't his typical style, but he'd discovered nothing about him was the norm when it came to Pamela Novak. From the moment he had first laid eyes on her, she had touched him in a way no other woman had ever done before, and that included Tammi.

He checked his watch again and as each minute ticked by so did his need to see her, be with her, hold her in his arms once more. He wanted to run his hands all over her and to taste her with his lips and tongue. He shifted in the seat as he felt his body get hard. It was cold outside, but the inside of his car was getting pretty damn hot.

Dillon tried to switch his concentration to something else, anything else, as he waited. His thoughts drifted to the conversation he'd had with Ramsey a few hours ago regarding the text message he'd sent. Ramsey had gotten an angry call from Carl Newsome. It seemed that Bane was hanging around the man's daughter again and making her dad downright unhappy to the point he'd threatened to do bodily harm to the youngest Denver Westmoreland if he didn't leave Crystal Newsome alone.

Dillon shook his head. For as long as he could remember, Crystal Newsome had been an itch his baby brother just had to scratch. If Bane didn't wise up and leave Crystal alone, that scratch might get him into hot water.

Dillon checked his watch again and after releasing a long breath, he opened the car door and got out. He couldn't recall the last time he'd sneaked around to meet a woman under the cover of night, but as he headed toward the entrance to the Dream Maker Drama Academy, he had a feeling that tonight such a move would be well worth it.

* * *

Pam's feet had touched the bottom stair when she heard the knock on the door. Without wasting any time, she moved in that direction. It was exactly eight o'clock.

As she got closer to the glass door, she could see Dillon through it. He was standing there staring at her with an intense look on his face. That look sent ripples through her body and made her shiver, although the temperature was warm inside. She nervously licked her lips as she opened the door and shivered even more when she felt a blast of cold air.

She quickly stepped back when Dillon walked in, and when he closed the door and gave her his dimpled smile, she felt heat bubbling up inside of her. As usual, he looked good. He had changed clothes and was now wearing dark slacks and a blue buttoned-up shirt. In place of his long coat he now had on a black leather bomber jacket.

She felt ridiculously happy to see him and for lack of anything else, she said, "It didn't rain today like I thought it would."

"No, it didn't rain." The warmth of his response matched the look in his eyes. As she stared deeper she saw that his dark depths seemed more hot than warm.

He glanced around and sensing his curiosity, she said, "Come on, let me show you around." She started to reach out and take his hand and then thought better of it. If she were to touch him now, any part of him, she would probably lose the little self-control she still had. For the next five minutes she took him on a tour of the academy and she could tell he was impressed with everything he saw.

"And the woman who used to live here was once a teacher of yours?" he asked, after she had completed her tour of the upstairs and was ready to show him the basement.

"Yes. Louise Shelton used to be my drama coach and was instrumental in my getting a scholarship to attend college in California. She died within a few months of my returning home after my father died. When she died she willed this place to me, with stipulations."

He lifted a brow. "What kind of stipulations?"

"That I could never sell it and that it would always be used for what it was intended, which was to be a drama academy. I don't have to stay here and run the school per se, but I have to make sure it is managed the way I know Louise would have wanted."

He nodded as he kept walking beside her. A part of her was aware they were wasting time when they both knew exactly what they wanted to do and why they had arranged to meet here at eight o'clock. She was willing to draw things out if he was; however, she doubted he had any idea of how being close to him, walking beside him, was messing with her senses and was stretching what little self-control she had to the limit. When they reached the basement stairs he slowed his steps to let her go first, and she could feel the intensity of his gaze on her again.

It took all she had to put each foot in front of her, being careful not to slip, knowing he was so close behind her, watching her every step. When she reached the bottom floor she turned to wait for him to join her.

*And to kiss her.*

She had a feeling he knew it. He probably had detected that fact by the way she was breathing, or by the way she was now looking up at him as he moved down the stairs toward her. No doubt it wasn't just one, but all of those things. And really, it didn't matter. What mattered was that he was intuitive enough to pick up on what she wanted and needed, and as soon as he joined her on the bottom floor, he placed his hands at her waist and pulled her into his arms. Before she could draw in her next breath, he leaned down and connected his mouth to hers.

Dillon figured he could stand there and sip on her all night.

*Then, maybe not.*

Plummeting into her mouth, tasting her like this, with such intensity, such greed and hunger, was making his entire body throb. Desire as thick as it could get, was spreading through him at a rate he could barely control.

He shifted his body, needing her to feel how aroused he was, which equated to just how much he wanted her. And just how much he needed her. He knew she was getting a clear picture when she wrapped her arms around his neck and shifted her body, adjusting it to his so that his erection was resting between the juncture of her thighs. And damn, it felt just like it was where it belonged, he thought.

*Well, not quite.*

Where it really belonged was deep inside of her. Hell, he was a man, a Westmoreland at that. He knew his male brothers and cousins that he'd grown up with, and he had met the male cousins from Atlanta. So there was no doubt in his mind they all had something in common when it came to basic primitive instincts. They all enjoyed making love to women.

He could imagine taking her all over the place. He wanted to make love to Pam in every room and every single position he could think of and then some. He could certainly get creative rather quickly. But first, this way, starting at her mouth, kissing her with a yearning that made him wonder where in hell a damn bed was when you needed one.

As if she sensed his agitation and the reason for it, she pulled her mouth away, took hold of his hand and led him through an area that looked like a soap-opera film set. They walked through a living room and dining room, caught a glimpse of a kitchen before going around a movable wall that led to a bedroom, one that was decorated with billowy white curtains at a fake window.

On a shuddering sigh she stopped by the bed, and Dillon gazed deep into her eyes. He could tell that she was about to get all nervous on him and decided to say the same words he'd spoken earlier that day. Words she seemed to understand and accept. "You give. I take. No regrets."

She stared at him for a moment and then he watched as her mouth curved into an easy smile. They would go through with their plans for tonight. No questions asked, no discussions needed. The main thing on his mind was getting inside of her, feeling her wetness surround him, clench him and milk him, which made him decide there was one subject open for discussion and he would initiate it. Birth control.

"I brought condoms," he said, patting the pocket of his slacks. There was no need to tell her just how many since it might scare her.

"And I'm on the pill." She bit nervously on her bottom lip and then added, "And I am not sleeping with Fletcher. I've never slept with him, in case you're wondering about that for health reasons."

*Fletcher.*

It was only then that he remembered the other man, which made him glance down at her hand. She had taken the ring off again. He wondered why she and her fiancé had never been intimate. Not that he was complaining.

He truly believed she was not a woman who could be in love with one man and sleep with another. That meant there was something about her engagement to Mallard that wasn't on the up-and-up. Sooner or later he intended to get some answers. But not now.

The only thing he wanted to get right now was some of her.

He suddenly detected that her scent had changed and, like a man acutely honed on the woman he wanted, he breathed her into his nostrils, a potent blend of perfume and body chemistry. It was an aroma that could drive a man wild and would make him want to get inside of her real quick and explode all over the place. But only after making sure she was ready to detonate right along with him.

For a long time after Tammi had left he had kept his guard up around women, and had only dated when he got a physical urge to mate as a way to relax, relieve stress and keep his abundance of male hormones in check. But there was something different about Pam, something he'd picked up on the first moment he'd seen her.

She sparked to life something inside of him and he knew making love with her was about more than just blowing off steam. More than great sex. It was about a connection he had never felt before with a woman. A connection on a plane so high it had his insides throbbing.

On a deep, shuddering breath he reached out and tilted her chin up, needing to plunge into her mouth once more, to intensify the connection he already felt. And when she automatically pressed closer to him, he deepened the kiss and slid his arms around her, holding her in a tight grip, as if he never wanted to let her go.

He gave full concentration to her mouth, just as he had done earlier that day. He'd once heard a woman say that you hadn't been kissed unless you'd been kissed by a Westmoreland. Dillon wanted to make sure after tonight that Pam thought the same thing.

So with thorough precision and a masterful meticulousness, Dillon took his time and put his tongue to work. He penetrated it into areas of her mouth that had her groaning, and then he flicked it around in a way that seemed to jar her senses—if the sounds she was making were any indication. He enjoyed kissing her, but moments later he knew he wanted more. Pulling his mouth from hers he took a step back to remove his jacket.

After tossing it across a chair he whispered, "Undress me and then I will undress you." He intended to save her—the best—for last.

A pair of uncertain eyes stared up at him in a way that had him asking, "You have done this before, right?"

He watched a lump appear in her throat as she swallowed, and then she said in a strained voice, "Which part?"

*Which part?* He lifted a curious brow before responding. "Any of it."

She shrugged her feminine shoulders. "I've had sex before, if that's what you're asking. While in college. Twice. But it wasn't good. Both times it was over before it got started. And I've never undressed a man."

She then lowered her gaze for a second before returning her eyes to his with a flush on her face. "I've said too much, haven't I?" she asked softly. "Given too much information?"

As far as Dillon was concerned, it definitely hadn't been too much information. What she'd just said was something he needed to know. Now he was aware of just what she needed and how she needed it. If any woman deserved to be made love to the Westmorelands' way, it was her. And he intended to do the honors. Proudly. Gladly. Tonight would be a night she wouldn't easily forget. In fact, he planned on taking things slow and making sure every aspect of the evening stayed in her memory forever.

"No, you've told me what I needed to know," he said.

In fact, he was sure there had to be more, like why the man she intended to marry hadn't done his job. But they would talk about Fletcher later.

"I'm going to make undressing me worth your while," he said, smiling at her, already imagining her hands on him, all over him. "Go ahead, baby, and do your thing."

She gave him a hesitant smile before reaching out, and the moment her fingers began working on the buttons of his shirt his stomach knotted, and it was all he could do to remember he was supposed to go at a slow pace and not be tempted to speed up the process. This first round would be hers and he intended to make it special for her, even if it killed him.

Pam pushed the shirt off Dillon's shoulders and marveled at how broad they were. She couldn't resist the temptation to touch them, amazed at the strength she felt in them. Then her hands slid to the dark hairs of his chest and she glanced down and saw his hard, flat abdomen. Dillon had a beautifully powerful body, she thought.

Deciding she wanted to check out other areas of that body, she trailed her fingers downward. The moment she did so, she heard his sharp intake of breath and glanced up to his face. The eyes watching her beneath lowered lashes were dark, smoky, sensuous.

Knowing they didn't have all night, she unhooked his belt and pulled it through the loops before tossing it to join his jacket and shirt on the chair. She glanced back up at him. "I need to take your boots and socks off before going any further," she said softly.

He smiled before sitting down on the bed so she could remove his boots and socks. When that was finished, she stepped back as he stood again. Instinctively, her hands went to his waist and she eased down his zipper. Tugging it down wasn't as easy as she'd thought it would be, mainly because of the size of his erection. It was hard to believe that he wanted her *that* much.

"Need help?"

She glanced up at him. "I'll be okay once I get this zipper past here."

He chuckled. "Here where?"

She couldn't help chuckling with him before replying, "You know where. And why do you have to be so big?" Too late. She couldn't believe she'd actually asked that.

Embarrassed to the core, she peered back up at him and saw the huge smile on his face. "This isn't funny, Dillon Westmoreland."

"No, sweetheart, that is the most precious thing anyone has ever said to me."

She knew he was teasing, of course, and after working with his zipper a few moments more it finally cooperated. She was able to tug his pants down his legs as he stepped out of them. Satisfied, she took a step back. There was only one piece left, his briefs. She frowned, wondering why she hadn't thought to remove them with his pants.

"It's not all that serious," he said in a deep, husky voice.

"Maybe not for you, but it is for me," she said, giving him a playful pout. "This is my first time and I have to get it right."

A smile curved his lips. "No, you don't. You can get it all wrong and I will still make love to you tonight."

His words, as well as the determined look in his eyes, did something to her, made her eager to remove his final piece of clothing. She was curious to unveil that part of him that had given her the most trouble. From the way the briefs fit him she had a pretty good idea of just how well-endowed he was. The rest of him was exceedingly toned, definitely virile and oh-so-male.

She inserted her fingers into the waistband of his briefs and gently tugged them down his hips, having no easier time getting them off than she had his slacks. But what removing them fully exposed to her eyes had been well worth the trouble. The man's body was perfect in clothes, but she was particularly enjoying this view of him out of clothes. She had seen a naked man before, but not one this well put together. Not one this large and hard.

"Is there a problem?"

She glanced up and met his gaze, suddenly feeling shy, awkward and unsure of her capabilities where he was concerned. "I hope not," she said softly.

"There *is* not," he countered. "Go ahead, feel your way. Touch it." And then in a lower voice he said, "Get to know it."

*Get to know it?* She had never fondled a man before in her life but, doing what he suggested, she reached out and first ran her fingers over the tip, fascinated by the feel of the smooth head. Then she traced with her fingertips a path along the sides, marveling at the swollen veins. And when she finally got the nerve to close her hand around him, he moaned out loud.

She quickly loosened her hand. "Sorry, I didn't mean to hurt you."

"It didn't hurt. In fact, just the opposite. Your touch feels good."

She smiled at that. "Really?"

"Yeah."

"Umm, in that case…" She began stroking her hand up and down the length of his thick erection. Her gaze held tight to his face and watched how his eyes became glazed and his lips seemed to tremble. She smiled, satisfied with her efforts and what they were doing to him.

"Not so bad for an amateur, wouldn't you say?" She beamed, feeling like she had accomplished something monumental and proud of herself for doing so. She allowed her hands to get more brazen while watching his erection get harder, and feeling it thicken in her hands.

"I have no complaints," he said in what sounded like a tortured moan. His physical reaction fascinated her, brought out a level of womanly pride that drove her boldness.

"When you're through having your fun then it's my turn," he said in a voice that to her ears sounded like an intoxicated slur.

She considered the wisdom of continuing what she was doing for too long and stole a peek at him from under her lashes. His eyes were closed and his head was tilted back at an angle that showed the veins in his neck. They looked like they were straining. Almost ready to pop.

"Hey, I'm merely doing what I was told. You said

to get to know it," she said defensively, but couldn't hide her smile.

Deciding she'd gotten to know him very well, she released him and stepped back and watched as he slowly regained control. Then he stared at her and muttered in a low, throaty voice, "Now it's my time to get you naked."

Getting her naked would be just the start, Dillon thought, looking at her and imagining just how she would look without her jeans and sweater. Even now she looked sexy, with her raven-black hair spilling around her shoulders, a few loose tendrils cascading around her face. Making love to her had been on his mind since leaving her house, and now that he was here, standing stark naked in front of her, knowing that soon, very soon, he would be inside of her sent his entire body into an intense throb mode.

"Come here, Pam," he murmured in a breathless tone, and watched as she didn't hesitate to cover the short distance between them.

When she was within close range, he reached out and snagged her by the waist and brought her closer to the fit of him, and was sure, without a doubt, that she could feel his hardness and his heat, through her jeans.

But he wanted more. He wanted to give her more. Wanted to let her feel more. And with that thought firmly planted in his mind, he reached out and pulled her sweater over her head. Moments later he slung it onto the chair. Her lacy black bra was sexy, but also needed to come off, and he proceeded to remove it. Like her sweater, he sent it flying to the chair.

"Good aim," she leaned closer to say, her breath warm against his throat.

"Thanks," he uttered raspily, his gaze giving her breasts full attention. Her breasts were full, firm twin mounds supported by delicate, feminine shoulders. As if a magnet was drawing his gaze, his eyes were pulled to the nipples and, unable to resist temptation, he took the pad of his finger to flick across both hardened tips.

But he wanted to do more than just look and touch. He wanted to taste them and, with that thought in mind, he leaned in and lowered his mouth to close over a quivering, delicious-looking peak.

"Dillon."

The moment she said his name he stuck out his tongue to run it across a nipple before pulling it into his mouth to suck in all earnestness. He didn't even try to change his stance when she lifted her hand to support the back of his head to keep right where he was, to continue what he was doing. Not that he intended to stop. The taste of her breasts was arousing him and, with an easy movement, he shifted his mouth to the other nipple to greedily ply it with the same attention.

By the time he lifted his head and met her gaze he could barely keep his entire body from trembling. A need for her, to make love to her, surged through him and he stooped down on bended knees to remove her shoes and socks. To maintain her balance she placed a hand on his shoulder and her touch sent his muscles rippling as sensations roared through him, made him clench his teeth.

After removing her shoes and socks, he stood, straightened his body to his full height and without saying a single word he reached for the waistband of her jeans. Somehow he managed to hold it together until she stood before him in nothing more than sexy, black, lacy, high-cut panties. They were panties he would be taking off her and he was fighting the urge to just rip them off her instead.

Getting back on his knees he began lowering her panties down her long, gorgeous legs, and sucked in a deep breath when her scent surrounded him. He shot a glance upward and saw the heated look of desire in her eyes.

It took all his strength to stand, and without wasting any more time, he reached out and swept her into his arms. Holding her gently he moved to the bed and together they tumbled back onto the covers.

## Chapter 7

Pam felt her stomach stir when she gazed up into Dillon's eyes. She had ended up on her back between his firm thighs, with him towering over her. At that very moment she felt several things. Captured. Ensnarled. His.

She forced the last from her mind immediately. How could a woman be engaged to one man and possessed by another? She didn't want to be confused by anything now, and she certainly didn't want to think about Fletcher. This was her time, this sensual interlude, her moment to seize something she might never have again.

*You give. I take. No regrets.*

And from the eyes bearing down on her and the arms locked on both sides of her, she had a feeling Dillon Westmoreland was more than ready to take everything she had to give. And there would be no time for regrets.

He began lowering his head and she lifted hers upward to meet his mouth. The moment they touched, he began devouring her with a hunger and need that she felt all the way to her toes. He had kissed her greedily before, but this was a different kind of ravenousness, one that bordered on insatiability. As if, no matter how many times he kissed her or how deep and thorough the kisses, he would never be able to get enough. However, that didn't mean he wouldn't try. And in this case, trying meant using his tongue to pleasure her in a way she'd never been pleasured before. No man before had taken so much time, had concentrated on so much detail during a kiss. It was a practice that he'd perfected and she was the satisfied recipient.

He gave all and held back nothing. Provoking her, tempting her, almost demanding of her to give back. So she did, by boldly returning his kiss with his same voraciousness. She wrapped her arms around his neck as he sank his mouth even deeper onto hers. Her response was wanton, her desires keen and her senses at the moment were shot to hell.

He broke off the kiss at the same time his hands began to move all over her as he held her gaze. Starting at the center of her throat, he slowly inched a path downward toward her chest. When he reached her breasts and ran the pad of his thumb across the protruding tips, pleasure, as sharp as it could get, rammed through her and she almost forgot to breathe. And when he leaned closer to replace his fingers with his mouth, she felt heat circulate then settle between her legs.

When he brought his tongue into the mix she gasped. Suddenly she felt full as if she needed to scream out, but could not. The most she could do was summon up enough energy to moan. Then his mouth released her breasts and he began trailing a heated path down to her navel with his tongue. He seemed fascinated with her belly button and she felt his wet tongue all around it. She shuddered as her stomach tightened and then relaxed, over and over again.

And when she thought he would be returning to her mouth, he shifted his body, lifted her hips and dipped his head. The moment the scalding tip of his tongue went inside her womanly core, she emitted a loud moan. At the same time, she heard his growl of male satisfaction. It was evident from the way he was using his tongue inside of her, that he enjoyed this type of lovemaking. He went about it with such ardent dedication that she was nearly in tears. She was pinned between his mouth and the mattress. She realized that he didn't intend on letting her go anywhere until he got his fill.

And he didn't intend to be rushed.

He was meticulous in his lovemaking, pushing her just to the peak, driving her close to the edge again and again. She couldn't suppress her response and groaned shamelessly, holding firm to his shoulders while she was his enjoyment. And even moments later when she let out a scream as a tide of pleasure came crashing down on her, his mouth remained locked on her, as if determined to savor every last bit of her.

It was only later, when she felt weak as water and was panting for breath, that he lifted his mouth to withdraw from her. He leaned back on his haunches, licked his lips and gave her a smile that made her come all over again.

There was nothing more beautiful than seeing a woman clutched in the throes of ecstasy, Dillon thought, as he studied Pam's features. And just knowing he'd been the cause sent desire clamoring all through him and made his already hard body feel harder.

With her glazed eyes on him, he eased off the bed to reach for his pants. Going through the pockets he pulled out several condom packets and tossed all but one on the nightstand. He then proceeded to put the one on, knowing Pam watched his every move.

He was a man who'd never had a problem with his nakedness and the thought that he was on display, exposed and being checked out from head to toe, didn't bother him in the least. The only thing on his mind was making love to the woman in that bed. And what a picture she made. Sexy. Naked. Exposed. It seemed that she didn't have a problem with nudity, either, and he was glad of that.

He returned to the bed and drew her to him, needing to hold her, needing to touch her, needing to kiss her. His mouth found hers again and he moved his hand downward toward her parted thighs. Inserting a finger inside of her, he captured her gasp right in their kiss.

He even swallowed her moan when his finger began moving inside of her, slowly with determined and well-defined strokes, glorying in her wetness, breathing in her aroused scent. All the while their mouths and tongues were mating greedily, and with a need that he felt in every part of his body, especially his throbbing shaft.

Not sure he could last much longer, he pulled away slightly to ease her back deep into the mattress as he shifted into position, simultaneously spreading her thighs and locking her hands above her head in his.

He changed positions again to get the lower part of his body in perfect formation, with the head of his erection right at her entrance. And then, while she watched him, he began lowering his body, surging inside of her. The moment his head came in contact with her heat he wanted to thrust inside, but felt that this was something he had to savor, even if it killed him.

And with every inch he pushed inside of her, he felt as if he was literally dying. She was tight and her body muscles clamped down on him, clutched him for all it was worth, and in response he released her hands to grip her hips, determined to go as deep inside as he could go.

A world of absolute pleasure began closing in on him, engulfing him with an urge to move. He cupped her bottom closer, so he could delve deeper, and with slow, steady strokes, he began staking his claim on her. Every time he slid inside of her and every time he slid out, he felt a sharp pull on his sanity, an increased dose of pleasure and a fortitude to drive into her the same heated, silken force that was driving him.

It worked. She began moving with him, joined him, clenched him, milked him to the point he felt everything was getting pulled out of him. He locked his legs with hers and then, while buried deep inside of her, he began flexing his lower body in a way to get as close as he could get, sinking into her deep, mating with her hard, thrusting into her rapidly. And when she screamed his name, he threw his head back when the same infused pleasure that ripped through her, tore through him.

And the name that he moaned from his lips was hers. The body he was exploding inside of was hers. And the lips he knew he had to taste at that very moment were hers.

Everything was about her, as well as her ability to make him feel things no other woman could make him feel was artfully and enticingly being transmitted in a satisfying way. Emotions he couldn't define, and not just on a physical plane, energized his muscles and made his hunger for her that much more intense. Making love with her wasn't just good, it was brutally good. So good he actually felt whipped. His senses shattered in a thousand pieces and, as sensations continued to race through her and spread into him, he felt a sense of fulfillment he knew that he could only find with her.

Pam wondered if she would have the ability to ever move again, and wasn't sure if she even wanted to. Even now she was wrapped in Dillon's arms, their legs entangled, their arms entwined and their bodies still intimately connected. She felt drained, worn out, deliciously sated in a way that almost made her purr.

The way he was draped across her, she didn't have to move her head to look into his eyes, since he was there, staring at her with the same amazement and sexual fulfillment in his eyes that she felt in her body.

This was what Iris had wanted her to experience at least once in her life and now she was glad that she had. This had been the ultimate in sexual satisfaction, the most gratifying, mind-blowing passion.

She had used muscles she hadn't ever used before, and she'd found every part of him, both working and nonworking, to have a definite purpose. She could only lie in awe, while her heart tried to slow down from beating so fast in her chest.

She felt cherished, protected and desired. Not only in the way he was looking at her, but at the gentle caress of his hand moving on her thigh, like he still had to touch her in some way, even in the aftermath of shared sexual bliss.

Pam moved her lips to say something but no words came out. It was just as well, because he leaned up and captured her mouth in his. She raised her hand to his cheek, needing to touch him, and to feel the movement of his mouth on hers beneath her palm.

When he finally broke the kiss she felt perfectly contented and when he finally released her, slowly pulled out of her to go to the bathroom, she felt a profound sense of loss. She watched for him to return and when he appeared, lounging naked in the doorway, his long, muscular legs braced apart, she thought his stance had a masculine sexiness that almost made her drool. Her gaze moved all over his body and the main thing she couldn't help but notice was that he was fully aroused again.

Seeing him in that state did something to her own body—made her feel alive, wanton, desired. His gaze scorched her, as he slowly scanned her entire body, lingering on her legs before moving upward to the juncture of her thighs. And there his gaze stayed, transfixed for a spell, and she felt the heat of it on her womanly core. She forced down a deep, shuddering breath when he began moving toward her and she couldn't help noticing the swell of muscles in his broad shoulders and the wide expanse of a strong, solid chest.

He paused by the bed, giving her a totally male smile while he proceeded to put on another condom. She watched the entire process, unable to force her gaze away. A heavy silence hung over the room.

And then she sat up in the bed and opened her arms to him. He moved, placed a knee on the bed, went into her arms and planted his mouth on hers. And as he adjusted their positions to ease her back deep onto the bed, the thought that continued to run through her mind was that tonight was their one and only time together. She desperately wished it could last.

A few hours later, they stood fully dressed together in the foyer of the academy. It was a little past midnight and time for them to part. Together they had stripped the bed and changed the linen. Then she had made them a cup of hot chocolate and they'd sat down at the kitchen table. Not much was said between them, as there was nothing left to be said. They were both deep in their own thoughts.

He had Jay Novak's journal back at the hotel, so he couldn't use the excuse of visiting her place to read it. But he wanted to see her again. Be with her again. In fact, he intended to be a part of her life.

He mentally scrambled to make sense of that decision and released a deep breath when he finally did. She had touched a part of him in a way he could not walk away from. She might have assumed this was a one-night stand, but as far as he was concerned that was not the case.

He didn't harbor any guilt that he was no better than Raphel in cutting in on another man's territory. If nothing else he had discovered, before even kissing her that first time, that she really didn't belong to Fletcher; at least not the way a woman should belong to the man she was about to marry—heart, body and soul. Totally and completely.

Now was still not a good time to bring up that fact and ask why she would even consider marrying a man she didn't love, a man who hadn't introduced her to passion. At first he'd thought he could get beyond that curiosity, deciding it was strictly her business. But that was no longer the case. Now it was his business, as well, mainly because as far as he was concerned Fletcher Mallard was not the man she needed.

He was.

Some may consider him thinking such a thing as arrogant, possibly even a little egotistical, and they probably would be right in their assumption, he thought. But something had happened tonight in that bed, something he couldn't dismiss. Every time he went inside of her, he'd felt more than just sexual pleasure. He'd felt a sense of belonging. He'd felt a connection he could not explain and a deep, abiding need to claim her.

As far as he was concerned he wasn't taking anything away from Mallard, because it was quite obvious that the man didn't have a claim on her anyway.

The only stamp Mallard had on her was the ring she had placed back on her finger. And, although he didn't particularly like the sight of it there, he would tolerate it for now.

His gaze moved from her hand to her face. She was staring out into the night. It was time to leave but neither was making an effort to do so. He knew he couldn't mention to her what he was thinking. For whatever reason she had decided to marry Mallard. He had news for her, but it wouldn't be delivered tonight. He would give her time to make her own decision about things—namely in his favor. And if she didn't, then he would intervene. He was the one who had introduced her to passion and he would be the one who would continue on with her lessons.

In the meantime, he would learn what kind of hold Mallard had on her to make her agree to a loveless and passionless marriage.

At that moment she looked up and met his gaze and he knew, whether she realized it or not, she was now his. That conclusion sent an immediate jolt to his nervous system, stimulated his brain and made every muscle in his body feel a strength of resolve he hadn't felt in a long time. He needed time to think, but for now, he'd just accept things the way they were.

Silently, he reached out and began buttoning up her coat. Surprised, she blinked, then smiled up at him while studying his face. "Thank you. You take such good care of me."

He smiled back, deciding not to tell her the reason he did so was because she belonged to him. Instead, he said, "You've been too hot to suddenly have to get cold."

She laughed and then reached out and placed her arms around his neck. "Yes, I have been hot tonight and all because of you. You're special, Dillon. I've known you for only a short time, but it seems like I've known you my entire life."

He understood what she was saying, because he felt the same way about her. He'd never been a man who would lay claim to a woman after sleeping with her just one time. But with Pam, things were different. He didn't know how, he just accepted that they were.

He felt his lips curve into a smile as he asked, "I never believed in that paranormal stuff, but do you think we could have been together in another life?"

He watched her brow furrow and then moments later the answer was in her eyes. "No," she said. "Nothing would have obliterated from my mind the kind of passion I felt tonight had I shared it once before with you," she said and smiled.

"What I shared with you tonight is something I've never shared before with any man. So there has to be another reason why I feel so free and uncontrolled with you."

He felt the same way. There had to be a reason why he felt free and uncontrolled around her as well. But whereas she might accept what they had shared tonight as a casual affair, he could not. If she figured he would just walk away, leave Gamble and head back to Denver without a second glance, then she was wrong. Dead wrong.

And to show her how wrong she was, he raised

a hand to her face and caressed her cheek. "Tonight was very special to me, Pam. I've never met a woman quite like you."

He could tell by the look in her eyes that she didn't know what to make of his words. That was fine because soon enough she would. He lowered his head and captured her lips in a slow yet greedy fashion. He felt her shudder beneath his mouth and when she tightened her arms around his neck, he deepened the kiss.

He wanted her. And he would have her. As far as he was concerned, she was already his. That was the Westmorelands' way. The ability to recognize his or her true mate when he encountered her or him, although they might initially try to deny it. He would be the first to admit some Westmorelands were stubborn, and he had discovered that trait wasn't confined to just the Denver clan. He'd been told that the Atlanta Westmorelands were just as bad.

He could now admit that he had made a mistake with Tammi in thinking she was the one. He felt certain there was no mistake with Pam. And for him to be so sure of that so soon might be a mystery to some, but not to him.

He slowly and reluctantly withdrew from her mouth, but for the moment he refused to release her from his arms. "I'm walking you out to the car and then I'm following you home to make sure you get there safely," he whispered against her ear.

She pulled back and a cautious look appeared on her face. "You don't have to do that."

"Yes, I do." For *reasons you can't possibly imagine,* he thought. But he simply asked, "Ready to go?"

"Yes, but…" She studied his face. "Tonight…"

She didn't continue, but nervously moistened her top lip with her tongue, an action that had him forcing back a rush of desire.

"What about tonight?"

"Tonight was tonight. Tomorrow remains the same. I'm engaged to Fletcher."

He looked down at her. A shaft of light from the fixtures in the parking lot came through the glass door and slanted across her face, making her look so beautiful he felt his heartbeat increase. He silenced the response he really wanted to make—one that clearly stated her engagement was evidently in name only and regardless, she was his, signed, sealed and so deliciously delivered. His stomach clenched just thinking about their lovemaking.

Her expression indicated she expected him to understand and to accept her words. There was no use telling her he wasn't about to do either. Instead, he knew he would do what he had to do. The first thing was to find out why she had gotten engaged to a man like Mallard in the first place.

So to bide his time, he pushed a strand of hair back from her face. "I know," he said.

Those two words were all he was capable of saying to her right now. "Let me walk you to the car."

She held back, refusing to move an inch as she studied his face for a moment. "You don't need to come to the house tomorrow, do you?"

He swallowed deeply. She was trying to cut ties now. She didn't have any regrets about tonight but she knew she couldn't continue. "No, I'll take the next couple of days and stay at the hotel and relax and read the journal. If you need me for anything, you know where to reach me."

She nodded and then moved toward the door. He walked by her side. He would give her two days and if she didn't come to him, engaged or not engaged, he would be going after her.

## Chapter 8

"We don't understand, Pammie. Why did Dillon stop coming for dinner?"

Pam glanced across the dinner table at Nadia, knowing how her baby sister operated. Nadia would ply her with the same question until she got what she considered a satisfactory answer. Pam wasn't sure that her response would be satisfactory, but judging by the three pairs of eyes staring at her, Nadia wasn't the only one waiting to hear what she had to say.

Pam could make it easy on herself and place the blame on the three of them by claiming they were the ones who'd scared him off, and that Dillon had been fully aware of their little matchmaking schemes at dinner and preferred to have no part of it. But telling her sisters that would not be the truth. Dillon had said on more than one occasion that he enjoyed her sisters' company and that they reminded him of his female cousins back in Denver. He had taken their shenanigans in stride and hadn't seemed bothered in the least.

"Pammie?"

Nadia's soft voice pulled her back to the moment and she glanced across the table. Before Pam could open her mouth to answer, Paige spoke up in a disheartened tone. "He doesn't like us any more than Fletcher does, does he?"

Pam was taken aback by her sister's assumption. "That's not true. Dillon really likes the three of you and enjoys dining with us, but he has our great-grandfather's journal and has been doing a lot of reading over the past couple of days. You must not forget the reason he came to town in the first place."

She took in a deep breath before continuing. "And as for Fletcher, you girls are wrong about him. He does like you."

"Then why is he planning to send us away after the two of you get married?" Nadia asked with a belligerent look on her face.

Pam was surprised by her sister's question. "Where on earth did you get such an utterly absurd idea? Fletcher is not planning to send you away after we get married."

Nadia's frown deepened and a worried look lit her eyes. "He is, too. He told Gwyneth Robards's father that he is, and her father told her mother, and Gwyneth overheard them talking and she told me."

Pam frowned. Gwyneth Robards was Nadia's best friend. Her father, Warren Robards, owned a slew of sporting goods stores across the state. He and Fletcher were good friends. Pam was not one to believe in gossip. She wished Nadia wouldn't do so, either. "Nadia, there's no way Fletcher would have said something like that."

"So, are you saying Gwyneth's father lied?"

Pam frowned. "What I'm saying is that Gwyneth apparently misunderstood what she heard from her parents' conversation. Again, there's no way Fletcher could have said that."

What she didn't add was that he knew why she was marrying him—to save her family home, to secure a future for her sisters and to keep the family together. Even if they were to lose their home, her sisters would return to California with her or they all would remain in Gamble and make do.

"Getting back to Dillon, Pam," Jill said. "I don't care how much reading he has to do, he has to stop and eat sometime. Did you invite him to dinner the last three nights?"

Pam nervously bit down on her bottom lip. She hadn't invited Dillon to dinner the first night because they had planned their secret meeting that night at the academy. And she hadn't invited him the past two nights because she had needed time to get herself together after their night of passion.

"No," she finally said. "Like I said, Dillon has a lot to read. He said as much the last time he was here."

"So you will invite him back?"

Pam's stomach knotted. Again, three pairs of eyes focused on her. "Yes, I'd invite him back but it's up to him whether he would come. Like I said, there's a reason why he came to Gamble and it's not to keep us entertained."

As if satisfied with her answer, her sisters resumed eating their dinner and the conversations then revolved around what had happened at school that day. She was glad their interests had shifted to other things, although hers remained on Dillon. Every time she thought about that night and all the things they'd done and shared, she would get all flushed inside, her body aching for a repeat. There was no doubt in her mind that if she were to see Dillon now, her body would weaken. If he were to make an attempt to kiss her, or even remotely suggest he wanted to take her to bed again, she would not be able to resist him.

She hadn't talked to him or seen him since that night. He had left a message for her on the answering machine yesterday indicating he'd decided to change hotels and had checked into one in Rosebud. Unlike Gamble, the neighboring city of Rosebud had a number of cell towers in close proximity so there was always a signal. She understood that he would want to stay connected to the outside world since he was a businessman.

He had provided the name of the hotel, which was only a ten-mile drive from Gamble. She had thought about calling him back to let him know she'd gotten the message, but had eventually talked herself out of it. She knew she would see him again, because eventually he had to return the journal. She was hoping that by then she wouldn't be thinking so much about how his kisses had felt on her lips, or just how good he'd felt going into her body. And then, how she'd felt when he was inside of her. She tightened her thighs together at the memory.

She licked her lips and then picked up her glass to take a sip of her cold tea, needing to relieve her suddenly hot throat. She forced her thoughts to shift to what Gwyneth thought she'd overheard about Fletcher's plan to send her sisters away. She'd ask Fletcher about the rumor when he called later that evening. She figured that he would be calling before she left for her evening class at the academy.

Halfway through dinner the phone rang and she pushed her chair from the table and crossed the room to answer it. "Yes?"

"How are things going, Pamela?"

A part of her wished she could feel some excitement, some fluttering of sensations anywhere in her body at the sound of Fletcher's voice, but that wasn't happening. Her heart slammed painfully in her chest at that realization. "Everything is fine, Fletcher. How are things with you? Is that problem in Bozeman getting corrected?"

"Yes, in fact, I have good news. I might be back in Gamble this weekend instead of next Tuesday."

She swallowed deeply and tried to put a smile in her voice. "That is good news."

"And do you know what would make me extremely happy, Pamela?"

She dared not try to guess. "No, what?"

"If you've decided on our wedding date by the time I return. I know you prefer waiting until February, but I want to marry this year, so a Christmas wedding is what I prefer."

All of a sudden she felt her stomach drop. Christmas was next month. "I can't possibly get things together by then."

"What do you need to do other than show up at the church? Besides, I hate to bring this up, but I'd like to satisfy that mortgage on your home as soon as possible. That's one of my wedding gifts to you."

Pam's eyes narrowed. In his own passive-aggressive way, Fletcher was reminding her of the reason she had agreed to marry him. "I'm sure you want that matter resolved and done with as soon as possible, right?" he added.

"Yes, of course."

"So will you have a date for me when I get back to Gamble?" he asked.

She stole a glance at the dining room table where her sisters were chatting away. They had happy looks on their faces and she was determined to keep it that way. They were smart, all three of them, and she'd made a promise to herself at her father's funeral to do whatever it would take to make sure they got the best life had to offer.

"Pamela?"

She breathed in deeply. "Yes. I'll have a date for you but I won't promise it will be this year."

He didn't say anything for a moment and then she heard the frustration in his tone. "Let's start with the date and I hope it's one we will both agree to."

Knowing he was probably about to ask her about Dillon, she quickly jumped in to say, "Nadia is bothered about something, Fletcher, and I'm sure it's all a misunderstanding, but I thought I'd mention it anyway."

"What?"

"She thinks you're sending her away when we get married. I assured her that wasn't the case and—"

"That has crossed my mind."

Pamela stopped talking in midsentence. Her hand tightened on the phone. "Excuse me?"

He must have heard the cutting anger in her tone. "Calm down, Pamela. It's not what you think. You have smart sisters and I think they're getting a wasted education going to that public school in Gamble. As you know, I went to a private school and I received a top-notch education. The best. And I know you want Nadia and Paige to get accepted into a good college. Going to a private high school will not only assure them a good education, but also entrance into the best colleges. That's what you want, right?"

"Yes, but—"

"And just think, they would be associating with people who will benefit them in the long run."

"Yes, but I'm not for sending them away from home," she whispered, so her voice would not carry to the dining room. She had just assured Nadia that she wouldn't.

"I know, which is why I'm looking into schools in Cheyenne. That's not too far away," he said, as if she would be glad to hear the news.

She moved away from the kitchen and into the living room, which would afford her more privacy. "As far as I'm concerned, if it's not here in Gamble then it's too far away."

"But we'll be looking out for their futures. There's a wonderful private school there that has excellent living facilities and great security."

Pam tried to keep a ripple of anger from consuming her. "You should have talked to me about this first, Fletcher."

"It was going to be another one of my wedding gifts. I know how much your sisters' futures mean to you."

Pam closed her eyes. "We can discuss this more when you return."

"I don't understand why you're upset. I'd think it would be what you wanted. At least I believe it's what you told me you wanted that day you accepted my marriage proposal."

Pam couldn't say anything. Was it really fair to get upset with him when she *had* said those things?

"If that's not what you want, Pamela, then no sweat. I want to do whatever makes you happy," he said in a throaty, low voice that did nothing but frustrate her even more.

"I know, Fletcher, and I appreciate everything you're doing, but we'll need to talk about this when you get back."

"Okay, baby. Have a good evening. And by the way, is Dillon Westmoreland still in town?"

She could actually hear the coldness in his voice. "No, in fact Dillon has left town," she said. What she'd just said really wasn't a lie because Dillon was no longer in Gamble. Fletcher didn't have to know he had merely moved to a hotel in neighboring Rosebud.

"I guess he got what he came for and decided to

move on. That's good. Maybe we won't be seeing the likes of him again anytime soon," Fletcher said cockily.

She frowned, not liking Fletcher's attitude. "I suspect he will be returning at some point since he still has my great-grandfather's journal." She figured she might as well prepare him now so he wouldn't go into cardiac arrest when he did see Dillon again.

"He can keep the damn journal for all I care. I just don't like the man."

Pam inwardly fumed. The journal was not his to decide whether Dillon could keep it or not. "Goodbye, Fletcher."

"Goodbye, Pamela, and I hope to see you Sunday."

Dillon smiled at all the voices he heard in the background of his phone conversation with his brother Micah. Micah, a graduate of Harvard Medical School who was only a couple of years younger than Dillon, was an epidemiologist with the federal government. Everyone often joked about Micah being the mad scientist in the family.

"So how long will you be home, or did you just drop in long enough to attend this weekend's charity ball?" Dillon asked Micah. His brother was known to travel all over the world doing work for the government. He had lived in China for an entire year during the bird-flu epidemic.

The charity ball he was referring to was the one the Westmoreland family hosted every year to raise money for the Westmoreland Foundation they had established to aid various community causes.

"I'm here for the ball and I'll be home at least

through New Year's. Then I'm off to Australia for a few months."

"Good to hear. I plan on flying in for the ball this weekend," Dillon said. A part of him really wasn't ready to put distance between him and Pam, even for a short while.

"I heard Sheriff Harper talked you into taking his sister Belinda as your date," Micah said in a teasing tone.

Dillon rolled his eyes. "It was either that or have Bane spend a night in jail for trespassing on the Newsomes' property in the middle of the night." He wasn't sure he appreciated his brother finding his predicament with Belinda so amusing. His brothers and cousins knew Belinda had had her eye on him as husband number three for about a year.

"So how is the investigation into Raphel's past coming along?"

"I'm finding out more and more information about our great-grandfather every day," Dillon replied.

Micah chuckled. "Just as long as it's nothing that can come back to haunt me with the State Department. I can barely handle the fact that he ran off with those other men's wives."

Dillon smiled. "I told you the real deal about Raphel and Lila. He did it to protect her."

"Yes, but we still don't know what was up with him and the second one, Portia Novak. It should be a rather lively discussion at Thanksgiving dinner this year and will be the first time in a long time everyone will be home."

After a few more minutes of conversation with

Micah, the phone was passed around to the rest of his brothers and cousins. Everyone wanted to know what information about their great-grandfather he'd been able to uncover so far. He didn't tell them everything he'd found out, but he felt he'd told them enough for now.

It was close to six in the evening when he finally said goodbye to everyone and hung up the phone. He glanced over at the journal he'd been reading over the past two days. He was surprised no one in the Novak family had taken the time to ever read the journal. If they had they would have learned just why Raphel had taken Portia away, and why Jay had given him his blessings to do so.

He glanced around the hotel room. It was totally different from the one he'd had in Gamble. It was a lot more spacious and the furnishings were early American instead of Victorian. Although CNN was alive and well on the big-screen television and the reception for his cell phone was perfect, he would be the first to admit that he missed the huge bathtub at the Gamble hotel. But he needed to be in a hotel that had fax and internet service. His firm was working on a huge multimillion-dollar deal and he needed to be available if a last-minute snag developed.

*And he needed to be someplace where if Pam wanted to pay him a visit, it wouldn't make the six o'clock news.*

He walked over to the window and looked out. It was cold outside but nothing like it had been the night he'd met Pam at her drama school. He sucked in a deep breath when he remembered that night and how it had changed his life. He hoped she'd gotten his message about changing hotels. The one in Gamble was closer to her place, but this one was only ten miles away.

She hadn't returned his call so a lot of things were going through his mind right now. Had she broken their rule about not having any regrets? Had Fletcher made it back to town? He didn't have answers to those questions, but the one thing he did know for sure was that if he didn't hear from her tonight, he would be making a trip into Gamble to see her. He still had her journal and tomorrow would be a good time to return it.

On the drive from Dream Makers back home later that night, Pam was trying, really trying, not to recall her conversation with Fletcher earlier that day. She was even trying, as hard as she could, to give him some slack and believe he had her sisters' best interest at heart when he'd made the decision they should continue their education in Cheyenne and not in Gamble. But for him not to have discussed it with her was totally unacceptable.

He of all people knew how close she and her sisters were. Did he honestly think she would let them go off and live at some private school, leaving their family and friends behind? And as far as she was concerned, there was nothing wrong with public schools. She'd gone to one and had done pretty damn well.

She reached out to turn up the dial for the heat a little. It was cold, although it wasn't as cold as it had been the last night she'd driven home from the academy. That was the night she had spent almost three hours in Dillon's arms. She couldn't help but smile just thinking about it.

She had talked to Iris but hadn't told her best friend a single thing. She hadn't needed to. According to Iris, there was something in the tone of her voice. She sounded relaxed. It sounded like she'd taken a chill pill. Pam chuckled as she remembered the conversation.

She passed a road sign that indicated the exit to Rosebud was coming up. She immediately felt a pull in the lower part of her body and it wasn't a gentle pull. It was a voracious tug. She tried to keep staring through her windshield, determined to keep her eyes on the road and to drive straight home. She then began experiencing flutters in her belly and her nipples pressing against her shirt felt sensitive.

The physical reactions her body was going through just knowing she was an exit away from Rosebud made her release a quiet moan. The hotel where Dillon was now staying was less than five miles from the interstate.

Dillon had given her his hotel room number when he'd left the message, but had made it seem as if he'd provided the number for informational purposes only. As if he'd wanted to assure her the journal was still safe and in good hands. Now she couldn't help wondering if perhaps he'd had an ulterior motive. Was he hoping to see her again, although she'd made it clear that what they'd shared that night was a one-night stand?

But the biggest question of all was why she was contemplating getting off at the next exit. And she knew the answer without thinking really hard about it. She was thinking of doing so because she needed to see him.

She needed to be with him.

She sighed deeply and as she took the exit to Rosebud she refused to question her sanity any longer. She was merely enjoying an indulgence that would be denied to her forever once she married Fletcher.

Dillon lay in his hotel room in the dark. He had dozed off, after eating a meal that room service had delivered and taking a bath. The television was on but he wasn't watching it. Instead his thoughts were on the woman he wanted.

He wondered what she was doing. Did she think about their night together as often as he did, or had she put it out of her mind? He had just shifted positions in the bed when he heard a knock at the door. Assuming it was housekeeping coming to turn down the bedcovers and to make sure he didn't need anything else before they retired for the night, he slid out of bed and into the jeans he'd placed on the back of the chair.

He opened the door slightly, just enough to make out his visitor and, when he did, sensations tore into him and forced air through his lungs. He quickly opened the door wide.

He refused to ask Pam what she was doing there. For a second he seriously doubted he had the ability to utter a single sound, so they stood there for a long moment and stared at each other, speechless. He did glance down at her finger. She had taken the ring off again. He looked back up into her eyes and felt his pulse rate increase.

Then she broke through the silence and smiled. "Are you going to invite me in?"

"Baby, I plan to do a whole lot more than that," he muttered thickly, his gaze not leaving hers.

He took a step back and she entered his hotel room. He closed the door behind her.

"I guess you're wondering why I'm here," she said in a quiet tone.

He shook his head. "We'll talk about the *why*'s later. Right now I just want to hold you. Make love to you. I've missed you."

"And I've missed you, too," she said honestly, wondering how she could miss him so much after two days, when she hadn't missed Fletcher at all and he'd been gone nearly twice that long.

Knowing they didn't have a lot of time on their side tonight, she took in his solidly muscular, naked chest and the way his jeans rode low on his hips. They were unsnapped and the zipper was barely up, which meant he had slid into them rather quickly. She hoped he was ready to slide out of them just as fast.

Feeling her heartbeat almost out of control, she shifted her gaze from him to glance around the room. Her great-grandfather's journal sat in the middle of a wingback chair.

She returned her gaze to him, knowing he'd been watching her intently and was probably waiting for her to make a move. She decided to do so. Moving away from the door she crossed the room to him and, the minute she stood in front of him, his arms easily slid around her.

"I hope I'm not interrupting anything," she said, reaching up and placing her arms around his neck.

He gave her a dimpled smile that was so sexy she felt her knees weaken. "Nothing at all. In fact I was just thinking about you."

"You were?"

"Yes."

And if to prove that point, he pulled her closer against him and she felt the erection he wasn't trying to hide. The magnitude of it resting snugly against the juncture of her thighs felt hard and hot. "And just what were you thinking about?"

"This." And then he swept her into his arms and kissed a startled gasp from her lips.

He took her mouth with a greed that made her moan in his arms as he placed her on the huge bed. And he continued to kiss her as she felt the heat of his body over hers. Whenever he kissed her like this, he had the ability to make her forget everything but him and how he was making her feel. Her thighs were nested between his and, although they were fully dressed, she could feel every hard and solid inch of him.

Slowly he withdrew from her lips, and as she stared deep into his eyes she caught the light from the lamp that brightened the eyes looking at her. And she knew at that moment that she could see a mirror of herself in his eyes. What she saw was a woman fiercely attracted to the man she was with and thinking she didn't want to be anywhere else.

"I want to show you how much I've missed you," he said huskily, kneeling before her while running a fingertip along the side of her face.

She met the intensity of his gaze, recalled every single thing he had done to her the previous time and felt her inner muscles clench at the thought he would be doing so again. That in itself made her lean up and whisper the challenge. "Then show me."

"With pleasure," he whispered close to her lips before taking those lips to begin a slow, sensuous mating that she felt as a gentle throb between her thighs. This kiss had all the high intensity, provoked the stirring sensations of the kisses they'd shared that night, but she could feel something different this time. It was there in the way he wielded his tongue in her mouth. He kissed her with a possessiveness that made every cell in her body become hypersensitive. And by the time he freed her mouth from his, she could only stare up at him, totally and fully at a loss for anything except the man gazing back at her. The look in his eyes clearly said he was claiming her. Here and now.

Warning bells sounded in her head. She knew what the outcome of her future had to be. He did not. She had to marry Fletcher—she didn't have a choice in the matter. It was something he would not understand and something she could not let him or anyone else prevent. It didn't matter what sacrifices she knew she was making. What mattered most to her were her sisters.

She hoped the vibes she was beginning to intercept from him were wrong and that he was not considering anything beyond what they had shared this week. Maybe she'd made a mistake in coming here tonight. Had removing her engagement ring made him think that she was willing to put aside her future with Fletcher? She had to make sure he understood that was not the case.

"Dillon?"

He reached out and placed a finger to her lips and, as if he comprehended what was going through her mind, said softly in a husky tone, "Although I don't have all the facts, I do understand, sweetheart, more than you know, and I think it's time for you to understand something, as well. Regardless of who you might be engaged to marry, you *are* mine."

Before she could comprehend his words, he lowered his mouth to hers in a kiss that was as potent and powerful as any intoxicating drug. And it was just as effective. Her mind and body became meshed in a mirage of sensations so forceful she gave up any desire to convince him to think differently.

She only recalled bits and pieces of him removing her clothes. But she did vividly remember the kisses he placed all over her naked body once he had completed the task. And she had committed to memory the sight of him removing all of his clothes, every single stitch, and then putting on a condom—almost a difficult task due to the size of his arousal—before returning to her.

Concentrated desire consumed her the moment he rose above her as he took her mouth again the way a hunter would go after his prey. Moments later he pulled away to use that same mouth to trace downward, to latch on to her nipples, sucking gently and causing flutters to stir within, to the point of being breathless.

And then he was there, close to her face, raising her hips, widening her thighs, lifting her legs to hug his shoulders, and then entering her in one smooth thrust that made her moan his name. But he didn't stop there. He continued to stroke her, inside and out, bearing down on her mind each time like he was bearing down on her body. And with each stroke it seemed to relay words he had not yet spoken, words she felt each time his dark eyes met hers, each time they breathed in and out together as one.

Sudden tears sprung to her eyes when she realized the depth, the intensity and then also the uselessness of the love she felt for him, all the way in her bones, in the air she was breathing. Yes, she had fallen in love with him. She'd once heard that a woman's body could and would recognize its mate, and the thought that this man was hers almost overwhelmed her, and touched her very soul.

He saw the tears flow down her cheek and leaned in to kiss them away, as if he had the ability to make whatever was wrong in her life right. She wished it was that simple, but knew it was not.

She looped her arms around his neck when his mouth moved from her cheeks to her mouth, and then she kissed him in all the ways she had dreamed of kissing him the past two nights.

He gave in, allowing her to lead, to take the kiss wherever she wanted it to go and to whatever degree of passion she wanted it to be. And when she felt the explosion that ripped through her body to ricochet to his, she couldn't hold back her scream of pleasure. And when she felt him sink deeper into her, tail-spinning into his own massive release, she clutched him tighter to her, locked her legs around his back, knowing that, regardless of what he thought and no matter that she now knew she loved him, this was all they would have together.

# Chapter 9

"I want to know why you are marrying a man you don't love," Dillon said raspily, close to her ear.

They lay locked in each other's arms, their bodies entwined, drenched in sweat from the intensity of their lovemaking. The aftermath of pleasure was so profound they were still fighting to get their heart rates back to normal while they savored what had to have been passion of the most explosive kind.

Dillon watched as her gaze widened at such a deliberate and bold question, and then his heart began pounding in his throat while he waited for her to respond. When she nervously licked her lips, he was tempted to lick right along with her but knew he had to hold back and listen to what she had to say. Tonight he wanted answers and wouldn't be satisfied until he got them.

And then, not surprisingly, fire crept into her eyes and she tilted her chin slightly. "You have no right to ask me that," she said.

A smile touched his lips. His woman was feisty when she needed to be and he liked that. He liked even more the thought of her as *his* woman. "I have every right, Pam. I'm a Westmoreland, remember. Raphel's great-grandson. I take what I think is mine regardless of whom it might belong to at the time. And you are mine. I told you that. And if you have any doubt of that take a look at the position you're in. I'm still inside you because it's where I want to be, where I know you want me to be."

She frowned. "Doesn't my engagement ring mean anything?"

He was tempted to laugh at that question. "No, not even when you're wearing it. And I notice that you don't hesitate to take it off when it suits you to do so," he said, knowing his words would stir her fiery anger even more.

At the moment he didn't care. He had fallen in love with her. If he hadn't been sure of it before, he'd known it as fact the moment she had taken the initiative and had plied him with her kiss. It seemed while she'd been ravishing his mouth with her tongue, emotions he had never felt before, deeper than he'd ever thought they could go, had consumed him, broken him down and reeled in his heart.

"Remember what I said? I give, you take and no regrets? I may have forgotten to mention that in rare situations, I claim. This is one of those situations."

She shifted to ease up but he had her leg pinned

beneath his. Her frown deepened and then she said, "It's complicated, so it won't do any good to tell you anything."

"Humor me. Tell me anyway."

She looked away from him but he heard her words nevertheless. "What makes you think there is something to tell?" she asked.

"Because you're here in this bed with me, and by your own confession a few nights ago, you've admitted you've never slept with Mallard, the man you're engaged to marry. And," he said, reaching out and tilting her chin upward, bringing her face back in focus to his so their gazes could meet, "you're not a woman who could be in love with one man and sleep with another."

"You don't know that," she all but snapped.

He continued to hold her gaze as he took her hand, led it to his lips and then placed a kiss on her knuckles. "Yes, I do."

For some reason deep down she actually felt that he did. No, she wasn't a woman who could love one man and sleep with another. In all actuality, he was the man she loved, but it would take more than love to help her now.

"Pam?"

She breathed in deeply and said, "I *have* to marry Fletcher."

He lifted a bemused brow. "Why?"

She hesitated for a moment before saying, "My father died and left a second mortgage on our home. Although I've worked out a monthly payment arrangement for now, which is being handled through my father's attorney, the bank in Laramie wants the loan paid in full within ninety days. I tried applying for a loan with a bank here in town but that didn't work out. Fletcher had offered to marry me to take care of it. And he's promised to make sure money is there when my sisters need it for college."

Dillon just stared at her. At first he wasn't sure he'd heard her correctly. Then to make sure he had, he asked in an incredulous tone, "You're entering into a marriage of convenience?"

She nervously licked her bottom lip. "No, not quite. He does want children one day, so it will not be a marriage in name only."

"If Mallard wants to impress you with kindness why didn't he just pay off the balance of the loan for you?" he asked, biting out the words through clenched teeth.

She looked surprised he would suggest such a thing. "I couldn't ask him to do that. I'm talking about a balance that's over a million dollars. Dad purchased adjoining land with the intention of reopening the dairy."

"Even if Mallard couldn't loan you the money, he could have cosigned for you to get it," he said, not accepting any excuses for the man. He could recall the number of times his signature had been on such a document for his family members. "And most banks require that loans of that amount be insured in case the borrower dies," he added. "Which bank holds the mortgage?"

"Gloversville Bank of Laramie. I guess somehow Dad got around it, which I still find rather strange. But I've checked with his attorney and he's gone over Dad's papers more than once. Dad didn't have the kind of insurance that would satisfy the loan. Mr. Gadling has been most helpful, working with the bank on my behalf, setting up the monthly payment arrangements where he receives the money from me to pay them."

Dillon heard what she was saying but it didn't make sense. In his profession he didn't know of any bank that would loan that much money without requiring that some kind of life insurance be purchased with it.

"So there," Pam pronounced.

She'd said it like that settled it, but he had news for her. It didn't. His gaze traced over her features. A part of him saw beyond what she was saying. It saw beyond what she thought she needed. She assumed she needed Fletcher Mallard. As far as he was concerned, she needed him. And unlike Mallard, he would deliver without any strings attached. It could only be then, after the matter with Mallard was dispensed with, that he would ask her to marry him, for all the right reasons two people should marry.

But still, something about the way her father's loan had been handled bothered him and he intended to check a few things out for himself on Monday. Deciding it would be best not to tell her what he planned to do, he lowered his head and tasted her lips instead, stirring the embers between lovers back to a roaring blaze.

And moments later, when he eased back inside her body, he knew he was where he belonged.


"Where do you get so much energy?" Pam asked in a whisper, while watching Dillon ease from the bed and head toward the bathroom.

He glanced over his shoulder and smiled at her. "You, Pamela Novak, give me strength."

He moved on toward his destination giving her a good view of strong, long legs and a nice, tight tush. He gave her strength, as well, she thought, closing her eyes and snuggling under the covers. She inhaled the masculine scent he'd left behind and knew at that moment, as crazy as it seemed, and unlikely as it could be, each time they made love she fell deeper and deeper in love with him.

Now he knew the whole story regarding her relationship with Fletcher, and although she had a feeling he didn't like it, at least she hoped he understood why she *had* to marry Fletcher. Shifting up in bed she glanced at the journal on the chair, just as she heard Dillon returning from the bathroom.

"Did you find out any more about why your great-grandfather ran off with my great-grandfather's wife?" she asked, trying to keep her focus on her question and not on his naked body.

"Yes, I found out," he said, walking over to the chair to pick up the journal and returning to the bed to hand it to her. "I marked the spot with a sticky note. Some members of your family had to have known the whole story, but I guess it was a family secret."

Pam lifted a brow before opening the journal to begin reading. A few minutes later she was lifting astonished eyes to his. "Portia was caught in bed? With another woman?"

Dillon nodded slowly. "Yes. And to protect her from the scandal it would have caused, the husband of the other woman and your great-grandfather decided it would be best to keep the matter between them. But it was decided both men would eventually divorce their wives, which during that time would have been a scandal in itself."

Pam nodded. "So since Raphel was about to leave Gamble anyway to head out to California, he and Jay came up with this plan to take Portia away so she could start a new life elsewhere. Do you think the other woman joined her later?"

Dillon shrugged. "Who knows? We're talking about the nineteen thirties. There's no telling how things turned out with Portia. But your great-grandfather did legally divorce her for desertion before marrying your great-grandmother. I'm glad to finally know why Raphel ran off with another man's wife for the second time."

Pam closed the journal. With the mystery solved, Dillon would be leaving Gamble. He had no reason to stay. "Both times Raphel came to the rescue of women who needed his help. Sounds like a high-caliber man, a real protector of women," she said.

His lips curved into a smile. "Yes, but so was Jay. He could have made things hard on Portia, but he was willing to step back and give her a chance to live her life the way she wanted to live it. Leaving with Raphel was still a scandal within itself, but it would have been far worse had the truth been revealed."

He took the book out of her hands and placed it on the nightstand before easing back into the bed with her. "I'm flying out in the morning to return home to take care of a few family matters, but will return by the end of the week," he said.

Confusion touched her face. "But why are you returning? You've gotten what you came for. You now know the reason Raphel ran off with Portia. He and Jay set the entire thing up to look that way to protect Portia's reputation."

"Yes," he said huskily, easing up on his knees in front of her and slowly advancing on her like a hunter stalking its prey. "That was the reason I came initially, but you're the reason I'll be coming back."

"B-but nothing has changed. I still need to marry Fletcher."

A dimpled smile touched his lips. "No, you don't. I'm a man known to make things happen instead of taking advantage of a situation like I think Mallard is doing, so I plan to offer you an alternative."

She lifted a brow. "An alternative?"

"Yes. I can't let you marry another man when I know that I'm the man for you."

She shook her head and gave a resigned sigh. She'd thought he understood, but he really hadn't understood at all. "Dillon, please listen to me, I—"

"No, I'm asking you to trust me," he said, gazing into her eyes with a plea that she felt all the way to the lower part of her belly. "I know that is a lot to ask when we've only known each other for a short period of time, but I believe there has to be another way out of this situation. A way in which you don't feel forced or obligated to marry Mallard or anyone else. I want you to trust me and give me time to find another way. Do for me what Jay did for Raphel. Trust me to make your situation better."

She stared deep into his eyes and then she said softly, "Fletcher expects me to have a date set for our wedding when he returns."

Dillon nodded. "When does he get back?"

"Sometime this weekend, probably Sunday."

"Then stall him. I need time to check out a few things," he said huskily. "Say you will trust me."

She continued to look into his eyes, searched his face for a sign of why she shouldn't trust him and knew she would not see one. "I will trust you."

A satisfied smile touched his lips. Raising his hands, he cupped the lower part of her face and leaned forward for their mouths, as well as their bodies, to mate once more.

# Chapter 10

"Pamela, I thought we agreed that you'd set a date for our wedding by the time I got back," Fletcher said, sitting down to the dinner table with her and her sisters.

He had called Sunday morning to say he would be arriving back in Gamble around noon and was eager to see her. She had invited him to dinner and the first thing he'd done, after giving her a hug and telling her how much he had missed her, had been to ask what day she had picked for their wedding.

"Maybe she's decided not to marry you after all, Fletch," Jill said, smiling sweetly over at him with a deliberate glare in her eyes.

"That's enough, Jillian," Pam said to her sister. Jill didn't know how true her words were. "I've been busy, Fletcher."

He frowned. "Too busy to plan a wedding that we both know needs to take place?"

She frowned back, wishing he wouldn't discuss such matters in front of her sisters. "We can talk about this later, Fletcher." She knew he didn't like putting off the discussion. In truth, she didn't, either.

Thanks to her sisters dinner hadn't been pleasant. They had practically ignored Fletcher. Having been gone for almost a week, he had wanted to be the center of attention and hadn't liked being ignored. Although she had tried rallying conversation around him, Nadia, Paige and Jill had not bought into her ploy. He hadn't been any better, often times mocking things they'd said. By the end of dinner her nerves were strained and she was ready for her sisters to retire to bed and for Fletcher to leave.

"Oh, I almost forgot," Fletcher said, breaking into her thoughts as she walked him to the door.

"My private plane made a pit stop at the Denver airport and I went inside to grab a copy of a magazine and noticed today's *Denver Post*. Your friend made the front cover with a very beautiful woman plastered by his side when they attended a charity function together this weekend. According to the paper, wedding bells might be in order for the couple," he said, smiling brightly. "I figured you'd want to see a copy so I saved the article for you."

She lifted a brow, confused. "What are you talking about?"

"This." He pulled the folded article from an inside pocket of his jacket and handed it to her.

She unfolded the article that had been neatly clipped

from a newspaper, and it took all she had to hold back a gasp from her lips. Before her eyes was the man she had fallen in love with, dressed handsomely in a tux with a very beautiful woman by his side. The two were smiling for the camera. Although there wasn't an article associated with the photo the caption read, "Is Romance Brewing for These Two?"

She swallowed and glanced back up at Fletcher who was watching her intently. "You seemed bothered by that photograph, Pamela. Is there a reason why?"

She lifted her chin and met his gaze. "You're wrong," she lied. "I am not bothered by it." In truth she was. She and Dillon had just spent time together a few nights ago. He had said he had to return to Denver. Now she knew why.

Fletcher smiled. "Now I think it's time I put my foot down regarding our wedding plans," he said, reaching out and catching her by the waist and pulling her closer to him. His move surprised her because he had never been so forward with her before. Being close to him did nothing for her or to her. It didn't have the same effect on her that Dillon had. Because she loved Dillon, and the thought that she meant nothing to him, that his words had all been lies, was too much.

"Put your foot down how?" she somehow managed to ask.

"I've been trying to be patient but more than anything I want you as my wife, Pamela. I'm aware you're not in love with me, but I believe over time that you will come to love me. I offered you marriage to help you out of a bad situation, but evidently you don't see it as such anymore. And maybe the thought of losing your home and securing your sisters' futures aren't the big deal they once were."

"That's not true."

"Then prove it. I no longer want a wedding date. Now I want an actual wedding. This week. A very private affair. Here on Friday. Make it happen or come Saturday our engagement is off."

Her eyes narrowed. "Are you forcing me into marriage?"

His smile widened. "No, sweetheart, it's your choice. Good night, Pamela." He then opened the door and left.

Pam stood in the same spot and stared down at the photograph in her hand. She angled her head to study the picture. Dillon was smiling. The woman was smiling. Had they been merely smiling for the camera or for each other, she wondered.

And come to think of it, the issue of whether or not there was a special woman in Dillon's life had never come up. She had never asked and he'd never offered any information. All she knew was that he was divorced, nothing more.

*But he had asked her to trust him while he checked out a few things. Came up with an alternative.*

She closed her eyes for a moment and leaned against the closed door. Had she read more than she should have into that request? Deciding the only person who could answer that question was Dillon himself, she crossed the room to use the phone, but then realized she didn't have his phone number. He'd never given her his number. Had there been a reason for him not doing so?

She glanced down at her watch. It wasn't quite nine o'clock and Roy Davis at the River's Edge Hotel would probably have information about Dillon on file. She would have to think of a good reason why she would need him to give it to her.

She released a long sigh when Mr. Davis picked up the phone. "The River's Edge Hotel."

"Mr. Davis, this is Pamela Novak. How are you?"

"I'm doing fine, Pamela, how about you?"

"I'm fine, but I was wondering if you could help me."

"Sure thing. What do you need?"

"Dillon Westmoreland's home number. I know he stayed at the hotel for a few days last week and I need to reach him. He left something here when he visited," she said.

"Hold on. Let me check my records."

It didn't take Mr. Davis but a few moments and he was back on the phone reading off a phone number to her.

"Thanks, Mr. Davis."

"You're welcome, Pamela."

As soon as she disconnected the call she quickly dialed Dillon's number. The phone was picked up on the third ring. "Hello?"

Pam's breath caught in her throat and her hands trembled as she hung up the phone. A woman had answered.

"So now, when are you going home?" Dillon asked the woman who was sprawled on the floor in front of his television set watching a movie.

He had come out of the shower a few moments before to find her there. Ramsey had warned him that he would regret the day he'd given Megan a key to his house. His twenty-four-year-old cousin Megan was an anesthesiologist at one of the local hospitals. She was okay to have around until she got underfoot. Like now.

"And why aren't you at your house watching your own television?" He walked through his living room on his way to the kitchen.

"It's a scary movie and I don't like watching these types alone."

He rolled his eyes. "Did I hear the phone ring a few moments ago?"

"Yes, a wrong number I think," she said, not taking her eyes off the television. "Do you mind if I crash here tonight?"

"Nope. I'll probably be gone when you wake up anyway," he said, opening the refrigerator.

That got her attention and she turned away from the television and glanced across the breakfast bar at him. "But you just got back."

"And I'm gone again. This time to Laramie. I have business to take care of there."

Dillon took a drink of orange juice right out the carton while thinking about his business in Laramie. He couldn't help but think about Pam. He missed her like hell. He had been tempted to call her but because Fletcher was probably back he had decided against it. He didn't want to make waves just yet. He hoped she trusted him enough so she could tell Mallard that she wasn't going to marry him at all. Dillon had promised to give her an alternative. An option in which she wouldn't feel compelled to marry for anything less than love. In a way he wished he'd never left Gamble or, better yet, had asked her to come home with him and be his date at the ball. But he had promised the sheriff that he would escort his sister. He'd felt obligated to keep his promise. He had pretended he had been having a good time, but had been missing Pam the entire time, which hadn't been fair to Belinda.

Then he'd really gotten ticked off to find his picture plastered on the front page of this morning's paper with a caption suggesting there was something between them. The last thing he needed was for Belinda to get any ideas, especially since he was in love with Pam. That's why he was determined to be able to offer an alternative solution to Mallard's marriage proposal, so that he could go to work to capture her heart the same way she had captured his.

Pam woke up early the next morning and, before she could talk herself out of doing so, she dialed Dillon's number again. Just like the night before, a woman answered. This time in a sleepy voice.

And again Pam quickly hung up the phone.

She felt a tug at her heart and knew she could not depend on Dillon to come through with an alternative solution any longer. He was back home and back into the arms of a woman who undoubtedly meant something to him. She had to remember that he had not promised her anything. *He gave. She took. No regrets.* But that still didn't stop every bone in her body from aching with the strain of heartbreak.

At least she had gotten a taste of passion that was so rich and delicious, she would savor it in her memories for years to come and they would be there to help her through the years ahead.

She drew in a deep breath. Her decision was made. She picked up the phone to make another call. This one to Fletcher. His voice, also sleepy, greeted her on the second ring. "Hello."

"Fletcher, this is Pamela. I'll make sure everything's set for our wedding on Friday evening."

Dillon had caught a plane early Monday morning to Laramie and went straight to Gloversville Bank from the airport. There he met with the bank president.

"Mr. Westmoreland, I recognized your name immediately," the man said, smiling from ear to ear. "Are you looking to do business in Gloversville?" he asked, offering Dillon a chair the moment he'd walked into the man's office.

Dillon was glad he had recognized Roland Byers as someone he'd once done business with a few years ago when the man had worked at a bank in Denver. "No, but I would like some information on one of your customers."

Byers raised a brow as he took the seat behind his desk. "Who?"

"Sam Novak. He passed last year and I'm helping his daughter close out his affairs. We were wondering why his loan wasn't paid off when he died. The balance was over a million dollars."

Confusion touched the man's face. "Umm, I don't see how that's possible. We require life insurance on all loans for that amount. Hold on a moment while I check. I can't give you any specifics of the loan due to privacy laws, but I can tell you whether it's still active."

Dillon watched as Byers called his secretary on the intercom and provided her with the information needed to look up the file. In less than five minutes the woman walked into the office carrying a folder, which she handed to Byers.

It took Byers less than a minute to glance through the papers, look over at Dillon and say, "There must be some mistake because our records are showing the loan is paid in full. That information, along with the appropriate papers, were given to Mr. Novak's attorney, Lester Gadling, almost a year ago."

"I can't believe you're actually going to go ahead and marry the guy," Iris said in a disappointed voice. "What about Dillon?"

Just hearing his name nearly brought tears to Pam's eyes. "There's nothing about Dillon. It was a fling, nothing more."

"But I thought he said he would—"

"I don't want to talk about it, Iris. Now, can you make it here by Friday?"

"Of course I can make it, although I prefer not to. But if you're determined to make a huge mistake, the least I can do is to be there and watch you make it."

The moment Dillon walked out of the bank and was seated in his rental car, his cell phone went off. He answered it immediately. "Hello?"

"Bane's in trouble. We need you home."

Dillon drew in a deep breath, released it as he shook

his head and snapped in his seat belt. "Okay, Ramsey. What has Bane done now?"

"Eloped."

"What the hell!" Dillon nearly exploded. "And please, whatever you do, don't tell me it's with Crystal Newsome."

"Okay, I won't. But I will tell you that Carl Newsome is going to make sure he goes to jail this time for sure."

Nothing like a death threat to get the Westmorelands together under one roof for something other than to eat or to party. Dillon glanced across the room and stared at his baby brother and wondered if Bane would ever outgrow his bad-boy mentality. You couldn't help but love him even when you wanted to smash his head in for not having a lick of sense.

Luckily, they had found him before Carl had, although it had taken nearly two full days to do so, and had included traveling to five different states. It had been obvious that he and Crystal hadn't wanted to be found. It had also been quite obvious they'd been having so much fun that they hadn't taken the time to swing by Vegas for a quick wedding after all.

That had made Carl Newsome somewhat happier. He hadn't needed to put out the expense for a quick divorce. Something had happened years before to make the Newsomes and Westmorelands modern-day Hatfields and McCoys. Something about a dispute over land ownership. As a result, Newsome would never allow his daughter to marry a Westmoreland.

Now they were all at the police station where Bane

had been charged with kidnapping, although Carl knew good and well that Crystal had gone willingly. Crystal had even said as much. She'd even gone so far as to admit to being the one who had planned the entire thing. She thought she was in love with Bane, but at seventeen her parents thought she didn't know the meaning of love. Bane thought he was in love with Crystal, as well.

"The judge has made a decision," Sheriff Harper said as he came back into the conference room and got everyone's attention. "Carl Newsome is willing to drop the charges as long as Bane agrees never to see Crystal again."

Bane, who had been leaning against the wall, straightened and angrily yelled, "I won't agree to a damn thing!"

Dillon rolled his eyes, shook his head and asked the sheriff, "And what if he doesn't agree?"

"Then I will have to lock him up and, since he violated the last restraining order with the judge wherein he promised not to set foot on Carl's property, we will transfer him to the farm for a year."

Dillon nodded as he looked across the room at his baby brother, held Bane's gaze a moment and then said to the sheriff, "He *will* agree."

"Dil!"

"No, Bane, now listen to me," Dillon said in a firm voice that got everyone's attention in the room. He had lost time in returning to Gamble and he wasn't too happy about it, especially now that he knew the attorney for Pam's father had lied to her.

"Crystal is young. You are young. Both of you need

to grow up. Carl mentioned he plans to send Crystal away to live with an aunt anyway. Use that time to finish college, get a job at Blue Ridge. Then in three to four years she will be old enough and mature enough to make her own decisions. Hopefully, by then the two of you will have college out of the way and can then decide what you want to do."

He saw the misery in his brother's features. "But I love her, Dil."

Dillon felt Bane's pain because he knew, thanks to Pamela Novak, the intensity of love. "I know you do, Bane. We all know you do. Hell, even the sheriff knows, which is why we've overlooked a lot of you and Crystal's shenanigans over the years."

It didn't take a rocket scientist to know that Crystal and Bane were sexually active. Hell, Dillon didn't want to recall the number of times he'd come home from work unexpectedly to find the two had cut school, or how he would get a call in the middle of the night from the sheriff after finding Bane and Crystal parked somewhere when neither Dillon nor Carl had been aware they were out of their houses.

"But it's time for you to finally grow up and accept responsibility for your actions. Go to college, make something of yourself and then be ready to reclaim your girl."

Bane didn't say anything for a moment as he switched his gaze from Dillon to stare down at the floor. Everyone in the room was quiet. And then he looked back at the sheriff. "Can I see her first?"

Sheriff Harper shook his head sadly. "Afraid not. Carl and Crystal and her mother left a short while ago.

It's my understanding they are taking her to the airport to put her on the next plane to an aunt living somewhere in the South."

Bane, with shoulders slouched in defeat, didn't say anything for the longest time and then he turned and walked out of the room.

Ramsey leaned against the door with a cup of hot coffee in his hand and watched Dillon pack. "You're leaving again?"

Dillon nodded as he continued to throw items into his suitcase. "Yes, I should have been in Gamble long before now, and I haven't been able to reach Pamela to explain my delay."

That had bothered him. He had tried more than once to phone her but either she was out or was not taking his calls and he couldn't understand why. He couldn't wait to meet with her father's attorney to find out just why he had lied to Pam, making her think that there was still an outstanding loan balance in her name. For some reason Dillon couldn't dismiss, he had a feeling Mallard was behind Pam's fictitious financial problems.

"Well, good luck. I hope your flight leaves on time. A snowstorm is headed this way."

"I heard," Dillon said, zipping up his suitcase. "That's why I'm heading out now. I'm hoping my plane can take off before it hits."

Ramsey took a sip of coffee. "I take it you're serious about Pam Novak."

Dillon smiled as he grabbed his coat off the rack. "Yes, and I intend to marry her."

\* \* \*

Dillon did get stuck at the Denver airport due to the snowstorm, and it was noon the next day before he arrived in Gamble. He was upset that he still hadn't been able to reach Pam. He hadn't spoken to her since last Friday and here it was Friday again.

Once he arrived in Gamble he went straight to Lester Gadling's office, deciding to let the man explain things before going to see Pam to let her know what he'd learned. He got to Gadling's office only to discover he was out to lunch, so Dillon waited.

It was close to three o'clock before Gadling returned and, when the secretary told him Dillon had been waiting for him, he looked at him nervously before asking if he had an appointment.

"No, I don't, but I need to talk to you about Sam Novak."

"What about Sam Novak?"

Dillon didn't like the fact the secretary was sitting there all ears. "I prefer talking to you about this privately," he said.

Gadling seemed to hesitate for a moment, then he asked, "And what relation are you to the Novak family?"

"A friend."

Moments later Dillon followed Gadling into his office and as soon as the door closed behind them, the lawyer asked nervously, "And what is it you want to know?"

Dillon didn't hesitate. "I want to know why you've led Pam to believe she owes a balance on her mortgage. I know she doesn't, so you better have a good answer for me, Mr. Gadling. And I want to know what happened to those payments she's been making to you every month."

"I don't have to tell you anything," the man said.

Dillon gave him the smile that all his family members knew meant business. "No, you don't have to tell me anything. I can always call the state attorney's office to let them know about attorney fraud."

That got Gadling's attention. He went around his desk and to Dillon's surprise pulled out a bottle of scotch, filled a shot glass and gulped the liquid down. "I didn't want to lie. It was Fletcher Mallard's idea. I am being blackmailed."

Dillon stared at the man for a long time and then sat in the chair in front of Gadling's desk. "I think you need to start at the beginning."

The man began talking and Dillon listened. Every so often Dillon's hands would clench into fists at how Mallard had manipulated both Gadling and Pam to get what he wanted. Pam actually thought Fletcher Mallard had come to her rescue, not knowing he had orchestrated the entire situation.

"So, there you have it. Mallard was so obsessed with marrying Pamela Novak he would have done anything to have her at his mercy."

Dillon's jaw twitched. "I'm going over to the Novaks' and bringing Pam back here. I want you to tell her everything that you've told me."

The man seemed surprised at his request. "That might be hard to do."

Dillon leaned forward. He refused to accept any

excuse from the man. "And just why might that be hard, Gadling?"

"Because she and Mallard are getting married today. In fact, the wedding is probably taking place as we speak."

# Chapter 11

"Please, Pammie, you don't have to marry him," Paige said with tears in her eyes.

"And why didn't you want to talk to Dillon when he called this week?" Nadia asked. "Why couldn't we pick up the phone when caller ID said it was him?"

Pam closed her eyes and looked across the room at Jill who hadn't said anything but whose eyes were narrowed. She then looked at Iris who looked just as upset. "Listen you guys, this is *my* wedding day."

She then turned her attention to Paige. "And I do have to marry him. You don't understand now but one day you will.

"The reason I didn't want to talk to Dillon this week is rather complicated, but I had my reasons," she said to Nadia.

She ignored Jill's undignified snort. "Come on, Reverend Atwater just arrived and we need to get this over with."

Pam glanced over at Iris, glad her friend had kept her mouth shut for once. Iris had been giving Pam an earful all morning. "Well, how do I look?" Pam twirled around the middle of the room in the new dress she had bought earlier in the week.

"Too damn good for that asshole," Iris said under her breath; however, Pam's sisters heard the comment. Pam frowned when her sisters fought to hold back their giggles.

"Okay, ladies, let's go," she said to everyone. "The minister is waiting."

Dillon didn't give a damn if he was going over the speed limit as he raced his rented car to the Novaks' place. Gadling's news that a wedding was going on and that Pam was the bride had sent him running to his car and tearing out of town at breakneck speed. It was a wonder the sheriff was not on his tail.

He had tried calling Pam before leaving Gadling's office but evidently someone had taken the damn phone off the hook.

He let out a deep breath when he finally pulled into her driveway and saw three cars parked in front of the house. He recognized the one belonging to Mallard but not the other two.

He had barely switched off the ignition before he was opening the car door and leaping out. At this point he cared less if he was late and she had already married Mallard. If that was the case then she would become a kidnapped bride, a feat a Westmoreland was gifted in crafting.

The minister's words floated over Pam, but her thoughts were on Paige. That morning, Pam had found her baby sister sitting on the side of the house crying. Paige was unhappy because today Pam would be marrying Fetcher Mallard. And Pam knew her other two sisters felt the same way.

Her father's death had left all three of her sisters in her care and at that very minute Pam realized their happiness meant more to her than anything else. And if marrying Fletcher was causing them this much distress then there was no way she could go through with it.

Reverend Atwater's words then rang out. "If any man can show just cause why these two people shouldn't lawfully wed, let him speak now or forever hold his peace."

She opened her mouth to put an end to the ceremony, knowing she couldn't let it continue, when a male voice boomed from the doorway of her home, loud and clear. "I can show just cause!"

Pam swung around and her heart literally jumped in her chest when she saw Dillon standing there with a fierce frown on his face. He was moving quickly toward her.

"What is he doing here?" Fletcher asked loudly through clenched teeth.

"Looks like he's coming for Pammie," Paige said smartly with a huge smile on her face, clapping her hands with glee.

Pam could only stare at Dillon, too shocked to move or say anything.

"What the hell do you think you're doing here?" Fletcher said, coming to stand in front of Pam, blocking Dillon's way.

A smile curved Dillon lips when he looked down at Fletcher. "What does it look like? I'm stopping the wedding. So move aside, I need to talk to Pam."

"I'm not moving," Fletcher snapped.

The curve in Dillon's lips widened. "I have no problem in moving you, trust me."

"Gentlemen, please," the minister was saying.

It was then that Pam found her voice. She moved around Fletcher to stand in front of Dillon. She met his gaze. "Dillon, what are you doing here?"

She saw the intense look in his eyes. "I asked you to trust me to come up with an alternative."

Pam's eyes narrowed. "I did until I called Sunday night and *she* answered the phone."

He raised a confused brow. "She who?"

"You tell me."

"Look, Westmoreland, I don't know why you're here but you're interrupting our wedding," Fletcher said in an irritated tone.

Dillon shifted his gaze from Pam to Fletcher and glared at the man. "There *won't* be a wedding." He then glanced back over at Pam and said, "We need to talk privately."

Pam stared at him for a moment and then took a step back. "No, we don't."

"If she doesn't want to talk to you, I do," Iris said.

When Dillon glanced over at her, Iris smiled. "I'm Iris, Pam's best friend."

When Pam shot her best friend a glare, Iris shrugged her shoulders. "Hey, what can I say? He's a cutie."

Dillon shifted his gaze back to Pam. "We do need to talk, Pam," he said, crossing his arms over his chest. "If you don't want to talk in private then I can very well say what I want right here. Fletcher and Lester Gadling lied to you. There is no balance owed on this house or land. Your father did have the necessary insurance to pay it off. Fletcher was blackmailing Gadling to claim otherwise. And those monthly payments you made on the loan were going to Mallard."

"That's a lie!" Fletcher said loudly. "How dare you come here spouting lies!"

"It is not a lie. Pam can verify everything I've said with Gadling. You weren't counting on her finding out the truth until after the two of you were already married, and by then you were hoping she would be so beholden to you that it wouldn't matter."

Pam turned to Fletcher, shocked at Dillon's allegations. "Is that true, Fletcher?"

Fletcher reached out and grabbed her hand. "Pamela, sweetheart. Please understand. I did it to give you all the things you deserve. I had to get you to marry me some way."

She angrily shook his hand off her and took a step back. The expression on her face was one of total rage. "You deliberately lied to me. Just to get me to marry you?"

"Yes, but—"

"Please leave, Fletcher, and don't come back."

He looked at her and then shifted his gaze to Dillon before moving it back to Pam. "Don't hold out for Westmoreland to marry you, if that's what you're thinking about doing," he snarled. "Remember that article I showed you? The one from the *Denver Post*. He already has a woman back in Denver, so I'm the best catch around these parts. When you want to renew our relationship, call me." He then turned and angrily stalked out of the house.

"Pam, we need to talk," Dillon said once the door had closed behind Fletcher.

She glanced up at him and narrowed her gaze. Placing her arms across her own chest, she said, "No."

His lips curved into a dimpled yet predatory smile and Pam had the good sense to step back. But she wasn't quick enough. Dillon reached out and swept her off her feet and into his arms.

"Put me down, Dillon!"

He gazed down into her angry face. "No. You are going to listen to what I have to say."

He then glanced at the minister's shocked expression before smiling at Pam's sisters and Iris. "Excuse us for a moment. We need to discuss something in private."

Ignoring Pam's struggles, he headed toward the kitchen and closed the door behind them.

"Put me down, Dillon!"

"Certainly," he said, sitting down in a chair and keeping her pinned to his lap. He looked down at her. "It seems I need to get a few things straight. First, that picture Fletcher was referring to that was in the *Denver Post* was about a date I had agreed to months ago. The woman, Belinda Harper, is the sheriff's sister. I owed him a favor for all the times he's helped me keep Bane out of jail."

When she didn't say anything, just continued to glare at him, he continued. "And the woman who answered my phone Sunday night was my cousin Megan. She stayed over at my place until Monday. In fact, I left her there to catch my flight into Laramie to check on things at Gloversville Bank."

Now, that got her attention. He watched as she lifted a brow. "She's your cousin?"

"Yes, I told you I have three female younger cousins. Megan, Gemma and Bailey."

He paused and added, "I would have gotten back to Gamble sooner, but we had trouble with Bane again, which I had to return to Denver to take care of. And then there was that blasted snowstorm that hit Denver. I got stuck at the airport."

Pam held his gaze. "You were trying to get back?" she asked as if still uncertain.

"Just as soon as I could. I made you a promise that I intended to keep. And then once I discovered the loan was actually paid off, I tried to call several times."

She glanced away, to look out of her secret window, before returning her gaze to his. "I didn't have anything to say to you. I wouldn't let my sisters answer your call."

"Because you thought I was involved with someone else." He'd made a statement rather than asked a question.

"Yes."

"And why did the thought of another woman bother you, Pam?"

She shrugged the feminine shoulders he loved so much. "It just did."

He leaned in closer. "Do you know what I think?" Before she could respond, he said, "I think it bothered you because you realized something. Those times that we made love, I made you mine. And you know something else you might as well go ahead and accept?"

"What?" she asked tersely.

"That I love you."

She blinked. "You love me?"

"Very much. I fell in love with you the moment I set eyes on you. And I want to marry you for all the *right* reasons. I want us, the Westmorelands and the Novaks, to be a family."

She hesitated, searched his gaze for the truth in his words. He could tell from her expression the moment she found them. A smile touched her lips. "I think Jay and Raphel would have liked that."

"So will you marry me? And I might as well warn you, marrying me means getting fourteen others."

She grinned. "I don't mind because marrying me means you'll get four. Oh, and there's Iris. She's like my sister."

A deep smile touched his lips. "The more the merrier. And I might as well warn you about my fifteen Atlanta Westmoreland cousins."

"Like you said, the more the merrier," she said, shifting in his embrace to wrap her arms around his neck. "I love you, too."

He leaned in closer as his gaze zeroed in on her lips. He kissed her there, slowly at first, then a little more hungrily. And when his tongue began dueling with hers, he almost forgot where the two of them were. He pulled away from her mouth and stood with her in his arms. He then placed her on her feet.

"I think we need to let everyone know there will be a wedding after all, but not today. We will set a date when we can get all the Westmorelands in one place."

He then leaned in closer to whisper, "I'm staying at the hotel in Rosebud tonight. Do you want to come spend some time with me later?"

A satisfied smile touched her lips. "Umm, I would love to. You give. I take. No regrets."

He chuckled as he pulled her into his arms. "Yes. No regrets."

## *Epilogue*

Pam glanced down at her wedding ring. It looked perfect on her hand. She then glanced up at her husband of ten minutes and smiled before looking around the huge, beautifully decorated ballroom at the Denver hotel. She and Dillon had decided to have a Christmas wedding and everything had turned out perfectly.

Her sisters were talking to some of Dillon's brothers and cousins and seemed to be in a very happy and festive mood. She couldn't yet distinguish which were Dillon's brothers and which ones were his cousins, since they all looked a lot alike. Even those who had traveled all the way from Atlanta. He had introduced everyone, but she was still a little fuzzy on names and faces.

And yet she had become immediate friends with Megan, Gemma and Bailey. They simply adored their oldest cousin and let her know they were more than pleased with the woman he had chosen as his wife. And then there were the wives of the Atlanta Westmorelands, with whom she was forming lasting friendships. Last night during the rehearsal dinner she had held in her arms the newest member of the Westmoreland clan, four-month-old Jaren.

There was no doubt in anyone's mind that Dillon's cousin Jared Westmoreland and his wife, Dana, were proud of their beautiful baby girl. While holding the baby Pam had glanced up and met Dillon's gaze, and from the look he'd given her, she had a feeling that he wasn't planning on wasting any time giving her a child of her own to hold.

"Ready for our first dance, Mrs. Westmoreland?" Dillon asked, whirling her around to face him, and bringing her thoughts back to the present.

She laughed. "As ready as I'll ever be, Mr. Westmoreland."

And then he pulled her into his arms as they glided around the dance floor. Her sisters were beaming happily and that made her feel good. They had been overjoyed to hear about her wedding plans. She and Dillon had wanted a small affair but with all those Westmorelands that was impossible.

They would live in Gamble until the end of the school year, and then once Jill left for college, Pam and her sisters would move into Dillon's home in Denver. Paige and Nadia didn't have any problems with moving and looked forward to making new friends. The house in Gamble would be a second home for them. Pam would be turning the day-to-day operations of the drama academy over to the very capable hands of Cindy Ruffin.

After a few moments a deep male voice said, "May I cut in?"

Pam glanced up into the face of the one cousin she remembered well, because he was a nationally known motorcycle-racing star, Thorn Westmoreland.

"Just for now," Dillon said jokingly, handing her over to his cousin. After Thorn, she remained on the dance floor through several more songs as each of Dillon's male cousins got a chance to twirl her around.

Finally, she found herself back in her husband's arms for a slow number. They would be catching a plane later that day to Miami, where they would set sail on a cruise to the Bahamas.

He pulled her tight into his arms and whispered, "At last," before lowering his head and latching on to her mouth, not caring that they had a ballroom filled with guests. When he finally released her mouth, she couldn't help but chuckle throatily. "That was naughty."

"No, sweetheart," he said, brushing his knuckles gently against her cheek. "That was this Westmoreland's way. Get used to it."

"I will." She went on tiptoe and captured his mouth with hers, deciding to show him that Novaks had a way of their own, as well.

\* \* \* \* \*

# HOT WESTMORELAND NIGHTS

# *Prologue*

Chloe Burton pressed her face to the windowpane as she watched the man sprint across the street. Her heart began pounding in her chest. He had to be, without a doubt, the most handsome man she'd ever seen.

She stared as he stopped to talk to another man in front of a feed store. He was tall, dark and every inch of sexy from the Stetson he wore on his head to the well-worn leather boots on his feet. And from the way his jeans and Western shirt fit his body, it was quite obvious he possessed powerful legs, strong arms, taut abs, tight buns and broad muscular shoulders. He had everything it took to separate the men from the boys.

And when he pushed back his hat, she saw dark eyes and a medium skin tone. Then she looked at his mouth and she couldn't help licking her lips at the sight of his. His lips were full, firm and luscious. She could imagine those lips and his mouth doing other things.

Just looking at him was enough to corrupt a woman's mind, she thought. Even from this distance, her body felt flushed, hot and unsettled. Nothing like this had ever happened to her while ogling a man in all her twenty-eight years.

Actually, over the past year the only male who had gotten her time and attention had been her *email*. And that was mainly because her last relationship with Daren Fulbright had been totally unsatisfying, a complete waste of the year she'd put into it, and she was in no hurry to get into another. No doubt there were some who thought she'd given up on love much too quickly, and perhaps that was true since these days she much preferred curling up with a good book during her free time than with someone of the opposite sex. And now, here she was practically drooling at just the sight of a man. He might be major eye candy, but the man was a complete stranger to her. Even so, the way he was standing with both hands in his jeans pockets, legs braced apart, was a pose she would carry to her dreams.

And he was smiling, evidently enjoying his conversation. He had dimples, incredibly sexy dimples in not one but both cheeks.

"What are you staring at, Clo?"

Chloe nearly jumped. She'd forgotten she had a lunch date. In fact she had forgotten everything once her sights had landed on the sexy man across the street. She glanced over the table at her best friend from college, Lucia Conyers.

"Take a look at that man across the street in the blue shirt, Lucia, and tell me what you see. Would he not be perfect for Denver's first issue of *Simply Irresistible* or what?" Chloe asked with so much excitement in her voice she almost couldn't stand it.

Chloe was the owner of *Simply Irresistible,* a magazine for today's up-and-coming woman. The magazine had started out as a regional publication in the southeast, but had expanded to a national audience during the past few years. By far the magazine's most popular edition was the annual "Irresistible Man" issue. The feature included a cover shoot and an in-depth story on a man who the magazine felt deserved the honor because he was simply irresistible. As the magazine had expanded, Chloe had convinced Lucia to come on board to manage its Denver office.

When Lucia didn't say anything, Chloe's smile widened. "Well?"

Lucia glanced across the booth at her. "Since you asked, I'll tell you what I see. I see one of the Westmorelands, and in this case it's Ramsey Westmoreland. And to answer your other question as to whether he would be perfect for the cover man on *Simply Irresistible,* my answer would be a resounding yes, but he won't do it."

Chloe raised a brow. "I take it that you know him," she said watching her friend closely.

Lucia smiled. "Yes, but not as well as I know the younger Westmorelands. There's a lot of them and he's one of the oldest. I went to school with his younger siblings and cousins. He has several brothers and male cousins who look just as good. Maybe one of them will agree to do it, but you can forget Ramsey."

Chloe glanced back out the window and knew two things. First, there was no way that she could forget him. Second, from the sound of things it seemed that Lucia was interested in one of those "younger" male Westmorelands. She could hear the wistfulness in her friend's voice.

"He's the one I want, Lucia," she said with both determination and conviction in her voice. "And since you know him, then just ask him. He might surprise you and not turn you down. Of course he'll get paid for his services."

Lucia laughed and shook her head. "Getting paid isn't the issue, Clo. Ramsey is one of the wealthiest sheep ranchers in this part of Colorado. But everyone knows what a private person he is. Trust me, he won't do it."

Chloe hoped she was wrong. "But you will ask him?"

"Yes, but I suggest you move on and find another man."

Chloe glanced back out the window. The man was the epitome of what she was looking for in her "Irresistible Man" issue and she was determined to have him.

"Um, I don't like that look on your face, Chloe. I've seen it before and know exactly what it means."

Chloe couldn't help but smile. She could only blame her smile on her father, Senator Jamison Burton of Florida, the man who'd raised her alone after her mother died of cervical cancer when Chloe was three. Her father was the one man she most admired and he'd always taught her that if people wanted something bad enough, they wouldn't give up until they got it.

She glanced out the window and watched as Ramsey Westmoreland ended his conversation and entered the feed store with a swagger that almost made her breathless. She *would* be seeing him again.

# Chapter 1

"I can't believe you're not posing for the cover of that magazine, Ram."

Ramsey Westmoreland didn't bother to look up from arranging a bale of straw in the lambing stall. He'd figured his youngest sister Bailey would show up sooner or later, because news traveled pretty fast within the Westmoreland family. And of course, Bailey made it her life's work to know everything about her five brothers, down to their every heartbeat.

"I'm not going away, Ramsey, until you tell me what I want to know."

He couldn't help but smile at the threat because he knew if he gave her an order to leave that she *would* follow it. She might like to express her emotions and display her defiance every once in a while, and God help him when she did, but when it was all said and done, Bailey knew how far to take things with him. He would be the first to admit that she had tested his limits plenty, especially during those years when she and their cousin Bane had been almost inseparable. The two thought getting into trouble was a way of life.

Since then Bailey had finished high school and was now attending college, and Bane had surprised everyone with his decision last month to join the military with the goal of becoming a Navy Seal. All was quiet on the Westmoreland front and Ramsey would be the first to admit, but only to himself, things had been a little boring.

"There's nothing to tell," he decided to respond. "I was contacted about doing that cover and I turned them down."

"Just like that?"

"Just like that." He figured she was probably glaring at him right now.

"Why, Ram? Just think of the exposure."

He finally decided to look up and the gaze that sharpened on Bailey was so keen, had it been anyone else they would have had the good sense to take a step back. But not twenty-one-year-old Bailey Joleen Westmoreland. Of his three sisters—Megan, who was almost twenty-five and Gemma, who was twenty-three—Bailey was the boldest and could test the patience of Job, so to try the patience of her oldest brother was a piece of cake.

"I don't want exposure, Bailey. I think the Westmorelands got enough exposure all those years when we had to deal with the trouble you, Bane and the twins got into."

Not an ounce of regret flared in her eyes. "That was then. This is now. And this would have been good exposure."

He almost laughed at that one. "Good exposure for who exactly?" he asked, getting to his feet.

He had a lot to do and little time for chitchat. Nellie, who'd had the responsibility of preparing the meals for him and the ranch hands for the past two years, had to leave suddenly yesterday when she'd gotten word that her only sister back in Kansas had emergency surgery for a ruptured appendix. She intended to stay and help out and it would be at least two weeks before she returned.

Ramsey understood and supported her decision, although Nellie's absence left him in a bind. Today was the start of shearing and with over twenty or so men involved, he was in desperate need of a cook to take Nellie's place. He had placed a call to one of these temporary employment agencies yesterday afternoon and was told they had just the person who would be perfect as a fill-in and the woman was to show up this morning.

"It would be good exposure for you and the ranch. It could put you in the public eye and let everyone know how successful you are as a sheep rancher."

Ramsey shook his head. Being in the public eye was something he could definitely pass on. He was close to his family, but when it came to outsiders he was basically a loner and preferred things that way. Everyone knew how much he enjoyed his privacy. Bailey knew it too, so he wondered, why was she harassing him?

"The ranch doesn't need *that* kind of exposure. I was

asked to pose for some girly magazine, Bail." He had never read a copy of *Simply Irresistible,* but the name alone made his jaw twitch. He could just imagine the articles that were between the covers.

"You should be flattered they want you on the cover, Ram."

He rolled his eyes. "Whatever." He then checked his watch for two reasons. This was Monday and he knew Bailey had a class at the university this morning *and* his temporary cook was ten minutes late.

"I wish you would reconsider."

He glanced back at her. "No," he said firmly. "And shouldn't you be in class about now?" He moved out of the barn and walked back toward the sprawling home he had finished building the previous year.

Bailey followed, right on his heels. He couldn't help but recall that she used to do that same thing when he took over the responsibility of raising her when she was seven and he was twenty-one. They'd lost both parents and a beloved aunt and uncle in an airplane accident. During that time she would rarely let him out of her sight. He fought back a smile at the fond memory.

"Yes, I have a class this morning, but I thought I'd drop by to talk some sense into you," he heard her say.

He turned around, placed his hands in his pockets. At that moment he couldn't stop the smile that touched his lips. "Fine. You've tried and failed. Goodbye, Bailey."

He watched her place her hands on her hips and lift her chin. No one had to warn him about Westmoreland stubbornness. Hers could be more lethal than most, but over the past twenty-one years he'd learned to deal with it.

"I think you're making a mistake. I subscribe to that magazine and I think you'd be surprised," she was saying. "It's not just a 'girly' magazine. It has a number of good articles for women, including some on health issues. However, once a year they feature a man on the cover. They try to find a man who's every woman's fantasy lover."

*A woman's fantasy lover?* Now that was a laugh, Ramsey thought. He was nothing more than a hard-working Colorado sheep rancher and since he'd doubled the size of his herd this past year, he couldn't recall the last time he'd been intimately involved with a woman. Working sunup to sundown, seven days a week had become a way of life for him.

"It will be my mistake to make, brat. I'll survive and so will you. Now scat."

A half-hour later he was alone and standing in his kitchen and clicking off his cell phone after talking to Colin Lawrence, a member of his shearing crew. Because of a snowstorm that had hit the area a few weeks ago, they were already behind in shearing and needed to get that done within the next two weeks in time for lambing to begin. Starting today everything would be moving rather fast to stay on schedule.

Colin had called to say a few of the pregnant ewes had somehow gotten out of the shearing pen and begun to wander. The dogs were having a hard time getting them back in the pen without stressing out the pregnant sheep. The last thing he needed was for any more shearing time to be lost, which meant that he had to get to the shearing plant on the north range as soon as possible.

He headed toward the door when he heard a car pull up outside. He glanced at his watch, agitated. It was about time the cook showed up. The woman was almost an hour late and that was not acceptable. And he intended to let her know about his displeasure.

Chloe brought the car to a stop in front of a huge two-story ranch-style structure and drew in a deep breath. She simply refused to take no for an answer regardless of what Ramsey Westmoreland had told Lucia. His refusal to be the cover story for her magazine was the reason she had ended a much-deserved vacation in the Bahamas to fly directly here. She intended to try to convince the man herself.

As she checked her GPS while traveling farther and farther away from Denver's city limits and heading into a rural area the locals referred to as Westmoreland Country, she had asked herself why on earth would anyone want to live so far from civilization. That in itself was a mystery to her. She hadn't passed a single shopping mall along the way.

Looking out the car's window, she couldn't get out of her mind the man she had seen that day a couple of weeks ago. That was why she refused to move on and select someone else. The bottom line was that she didn't want anyone else. Ramsey Westmoreland was not only the man made for the title of *Simply Irresistible,* but he *was* simply irresistible.

Once she had turned off the main road, she saw the huge wooden marker that proudly proclaimed The

Shady Tree Ranch. Beside it another smaller marker read *This is Westmoreland Country*. Lucia had said each of the fifteen Westmorelands owned a hundred acres of land where they had established their private residences. The main house sat on three hundred acres.

Once she turned off the main road, there had been several turnoffs, each denoted by smaller brick makers that indicated which Westmoreland the private drive-way belonged to. She had traveled past Jason's Place, Zane's Hideout, Canyon's Bluff and Derringer's Dungeon before finally reaching Ramsey's Web.

She had done her research and knew everything she needed to know about Ramsey Westmoreland for now. He was thirty-six. A graduate of Tuskegee University's agricultural economics program, and had been in the sheep ranching business for about five years. Before that he and his cousin Dillon, who was older than Ramsey by only seven months, had run Blue Ridge Land Development, a multimillion-dollar company started by their fathers. Once the company had become successful Ramsey had turned the management of Blue Ridge over to Dillon to become the rancher he'd always wanted to be.

She also knew about the death of his parents and aunt and uncle in a car crash while Ramsey was in his final year of college. For the last fifteen years, Ramsey and Dillon had been responsible for their younger siblings. Dillon had gotten married three months ago, and he and his wife Pamela split their time between Dillon's home here and Pamela's home in a small town in Wyoming.

As far as Chloe was concerned, Ramsey Westjmoreland was a success story and the type of man that women not only would want to fantasize about, but also one they would want to get to know in the article that would appear in her magazine.

She couldn't stop the fluttering in her stomach thinking that she was on property he owned and she would be seeing him again. If he had the ability to wreck her senses weeks after first setting eyes on him, she could just imagine what seeing him again would do. But she intended to handle herself as the professional that she was, while at the same time trying to convince him that sheep produced wool that eventually got weaved into articles of clothing—dresses, coats, jackets and such—that were mainly purchased by women.

She took another deep breath and opened the car door and got out at the same time the front door was slung opened and the man who'd tormented her dreams for the past couple of weeks stepped out on the porch with a scowl on his face, and said in a firm voice, "You are late."

Ramsey tried not to stare at the woman but couldn't help it. And this was supposed to be his temporary cook? She looked more like a model than a damn cook. There was no doubt in his mind that she would be able to generate plenty of heat in the kitchen or any other room she set foot in.

She was definitely a beauty with dark brown curly hair that flowed to her shoulders, dark brown eyes that looked seductive rather than contrite and a perfectly shaped mouth. And seeing her dressed in a pair of jeans that hugged her hips and pink blouse beneath a black leather jacket, made her look ultra-feminine and made him blatantly aware of his sexuality, while reminding him of just how long it had been since he'd been with a woman.

Ramsey hadn't expected this gut-stirring lust. He didn't need the attraction nor did he want it. It would be best for all concerned if she just got back in her car and returned to wherever she'd come from. But that wasn't possible. He had over twenty men to feed come lunchtime. He had managed to get through breakfast and thank goodness no one had complained. They had understood Nellie's emergency and had tolerated the slightly burned biscuits, scorched eggs and the overly crisp bacon. He had promised them a better meal for lunch. When they saw this woman they would definitely think *she* was a delicious treat.

"Excuse me. What did you say?"

He glanced across the yard where she was still standing by her car. Feeling frustrated as hell and fighting for control he walked down the steps, not taking his eyes off her. "I said you are late and your pay will be docked accordingly. The agency said you would be here at eight and it's now after nine. I have twenty men you'll need to feed at lunchtime. I hope there won't be a problem because I have plenty to do this morning and the agency assured me that you knew your way around a kitchen."

Chloe resisted the urge to ask what he was talking about. Instead she spoke up and said, "Yes, I know my way around a kitchen."

"Then get to it. I'll be back for lunch and we can talk

then, but I can tell you now that one of my pet peeves is tardiness," he said, moving toward his truck.

From what Chloe gathered he was expecting a cook who evidently was late in arriving. She should speak up now and explain to him that she was not the cook but he seemed to be in such a hurry. "Wait!"

He paused, turned sensual dark eyes on her and she felt a heated sensation rush up her spine at the same time she felt the tenderness in the nipples pressed against her blouse. "Look, lady, I don't have time to wait. I'm needed over at the shearing plant as we speak. You'll find everything you need in the kitchen."

His voice was hard, yet at the same time it sounded sexy. And she couldn't believe it when he hopped into his truck and pulled off. She couldn't do anything but stand there and watch him leave.

So much for having her say to convince him to do the magazine cover. For crying out loud, he thought she was a cook of all things. What she should do was to just get into her car and leave and come back another time, she thought. But where was this cook he was expecting? And did she hear him correctly when he said that come lunchtime there would twenty men to feed?

Chloe rubbed her hands down her face. Surely there was someone she could call who had his cell—who could get word to him of the grave mistake he'd made.

She turned toward the front door. He had left it wide open on the assumption that she would go inside, and at the moment she didn't have the common sense not to do so. If nothing else she could call Lucia. There was a chance Lucia knew how to contact a family member who would get word to him.

As Chloe walked up the steps it was easy to tell with the fresh-looking paint around the trim, white siding and brick sides that this was a relatively new house. There were a lot of windows facing the front, which provided a good view of the mountains and that were perfectly positioned to take advantage of the sunlight whenever it did appear, which wasn't too often this time of year. The porch wrapped around the front of the house, and the rocking chair and swing looked inviting enough to sit in the afternoons and just relax, even now in March when the weather was still cold.

And speaking of March weather, she tightened her jacket around her and walked into the living room, closed the door behind her and turned around. The place was huge and in the midst of the room, a spiral staircase led to the upstairs. There wasn't a whole lot of furniture in the room, but what was there looked rugged and sturdy. Few pictures hung on the wall and they were classic Norman Rockwell. The floor was hardwood with several area rugs scattered about.

She was about to walk through the living room to where she figured the kitchen was located when the phone rang. She quickly moved toward it, hoping it was either Ramsey Westmoreland or someone who knew how to reach him.

"Hello."

"This is Marie Dodson at the employment agency. May I speak with Mr. Ramsey Westmoreland, please?"

"He isn't here."

"Oh. Then please let him know there was a mix-up and the woman who was supposed to show up at his place this morning as a live-in cook for two weeks was sent somewhere else."

Chloe nodded and tapped her perfectly painted nail against the pad beside the phone. "All right, I'll be sure to tell him."

"He told me that his regular cook had to leave town unexpectedly due to a family emergency. I do hate leaving him in a bind like this with so many men to feed," the woman said with regret in her voice.

"I'm sure he will understand," was the only response Chloe felt she could make. "As a matter of fact, I think he's made other arrangements," Chloe added.

Moments later she was hanging up the phone, hoping that Ramsey Westmoreland *would* understand. But with what she guessed would be twenty hungry men come lunchtime, she wasn't so sure.

At that moment an idea flowed through her mind. Although her father had spoiled her rotten, he was a person who never forgot where he came from and believed in helping those less fortunate. That had been the main reason why she had spent her summers while home from college working at the homeless shelters. And since she enjoyed cooking, for three full summers while all her friends had spent time on the Florida beaches, she had volunteered her time helping out in the shelter's kitchens where large amounts of foods had to be cooked and served.

Mama Francine, who had worked as a cook at the shelter for years, had taught her all she needed to know, regardless of whether Chloe had wanted the education. Now it seemed all Mama Francine's cooking instructions about how to prepare food for a large group hadn't gone to waste.

Chloe tapped her finger to her chin. Maybe if she helped Ramsey Westmoreland out of this bind with lunch today, he just might be grateful enough to return the favor by doing her cover story. Especially if she made sure he felt he owed her big time. She smiled, liking the thought of that.

After glancing at her watch she took off her jacket and rolled up her sleeves as she headed toward the kitchen. One good favor deserved another and she was counting on Ramsey Westmoreland seeing things that way.

## Chapter 2

Ramsey's jaw tightened as he slowed his truck to a stop. He had been in such a hurry to get out of the woman's presence that he hadn't taken time to even ask for her name. All he could think about was how his testosterone level had suddenly kicked into gear and that a sexual hunger, unlike any he'd ever experienced before, had begun sliding up his spine.

And the woman was his cook? A live-in cook for two weeks? How in the hell was he supposed to handle something like that? He couldn't imagine sharing space of any kind with her. There was something about her that drew him, made him think of things he hadn't thought of in a long time, had no business thinking about now. Lustful things.

Crap!

He slid the truck into gear to start moving again.

What he should do is to turn around, go back and tell her as nicely as he could that she wouldn't work out. Then he'd call the employment agency and request that they send out a replacement.

He checked his watch, wondering how much time it would take to get another cook out to his place. Would the agency be able to find someone else right away? At least in time for lunch? Probably not, which meant he was stuck with the woman at least through today. But what if the agency couldn't find anyone else by tomorrow? What then?

He brought the truck to another stop and rubbed his hand down his face. This wasn't good. The shearers had been at it since six that morning after eating the pitiful breakfast that he had prepared. And he of all people knew his men worked hard and expected a good meal at lunch to keep going until the end of the day. And as their employer it was his job to make sure they got it.

As he turned his truck toward the area where the shearing plant was located he set his jaw in determination as he thought about the challenges that lay ahead with his new cook. He grabbed his cell phone off the seat beside him and figured that maybe he should call the house and check on her, make sure things were running smoothly, and then he quickly decided against it. Although he hadn't given the woman time to say much of anything, he had liked the sound that had flowed from her lips with the few words that she'd spoken.

She looked young, maybe a year or two older than his sister Megan who would be turning twenty-five in a few months. Why would a woman that young want to be a ranch cook? The scowl on his face deepened. Sniffing behind any woman was something he hadn't done in a long time and was something he wouldn't be doing now.

A satisfied smile touched Chloe's face as she glanced around the huge kitchen thinking she had somehow pulled it off. Granted she'd had to call Mama Francine and the older woman had walked her through the peach cobbler recipe, but once Chloe had begun moving around, getting familiar with her surroundings, she had felt within her element. She had made herself at home. She enjoyed cooking, although she would prefer not doing so on a constant basis for a small army.

Ramsey Westmoreland had a well-equipped kitchen with beautiful granite countertops and a number of shining stainless steel pots hanging from a rack. There was an industrial-size refrigerator, a large stove and a spacious walk-in pantry filled to capacity and in neat order. She had been able to find everything she had needed without any problems.

She had glanced through the cook's log that was kept on the kitchen counter. She saw that on most Mondays the men were fed chicken and dumplings, string beans and bread pudding for lunch. To Chloe's way of thinking that menu sounded bland and she had a mind to fix something different. She'd decided on lasagna, a tossed salad and Texas toast. For dessert she figured the peach cobbler would do the trick.

And she had set the table differently. Although she figured when it was time to eat a hungry man didn't care how the table looked, she decided to spruce things up with a different tablecloth, a springy yellow instead of the plaid one that had been on the table and appeared to have seen better days.

It seems that knowing he would always feed a huge work crew, Mr. Westmoreland had built a spacious banquet-size dining room off from the eat-in kitchen with tables and chairs to comfortably accommodate around fifty people. To her way of thinking, it was a smart move and showed just how much he cared for his employees. They would feel important enough to eat under the boss's roof instead of them being relegated to eating in the bunkhouse. To her that said a lot about the kind of employer he was.

She checked her watch. With less than fifteen minutes left she figured it was time to place the serving dishes on the table when she heard a vehicle pull up outside. She glanced out the window and saw it was the truck Ramsey Westmoreland had been driving that morning.

She stiffened, then drew in a deep breath, fighting for control and refusing to come unglued. No matter how handsome the man was, the only thing she wanted was for him to agree to do her magazine cover. She glanced out the window and saw he hadn't gotten out the truck yet and figured because he had arrived that his men were probably not too far behind.

With that thought in mind she moved to the stove to go about getting everything prepared.

Ramsey leaned back in the leather seat and stared at his house, not sure if he was ready to get out of the truck and go inside. He sniffed the air and then out of curiosity he rolled down the window.

Was that something Italian? He inhaled sharply thinking that it certainly smelled like it. When was the last time he and his men had something besides chicken and dumplings on Monday? Nellie was a fantastic cook, but she detested change. When it came to lunch his men could expect chicken and dumplings on Monday, shepherd's pie on Tuesday, chili on Wednesday, beef stew on Thursday and baked chicken on Friday. Nellie was known to keep things simple.

Deciding he couldn't sit in his truck forever, he opened the door to get out. By the time he rounded the front of his truck his front door opened. He stopped walking, literally froze in his tracks as he stared at the woman who stepped out on the porch.

His eyes hadn't played tricks on him that morning. She was a pleasant sight for the sorest of eyes and so stunningly beautiful that he felt every male hormone inside his body shift into overdrive. He struggled, unsuccessfully, to control the attraction he felt toward her. But when a knot twisted in his stomach, he knew he had to get her gone and off his property as soon as reasonably possible. Her being here for any amount of time was not going to work.

Chloe was going through her own issues as she studied the fierce frown on Ramsey Westmoreland's face. She wondered what had him so uptight. She had been the one who'd spent the last two hours in the kitchen over a hot stove, so she saw no reason for what she perceived as an unpleasant demeanor. If he knew the real deal and how she had helped him out of a sticky situation he would be kissing her feet.

And speaking of kissing her feet…

Her mind paused, got stuck on that thought as a vision played out in her head of his actually kissing her feet before his mouth traveled upward to tackle other parts of her body. The very idea made her tighten her hands into fists at her sides at the same time a wave of heated desire suffused her senses.

Jeez. She had been dealing with all kinds of emotions and sensations since entering the man's home, and for her misery he owed her big time.

Yet at the moment, Ramsey Westmoreland was more than a little intimidating. Chloe wasn't sure if she wanted this man indebted to her in any way. He had the look of a man who shared humor only when it suited him. A man who wouldn't hesitate to offer his opinions and not necessarily in a tactful way. He would tell you exactly what he thought. And she had a feeling that he was not a man who made foolish mistakes, or one who could easily be led around by a woman. The latter perversely bothered her because she was used to being in total control of any relationships she got involved in. But then, she and this man were not involved.

Deciding they had wasted enough time sizing up each other, she spoke up. "You were in such a hurry to leave this morning that I didn't get a chance to introduce myself. I'm Chloe Burton."

"You were late this morning."

She couldn't help the frown that settled on her face. Was he thinking of reminding her of it at every turn? Evidently he had very little tolerance for certain things.

"No one told me that once I left Denver's city limits that I would be headed for the boondocks, away from normal civilization. You're lucky I made it here at all. So the way I see it is you really should be counting your blessings, Mr. Westmoreland."

Chloe could tell by the way his brow lifted that he was somewhat surprised by her flippant tone. She noted his rigid stance and drew in a fortifying breath, thinking he really shouldn't be so uptight. Life was serious, but there was no reason to take it to the edge. Her father had been that way until a heart attack brought on by stress had nearly done him in a few years ago.

"So when can I expect the other men? I made a feast," she said, deciding to change the subject.

His gaze narrowed at her with shimmering intensity. "They'll finish up and should be here any minute, so we need to talk before they arrive."

Chloe decided then and there that she didn't want to talk. His voice was just like the rest of him, sexy as hell. There was richness to his Western accent that caused a tightness in her throat. Being in his presence for the past few moments had frazzled her nerves, had blood pounding through her veins and had unceremoniously reminded her of the hormones he'd awakened since the first time she had set eyes on him. It also stirred warm emotions, confusing feelings she hadn't felt in a while…if ever. That was not good.

"What do we have to talk about? You've made it clear I was late and my pay would be docked. What else are you out for? Blood?"

Ramsey tensed. Evidently at some point the woman had forgotten that she was the employee and he the employer. Maybe her past employers found her attitude amusing, but he didn't. He opened his mouth to state such a thing, but closed it when he heard the trucks pull up, which signaled the arrival of his men.

"We'll have to wait and talk after lunch," he said tersely. And then without saying anything else, he turned and headed toward the bunkhouse to wash up for lunch.

Ramsey leaned back in his chair thinking he had eaten lasagna before but never this delicious. And from glancing around the room at his men, he figured they were thinking the same thing. And there had been more than enough, which was a good thing because a number of the men had asked for seconds.

And he hadn't been able not to notice that he wasn't the only one who enjoyed seeing Ms. Burton work the room as she made sure everyone had everything they needed. Initially he'd been amused when the guys first arrived and a number of them, once they'd noticed there wasn't a ring on her finger, had tried their hand at flirting. But she had maintained a degree of professionalism that had impressed him. Even Eric Boston and Thelon Hinton, the two hard-core womanizers in the group, had pretty much backed off when it became obvious that she wasn't returning their interest. That surprised him because those two had a reputation in Denver of being sought-after ladies' men.

Another thing that had impressed him about Chloe Burton was the way she had set up the employee dining room. It was obvious she had taken the time to spruce

things up a bit, changing the decor of the men's surroundings. Changing the menu had also been a plus.

He had good men who worked hard. Moreover, they
would be putting in long hours during the next two
weeks. Most had been with him since he'd started the
operation and were family men who went home for
dinner and returned for work each day. After shearing,
which occurred once a year, some of his men would
turn their attention to lambing, while the others would
resume their roles as sheepherders.

"I see you can't keep your eyes off her either, Ram."

Ramsey shot a sharp glance over at Callum Austell.
When Ramsey had decided to become a sheep rancher
he had flown over to Australia to spend six months
on one of the country's largest sheep ranches. It was
there that he'd met the Aussie, who happened to be the
youngest son of the ranch owner. Callum had agreed
to come to the States to help Ramsey start his operation. Now three years later, Callum was still here with
him. He was the one who'd basically taught Ramsey
everything he knew about sheep. He considered Callum a good friend.

"You must be seeing things, Aussie," was Ramsey's
reply, even though he knew Callum was right. Okay,
so he was looking at her, but because he was her employer he needed to make sure she did her job right and
that she conducted herself properly. He had twenty-five
employees year round and not including Nellie, they
were all men. And he was a hands-on boss, so he was
familiar with everything that went on with his ranch
and if needed, he could fill in for any of his men.

"I think not, but if you want to convince yourself of

it, then go ahead," was Callum's comeback. "All I got to say is that you should be impressed with the way she handled Eric and Thel. I think she might have broken their hearts."

Ramsey couldn't help but snort at that. If that was true, it was about time some woman did. He glanced down at his watch. Lunch was almost over and the men, knowing his policy about punctuality, were standing to leave and were giving Chloe Burton all kinds of compliments. He stood as well, but unlike his men he had no intentions of going anywhere until he had a talk with his cook.

After grabbing his hat off the hat rack, Callum rounded the table and halted in front of Ramsey and studied his features. "I hope you don't plan on ruining things for the rest of us. We like her cooking. And we like her. We would like to keep her around, at least until Nellie comes back."

Callum had quietly spoken his words, just for Ramsey's benefit. Without glancing over at Callum, Ramsey said, "We'll see."

And for now that was all he would say on the matter. Yes, the woman had impressed him and his men with her cooking skills, and yes, she had carried herself in a professional way. But Callum had been right. Just like his men he hadn't been able to stop looking at her and that wasn't a good thing. He had been sitting at the table eating his lasagna and imagining eating her instead. His mind was so filled with lust it wasn't funny, and the flame that burned deep inside him wasn't amusing, either.

He glanced over his shoulder and saw the last of the men had gone, all but Callum, who threw him a daggered look before walking out the door and closing it behind him. Ramsey pulled in a deep, frustrated breath. The impression Chloe had already made on his men was not a good thing. Even if she stayed for two weeks she would have to leave when Nellie returned anyway.

He heard the rattling of the dishes and glanced over at Chloe, watching her as she cleared the table. His gaze slowly swept over her figure, liking the way the jeans fit across her backside. He figured her height was probably around five-eight and he would bet all the wool his sheep would be producing this year that she had long beautiful legs. The kind that would be a killer pair in a miniskirt.

He shook his head thinking about his fetish for seeing women in short skirts. He was a leg man all the way. So why was seeing this woman in jeans having basically the same effect?

Really it didn't matter because he planned to let her go as soon as he could get in a replacement. Temptation was temptation and he would hate to suddenly develop sleepwalking tendencies knowing she would be in the guest bedroom down the hall from him.

Hell, such a thought no matter how tempting, didn't sit well with him, mainly because he made the Double Creek Sheep Ranch one of the most successful in the United States. He'd done so by staying focused on what needed to be done and not by getting caught up in a woman. He didn't intend to get caught up on one now.

He leaned against the counter, deciding not to interrupt what she was doing just yet. Not when he had her within his scope. Whether he liked it, he was enjoying the view.

The man was agitated about something, Chloe could sense it, but at the moment she refused to let him get on her last nerve. She had plenty of work to do and didn't have time for a confrontation. After she was finished clearing the table she would break the news to Mr. Westmoreland that she was not his cook, that she had done him a favor and that she expected one in return.

The room was quiet, but she could hear his breathing, strong and steady. But even though she refused to look over at him, she was well aware he was looking at her, checking her out. And she knew he was paying a lot of attention to her backside, probably had his gaze locked on it real tight, which would account for the heat she actually felt on that part of her anatomy. She'd been told by more than one man that she had a nice derriere, curvy and shapely, just the way a man liked. *Whoopie,* she thought sarcastically.

But still, she would be the first to admit that just the thought that Ramsey Westmoreland's gaze was on her bottom almost made her breath catch in her throat. His eyes, whenever she looked into them, were filled with intensity and she could actually feel that intensity now focused directly on her.

Not able to stand it a minute longer, she swung around and frowned deeply. "We can talk now."

His dark eyes remained steady on her, even when he nodded and said, "All right. First I want to say you did a heck of a job with lunch today. The men were impressed and so was I."

She blinked. A compliment hadn't been what she'd been expecting. The man definitely had a way of delivering it with mixed emotions. His words were syrupy and sweet, while the texture of his voice was brooding. "Thank you, I'm glad everyone enjoyed it."

"They also enjoyed you." At the lift of her brow he clarified and said, "Enjoyed you being here I mean."

She wondered where he was about to go with that comment and figured she would know soon enough. "I enjoyed being here as well," she responded as she placed the dishes in the sink. It was time to come clean and let him know her real purpose for being there. "Mr. Westmoreland, I think that you—"

"Ramsey. I prefer you call me Ramsey. Everyone around here does. Some even call me Ram."

She couldn't help but smile at that.

"You find something amusing, Ms. Burton?"

She met his gaze and her smile widened even more. "You can call me Chloe, and what I find amusing is the fact that a ram is a male sheep and you are in the sheep business. Unique, don't you think?"

He shrugged muscular shoulders. "Never gave it much thought."

She lifted a brow. "Are you trying to tell me that no one has ever made the connection before?"

"If they did, they knew better than to mention it."

Chloe wanted to just throw her hands up in the air and give up. It was quite evident that even when they were trying to hold a civil conversation they had the ability to rub each other the wrong way. That made her wonder about him, the man she wanted to be on the cover of *Simply Irresistible*. He looked better than chocolate cake oozing with deep, rich chocolate icing—her favorite—but it was becoming quite evident he was a complex man. She couldn't help wonder what made Ramsey tick? What would it take to make him become relaxed, more laid-back? she wondered. Although she could see that around his men he was pretty mild-mannered and friendly. It was obvious they had a good working relationship while maintaining a degree of respect. That meant he was reserving his uptightness mainly for her. She wondered why.

The research she'd done indicated he dated when the mood or the urge probably hit him. Yet he didn't have any steady woman in his life. His last serious relationship had been with the woman he'd become engaged to, a woman by the name of Danielle McKay. However, she had ruined what was to have been his wedding day by stopping the minister in the middle of the wedding and walking out. That had been over ten years ago. Surely he'd gotten over that incident by now.

In addition to the cover photo for the magazine, she wanted an interview with him and had a feeling getting him to talk would be just as difficult as getting him to agree to the cover photo. Talk about pulling teeth. She had planned to send one of her seasoned reporters to talk to him and now she could clearly see that just wouldn't work.

Suddenly an idea popped into her head. She might as well go about killing two birds with one stone. She wanted him to do the magazine cover and she wanted an article on him as well. His profession intrigued her.

For instance, why had he gotten into sheep ranching versus cattle or horse ranching?

An insider's view of his operation might be good reading information to her readers. And the best way to find out everything she wanted to know about him was to hang around and get to know him for herself. The man was without a doubt masculine perfection and she wondered if there was more to Ramsey Westmoreland than a handsome face and a hard, muscular body.

Chloe nibbled on her lower lip. Now was the time to come clean and tell him the truth, but something was holding her back from doing so. He owed her for lunch today and she intended to collect, but she wanted more from him than just the photo cover. She wanted to interview him for a piece in the magazine as well. Women loved wool and she could do an article informing them of the entire process of getting it off the sheep and into the stores. At lunch a number of the shearers had explained how things were done, but she wanted to hear it from Ramsey.

"What made you get into sheep ranching?" she decided to ask. There was no sense in wasting time getting the information she needed.

She glanced over at him when he didn't say anything and felt heat thrum through her body when he shifted his gaze to her face. From his expression she could tell he was surprised by her question.

"Why do you want to know?"

He was a suspicious sort and she would add that to the list of his characteristics. "I'm just curious. You have a big spread and a good number of men to help you run things. Most people around here have cattle or horses, but you have sheep. Why?"

Taking his time, Ramsey pondered Chloe's question. It was one he had asked himself many times and whenever he did he would always come up with the same answer. "Being a rancher was a dream my father and I shared from the time he took me with him to visit a friend of his in Maryland who owned a sheep farm. I couldn't have been any more than twelve at the time. In college I majored in agriculture economics, so I would know everything there was to know about farming and ranching, although my plans were to join the family's real estate business like everyone else. It was Dad's intent to one day retire and just have a small flock of sheep, but he died before he had a chance to fulfill his dream."

"I'm sorry, Ramsey."

She had spoken quietly and he saw his sorrow reflected in her eyes. He quickly wondered why he had shared that with her. He wasn't sure why he had answered her question at all. What was it about her that had made him feel comfortable enough with her to bare his soul? "Look, Chloe, what I need to talk to you about is—"

At that moment his cell phone went off. "Excuse me," he said before fishing it out of his back pocket. "Yes?"

She watched, nearly mesmerized as a huge smile touched his face, curving his lips. If she hadn't seen it, she would not have believed it. Did he reserve his frowns just for her?

"Dillon, when did you get in?" He paused. "No problem, I'm on my way."

He quickly returned the phone to his jeans pocket and glanced over at her. "I need to run. We still need to talk. I'll be back in an hour or so." He turned to move toward the back door.

"I'll be gone by then."

He stopped and pivoted around and lifted a questioning brow while staring at her. "Gone where?"

There were those intense eyes again and she drew a breath. "Back to town."

He leaned back against the counter again. "Did the agency not tell you that I hired you as a live-in cook? The men will be expecting another meal in the morning around five."

"Five!"

"Yes."

She looked at him suspiciously. "Did your other cook live here?"

"No. But then I didn't have to worry about her getting here early enough to have breakfast ready for my men. Nellie and her husband have a house less than ten miles away. She arrived every morning at three and left in the late afternoon."

He then lifted a brow. "Just what did that employment agency tell you? This is shearing time here at the ranch and it happens only once a year. I own over three thousand sheep and have only a two-week window to get the wool off. Unlike a lot of sheep ranchers who hire a sheep shearing crew from year to year, my men are trained to do all the job duties here. That means they will work around the clock. I have to make sure they eat a hearty breakfast and are fed a good lunch. I can't wake up tomorrow morning and worry about whether you'll show up."

"I'll be back in the morning," she heard herself say. "I promise."

Ramsey frowned. Hadn't he made up his mind that they could not stay under the same roof? Wasn't it his intent to talk to her about remaining as his cook only until he'd found a replacement? So why was he making a big deal of her staying over tonight? He should be overjoyed that she was leaving.

He inwardly shrugged and figured he only cared because of his concern that she would not be here on time in the morning to feed his men. "I'm going to need you here on time, Chloe," he said in a voice that sounded pretty damn curt even to his own ears.

"I said I would be here, didn't I?" she all but snapped back in a tone that said he would get just as good as he gave.

His glare locked on her face and then he nodded stiffly. "I'm taking you at your word. Lock the door behind you when you leave and I'll see you in the morning." He then headed for the door.

He turned and met her gaze one more time and she didn't release her breath until the door had closed behind him.

## Chapter 3

"Please tell me you're joking, Clo."

Chloe sat her luggage down near her feet and turned to Lucia who had a worried look on her face. Chloe had decided to return to Ramsey's place tonight instead of trying to find her way there again in the early morning when it would still be dark outside. "Come on, Lou, it's not that serious. I'm doing Ramsey Westmoreland a favor and in the end he will be doing me a favor."

Lucia rolled her eyes. "He won't see things that way when he finds out what you're really about. You're not only invading his privacy, but you're also being deceitful."

"I'm not."

"You are, too, and all hell is going to break loose when he learns the truth. I live in this town, you don't. You'll be back in sunny Florida and I'll be here feeling the heat of the Westmorelands' wrath. When it comes to anyone messing with one of them, they all stick together."

Chloe crossed her arms beneath her breasts and gave her best friend a pointed look. "And which Westmoreland are you concerned with pissing off, Lucia?"

Chloe knew she had hit the jackpot when Lucia dropped her gaze and began looking everywhere but at her. "I don't know what you're talking about."

Chloe had no intentions of believing that. "Yeah, right. You don't want to make waves with the Westmorelands for a reason, so fess up. Which one is it? Ramsey?"

"No," Lucia said quickly. "It's no one."

Chloe didn't believe that any more than she believed there was a lost colony off the California coast. "Okay, Lou, this is Clo. You can't lie straight even on your best days, so I'm going to ask you one more time, who is he and don't waste my time telling me he's not a Westmoreland."

Reluctantly, Lucia met her gaze and then in a quiet and flat voice she said, "It's Ramsey's brother, Derringer."

Chloe raised a brow. Her best friend's expression was filled with so much love it almost hurt her to look at it. "Derringer Westmoreland? When did all this take place?"

She had known Lucia since her first year of college and the man's name had never come up, yet judging by the expression on Lucia's face whatever she felt for the man ran deep and had been there a long time.

A faint smile touched Lucia's lips. "I've loved him forever."

Chloe was shocked. "Forever? And I'm just hearing about him?"

Lucia shrugged. "There was never a point. My crush began in high school, but he saw me as nothing more than one of his sister's friends. I thought I'd gotten over him when I left for college but since returning home four years ago I've discovered that isn't the case."

Lucia's face warmed when she said, "Last month I ran into him, and for the first time in years we were close enough to speak." A smile then touched her face. "And he asked me—"

"Out on a date?" Chloe asked excitedly.

"I wish. He dropped by my dad's paint store and I was working behind the counter and Derringer asked me to hand him a can of paint thinner."

Chloe couldn't help the grin that curved her lips. Evidently that little incident had made Lou's day. Just being around Ramsey Westmoreland put a spark in *her* day. Now where had that thought come from? Chloe wondered.

"Now that I know how you feel about Derringer Westmoreland, I will tell Ramsey the truth as soon as reasonably possible. I still want to make him feel indebted to me first for a while and then I'll level with him and come clean."

Lucia nodded. "I know how much having Ramsey on the cover of your magazine as well as doing that article on him means to you."

Chloe met Lucia's gaze and smiled. "Yes, I don't

want you to worry about it because I believe in the end we'll both get what we want."

Ramsey looked up from the breeding charts he had spread over his desk and considered going into the kitchen to eat that last bit of peach cobbler that had been left from lunch. It had been so delicious his mouth was beginning to water just thinking about it.

And his mouth was beginning to water just thinking about something else as well. More specifically, someone else. Chloe Burton. Talk about looking yummy. He threw his pencil down and leaned back in his chair. At that moment he couldn't help but think about snug-fitting jeans that covered a curvaceous backside and a blouse that fit perfectly over a tempting pair of breasts. He was getting aroused at the memory.

*Damn.*

Deciding he needed a beer more so than any peach cobbler, he got up to make his way to the kitchen. Moments later he was leaning against the counter and tipping the bottle to his lips and taking a much-needed drink. Lowering the bottle he then glanced around the room and for the first time noticed just how large and quiet his home was. Usually he welcomed the silence, but for some reason it bothered him tonight.

He studied the ceramic floor as he thought about his great-grandfather, Raphel Westmoreland, who had owned over eighteen hundred acres of land on the outskirts of Denver's city limits. When each Westmoreland reached the age of twenty-five they were given a one-hundred-acre tract of land. It was why he, his siblings and cousins all lived in close proximity to each other. As the oldest cousin, in addition to receiving his one hundred acres, Dillon had also inherited Shady Tree Ranch, the Westmoreland family home. The huge two-story dwelling sat on three hundred acres and hosted the majority of the family functions. Since Dillon had married Pamela it seemed the Westmorelands had reason to celebrate a lot. Everyone adored Dillon's wife, found her totally different from his first wife, and had welcomed Pamela and her three sisters into the family with open arms.

He lifted his head when he heard a knock at his door and glanced up at the clock on the wall. It was close to eleven, but that didn't mean a damn thing to any of his siblings or cousins. They felt they had a right to come calling at any time. He shook his head as he made it to the door, thinking it was probably his sister Megan. She was twenty-four years old and an anesthesiologist at the hospital in town.

Without bothering to ask who it was, he slung his front door open to find Chloe Burton standing on his porch and tightly gripping a piece of luggage. He was so surprised to see her that he could only stand and stare.

He could tell by the way she was nibbling on her lower lip that she was nervous, but that wasn't what held his attention, although the action caused a tightening in his gut. What had him transfixed was her outfit. She had almost ruined a saucy minidress by wearing leggings. He would have loved to see her bare legs and almost sighed in disappointment. But then he had to admit she still looked gorgeous and sexy as hell. Good enough to eat after first lapping her all over. He swallowed knowing at that moment that he was in trouble.

"I know I said I'd come back in the morning, but I figured not to take any chances getting here late. Besides, I need to get things set up, if the men eat at five. I'll need to be in the kitchen at least by four. So…here I am."

Yes, here she was, and although he wished otherwise, ideas continued to pop up in his head, literally pound his brain, regarding all the things he'd like to do to her. Even now he wished like hell he could ignore the ache that was stirring in the lower part of his body, as well as the heavy thudding doing havoc to his chest. But he couldn't.

She stared at him and he stared back at her as his insides began filling with lust of the thickest kind. He should have followed his mind earlier and contacted the employment agency to see if they could send in a replacement by morning, but he had failed to do so mainly because deep down he really hadn't wanted to. He grudgingly admitted that he had been looking forward to seeing her in the morning. But she was here now and he wasn't quite sure just how to handle her unexpected arrival.

He watched as she raised her brows. "So are you going to let me in or do I get to stand out here all night?"

At that moment he couldn't help but quirk his lips in a smile. She was almost as bad as Bailey with her sassy mouth. A mouth that at that moment snagged his gaze. Breath slammed through his lungs when she took that time to moisten her lower lip with the tip of her tongue.

He fought the heat flaring in his midsection. "Yes, I'm going to let you in," he said, reaching out and taking the luggage out of her hand and stepping back and moving aside.

"I appreciate it," she responded, stepping over the threshold.

When she walked past him every cell in Ramsey's body began throbbing as he took in her scent. Whatever perfume she was wearing was lethal and could wrap a man up in all kinds of sensuous thoughts.

She glanced over at him. "So where's my room?"

He gave her a tight smile. "Upstairs. Please follow me." A part of him wished he was leading her to his bedroom instead of the guest room. Damn, he needed another beer.

They walked up the stairs and when they reached the landing they walked down the hall. "Nice place."

He glanced over his shoulder. "I'm sure you've seen it before."

She arched her brow. "No, I haven't. Earlier today when you left your door wide open, I had no reason to snoop around up here. My job was in the kitchen area and no other part of your house."

He wondered if she could be believed, and when he glanced over his shoulder again he couldn't help but note how she was checking out several of the bedrooms they passed. Maybe she hadn't come *snooping* after all. He had five guest rooms all with their own private baths. At twenty-three, Gemma was the interior designer in the family. She had been more than happy to spend his money to lavishly decorate each of his bedrooms. And she was dying to get started on the rooms downstairs once he gave her the go-ahead. That wouldn't be for a while. He was still recovering from having her underfoot when she'd done the upstairs.

"Sorry, my mistake," he apologized by saying.

When they reached the bedroom that she would be using, he stood back to let her enter. He could tell from her expression that he had made a wise choice. She liked it, which meant she was a frilly, lacy and soft colors kind of girl. While she was standing in the middle of the room, scanning the room in awe, he placed her luggage on the bed.

His first inclination was to bid her good-night and leave her standing right there, but something about the expression on her face stopped him. She actually seemed absorbed. He somehow understood. Gemma's interior design work could do that to you. He would be one of the first to admit that his sister was good. The money used to send her to college had been well spent.

He doubted there was ever a time Gemma hadn't wanted to be an interior designer. He could vividly recall how she had made curtains for his first car—a bright red Chevy—when she was eight. To not hurt her feelings he had mounted the things in the car's rear window hoping that none of his friends saw them.

"Whoever decorated this part of your home did a fantastic job," Chloe said, as her gaze returned to Ramsey.

Chloe noted that he was looking at her again, with the same intensity that he'd looked at her earlier that day. And as she stared back his gaze never wavered, it held hers deep within its scope. Without words, with barely a breath, something was taking place between them. She wished she could dismiss her theory and believe she was just imagining things, but there was no make-believe with the heat consuming her body. Her breasts suddenly felt swollen and her nipples seemed tender against the fabric of her dress.

Her gaze moved from his face and scanned his body downward and was glad to see she was not the only one affected by the moment. He was aroused. Fully. There was no way he could hide it and he wasn't trying to. Her gaze shifted back to his face and what she saw in the depths of his eyes almost took her breath away. There were promises of hot, lusty nights, more pleasure than she could probably stand, kisses that would start at her mouth and end between her thighs and an explosion that would shatter every single thing within her. She paused for breath at the thought that those were real promises she saw in his gaze and not a figment of her imagination.

Then she also saw something else in the depths of his eyes beside those promises. She saw a warning. If she couldn't stand the heat, then she needed to stay out of the kitchen. At that moment she pulled in a wary breath. Was Ramsey Westmoreland the one man she could not handle?

"I'll leave you alone to unpack," he finally said, breaking the intense sexual tension that surrounded them. "You have your own bathroom, which I believe you'll find more than sufficient."

She nodded. Her ability to speak had escaped her.

"Good night, Chloe. I'll see you in the morning."

She could only stand and stare after him as he left the room.

\* \* \*

There was no doubt about it. He had to get her out of his house, Ramsey thought, as he paced his bedroom hours later. What had happened in the guest room tonight was uncalled for, but still pretty much unclear. He had come within seconds of crossing that room, bending his head and taking her mouth with his to satisfy the hunger he felt. The hunger he was still feeling. The thought of his tongue mingling with hers while he held her tight against the heat of his chest caused the hot stab of arousal to nearly knock him to his knees.

And where on earth had such passion come from? It had nearly taken over him, transformed his brains into mush and had filled his mind with naughty thoughts of all the things he wanted to do to her. He pulled in a deep breath deciding he needed to analyze the situation. He needed to determine just how they had come to this point.

He would be the first to admit there had been a strong sexual attraction from the first moment he'd laid eyes on her. A rush of hot blood had shot through his veins, had hammered away at his insides, and an awareness as profound as anything he'd ever encountered before had zinged through him with the force of a volcano erupting. Every nerve, every bone and every muscle in his body had been affected.

And things hadn't gotten any better during the lunch hour when he hadn't been able to keep his eyes off her just as Callum had claimed. And he had a feeling that the reason Eric and Thel had probably backed off hadn't been because of any feeling of defeat where she was concerned. They had retreated because they'd picked up on his interest. If Callum had noticed his staring at her, then there was a strong possibility others had as well. And because doing such a thing was so unlike him, they probably figured he was being territorial. Had he been?

He rubbed his hands down his face as he uttered a frustrated curse. She was probably in her bed, sleeping peacefully between the sheets, while he was the one walking the floor with an erection that was keeping him awake. He seriously considered going into her room, getting her up and asking her to leave. How crazy was that? To even contemplate doing such a thing showed just how close to the edge he was.

Of his four brothers he was the one who could generally take a woman or leave her just where she stood. His love 'em and leave 'em attitude unnerved his siblings who thought he spent more time sleeping with his sheep than with women. Considering the time he'd done duty as a sheepherder over the past year, that accusation was not a lie. But it really wasn't any of their business. And he had been quick to point out—especially to his brothers and male cousins—that they were spending enough time chasing women without him, boosting profits for the condom industries and making it quite obvious they were men on the prowl the majority of the time. He cringed at the reputations some of them had.

And he had been quick to assure them that his decision to not bed women as often as they did had nothing to do with Danielle McKay, the woman who had walked off, leaving him standing at the altar ten years ago at a church filled with over two hundred guests.

The really sad thing was that his family had liked her, until they'd discovered the truth as to why she had walked out on him in front of everyone with an "I'm sorry," instead of an "I do."

She had later confessed to having an affair that had resulted in a pregnancy. To her credit, at least she'd had the decency to not go through with the wedding instead of passing the kid off as his. But what his family hadn't known and what he'd kept hidden was that it had been a sense of obligation and not love that had driven him to ask Danielle to marry him in the first place. So in reality, her calling off the wedding had been a blessing in disguise.

He pulled in a deep breath. If anything, thoughts of Danielle should have reduced the size of his erection but they hadn't. That meant thoughts of Chloe outweighed thoughts of Danielle by a large margin. He doubted Danielle ever got him this aroused without even touching her. As far as he was concerned, this sort of physical reaction to a woman had to be cruel and unusual punishment.

Ramsey moved toward the bed, swearing with every step. He had to get up just as early as Chloe did. There were early morning chores that had to be done. Already a few of his nosy family members had called asking questions after a number of his men had bragged about his new cook and how pretty she was. News carried in Westmoreland Country and no doubt some were anticipating his next move and taking bets as to how quick he would be getting her from under his roof.

As far as he was concerned that was a no-brainer. She was definitely on her way out of there. He was determined that no matter what, he would be contacting the employment agency about finding him a replacement.

# Chapter 4

When Chloe heard a sound behind her she didn't stop beating the huge bowl full of eggs because she knew who it was. She was determined that nothing about Ramsey Westmoreland was going to unnerve her today. After all, he wasn't the only man alive with a lot of sexual appeal, although he happened to be the only one who seemed to hold her interest.

She considered turning around to greet him and then decided because he was the one who'd entered the kitchen, he should be the one to make the gesture. If he didn't, it wouldn't be any sweat off her back, namely because she didn't have any sweat left after those naughty dreams last night where he'd had a starring role.

"Morning."

Okay, he'd done the proper thing and spoke first, but

did he have to do so with such a deep huskiness in his voice? Such raw sexuality in his tone? It had only been one word for crying out loud. Yet the sound that had emitted from his lips was sending shudders through her body and had the potential to do other things she just didn't want to think about this early in the morning. It wasn't even four yet. And it was going to be a busy morning and an even busier noon.

Reluctantly, she turned around, deciding she would at least return his greeting. "Good—"

She swallowed the other word. And was that a moan she'd heard that had just passed her lips? Ramsey West-moreland had the nerve, the sheer audacity to be standing in the middle of the kitchen putting on a shirt. At least now he was buttoning it up. But not before she'd caught a glimpse of his naked chest, ultra-fine biceps, sculpted shoulders and muscular arms. And it didn't help matters that his jeans were riding low on his hips and he was barefoot. It was quite obvious he had just taken a shower and had shaved. But still, he had that early-morning take-me-as-I-am look and she was tempted to do just that.

She wished she had the strength not to let her gaze hone in on such a powerful muscled body, but you could call her weak and she would answer. She was seeing firsthand why she wanted him as her *Simply Irresistible* man.

His gaze met hers when he'd noticed her looking and held on to her eyes until the last button was done. What a pity, she thought. She had enjoyed the show.

"I can't believe you beat me up," he said, now slipping a belt through the loops of his jeans.

Chloe wondered if it was the norm for him to get dressed in the middle of his kitchen. "I couldn't sleep," she decided to say. "Unfamiliar bed." There was no reason to tell him what had really kept her awake.

"But you did get enough sleep to function this morning," he stated. "The men will be hungry," he added.

She snorted, not caring how it sounded. "Mama Francine said men are always hungry. Even when their stomachs are full."

He leaned against the counter. "And who is Mama Francine?"

Too late she realized she might have said too much, but quickly decided telling him about Mama Francine wasn't giving anything away. "She's the person who taught me how to cook."

He nodded and she turned back to her eggs. She wasn't sure how many men would want their eggs scrambled, but she wanted to have the mixture ready just in case. And Mama Francine had taught her how to flip eggs, so those who didn't want their egg scrambled could tell her just how they liked it.

She heard him move, but refused to look up again. Besides, she knew he was moving toward her with a slow walk and glancing around inspecting everything while doing so. And with every step he took closer to her she felt his heat. It was even more powerful than what the stove was generating.

"I'm impressed."

She couldn't help but smile as she glanced over her shoulder. "Again?"

"Yep. You're serving both bacon and sausage."

She lifted a brow. Curious. "Something's wrong with that?"

He shrugged. "No. It's just that usually Nellie did one or the other."

She gazed him a pointed look. "Well, I'm not Nellie."

His heavy-lidded eyes raked over her. Slowly. Thoroughly. Then he said in a voice drenched with masculine awareness. "I can see that."

She didn't know what to say to that, so she said nothing at all before turning back around, placing the egg mixture aside to give attention to the pan of biscuits.

She knew he was staring at her legs and was tempted to pull her skirt down. However, doing so would give him the impression she was uncomfortable with what she was wearing. She wasn't nor should she be. It was a decent length and, therefore, it was appropriate. It hit just a little above the knee, but she was wearing leggings underneath. If he were to see her in some of the other outfits she owned, the ones that barely covered her thighs, he would probably be shocked.

"And we're getting homemade biscuits, too?"

She couldn't help the grin that touched her lips when she moved to open the oven door and slide the pan of biscuits inside. "Another abnormality?"

"Around here, yes."

That made Chloe wonder why this Nellie didn't prepare more of a variety of foods for breakfast. After closing the oven door she turned around, trying to ignore how responsive certain parts of her body were to Ramsey's nearness. He looked like he needed another five hours of sleep to do him justice, yet at the same time he looked sexy as sin. "May I ask you a question, Ramsey?"

He shrugged those massive shoulders again. "Depends on what you want to know."

She crossed her arms under her breasts and wondered if that had been a good thing when his eyes, half-asleep or not, followed the movement and seemed to be staring right through the material of her blouse to her nipples. At least the nipples thought so and were tingling at the attention they were getting. They were tingling and getting hard all at the same time.

"I want to know why this Nellie didn't offer more of a variety to the men at breakfast time."

She watched as a grin quirked his lips. "If you knew Nellie you wouldn't have to ask that question."

She rolled her eyes. "I don't know Nellie, so I'm asking it."

He tilted his head to the side, focusing those ever-so-intense eyes on her. And weakling that she was, immediately felt her body's response to his gaze. She wondered if he could detect it. It seemed so unreal that she would react to him this way when Daren couldn't get a spark of response out of her no matter how much he tried. But then, he hadn't tried too often. He'd been more interested in building his political future by parading Senator Burton's daughter out in front of those he felt he needed to impress. And when they were alone he was more into surfing the internet for political blogs than getting into her. And those times when he had given her his attention, he might as well not have bothered. To say Daren hadn't had a romantic bone in his body was an understatement. However, the final straw came when he'd actually suggested they participate in a threesome. He claimed that kind of sexual kinkiness was a total turn on for him. For a man who couldn't even handle a twosome to fix his mouth to propose such a thing was too much. She'd sent him packing with the few items he had kept at her place and with a clear understanding not to come back.

Since then she had to focus all her energy—sexual and otherwise—into making her magazine a success and refused to think about having any type of a relationship with a man, and now, here she was, behaving like some supercharged, highly-sexed woman, ready to unzip his pants and jump his bones.

"Nellie figured that for breakfast she would give them just the basic, enough to get by so they could really be hungry by lunchtime," he interrupted her thoughts by stating.

She raised a brow. In her opinion that didn't make much sense. "Wouldn't they be hungry at lunchtime anyway?"

"Yes."

Chloe opened her mouth to say something, then snapped it shut, deciding to leave it alone. She and Nellie were two different people and the way the woman ran her kitchen was none of Chloe's business. Chloe's concern, her aim, was to make sure by the time she confessed who she was, Ramsey would feel he was irrevocably in her debt. And if offering the men who worked for him a variety at breakfast was going to get brownie points with him, then so be it. Besides, after listening to the men yesterday, it was quite obvious that most of them would like a home-cooked meal and she had no problem giving them one. Besides, being back in the kitchen had made her realize just how much she enjoyed cooking.

She heard the sound of a vehicle pulling up. "Sounds like your men are starting to arrive."

He shook his head. "No, it's Callum. He always arrives earlier than the others. He and I usually have business to discuss in the mornings."

She nodded. She had noticed the man yesterday and could tell he and Ramsey had more than just an employer-employee relationship. They seemed to be close friends. "He's from the Outback, isn't he?"

Ramsey had moved to where the coffeepot was sitting to pour a cup of coffee. He took a sip and frowned. The woman could even make damn good coffee. "Yes," he finally said, answering her question.

Few people, including some members of Ramsey's own family, knew that Callum was a millionaire in his own right and owned a vast amount of land in Australia. He had several sheep ranches in Australia that were run by a very efficient staff. There was no need to tell her that the Aussie donated to charity the salary he earned as Ramsey's ranch manager.

Callum, at thirty-four, was the product of a wealthy white Australian father and an African American mother. His family had made billions in the sheep ranching business. Another thing she didn't need to know was that the only reason Callum was still hanging around here instead of moseying it back to Australia was because he didn't plan to leave without Gemma going with him.

Callum knew Ramsey well enough to know that

when it came to his three sisters, Ramsey was a tad overprotective and would stop any advances on Megan, Gemma or Bailey cold. It had taken the Aussie a full year to convince Ramsey that his intentions toward Gemma were honorable and that he loved her and wanted to marry her. Both Ramsey and Dillon had given Callum their blessings for a marriage; however, they'd made it clear the final decision would be Gemma's. His sister had never given any indication that she was the least bit interested in Callum and was virtually clueless in regards to Callum's interest in her. As far as Ramsey was concerned maybe that was a good thing because Gemma was known to be a handful at times and would definitely have a lot to say about it; especially when she'd stated on more than one occasion that she never intended to ever give her heart to any man. That meant the Aussie had his work cut out for him if he intended to win her over.

Ramsey glanced around the kitchen before returning his gaze to Chloe. "It seems that you have everything under control."

"Sorry you thought that I wouldn't."

The mockery of her words had him frowning. Something told him that when it came to an attitude, hers was worse than his sister's. "It's not that I thought you wouldn't, Chloe. I think you more than proved your capabilities yesterday."

She lifted her chin. "Then what is it with you?"

He could pretend he had no idea what she was talking about, but he didn't. If the truth be told, he was the one with the attitude and was well aware it had probably been the pits since their initial meeting. He wasn't used to having to deal with a woman who made men pause when she walked into a room. A woman who wore her sexuality like it was a brand with her name on it. A woman who even now had blood surging through his veins.

And a woman he wanted to kiss.

His heart was racing at the very thought of locking his mouth with hers, and he knew at that moment if she stayed another night under his roof he would be doing that very thing if for no other reason than to get her out of his system. It would only be right to give her fair warning.

"How old are you, Chloe?"

From her expression he could tell she was wondering what her age had to do with anything. "I'm twenty-eight."

He nodded slowly, while his gazed continued to hold hers. "Then I would think you'd know what it is with me. But just in case you don't have a clue, I'll show you later."

Chloe felt a slow burn in her midsection followed by the feel of her heart thudding erratically in her chest. The meaning behind his words was pretty clear. If it hadn't been, then his eyes would have spelled things out for her. She could see the promises in the dark depths. Promises he wasn't trying to hide. Promises he intended to keep.

Before she could level a response the back door opened and Callum Austell walked in. He looked first at her and then at Ramsey. The smile that touched the man's lips would have been too deadly sexy if she hadn't thought Ramsey had a monopoly on sexiness.

"Ram. Chloe. Did I come at a bad time?" Callum asked in a low tone.

Chloe watched an irritated frown touch Ramsey's features and she drew in a deep breath. Lucia had warned her that he was a private person and she wasn't sure just how he felt about his friend picking up on the sexual tension flowing between them. It was tension so thick you could probably cut it with a knife and then spread it on bread. Deciding she needed to play off Callum's words, make the man think he was wrong in his assumption, she turned to Callum, opened her mouth to speak, but Ramsey beat her to it.

"No, you didn't come at a bad time. Come on, Cal, let's have that meeting." He then sat the coffee cup he'd been holding on the counter with a thud and headed out of the room. He stopped and glanced over his shoulder at Callum who had halted beside her.

"You sure look nice this morning, Chloe," Callum said in a husky tone with his deep Australian accent.

Chloe glanced up at the handsome man whom she figured was a year or two younger than Ramsey and couldn't help wondering what he was about. Had he just delivered a polite comment or a blatant flirtation?

"You're wasting my time, Cal. Are we meeting or what?" Ramsey called out in a sharp tone.

Callum looked across the room at Ramsey and smiled. "We're meeting."

And then he moved to follow Ramsey out of the room.

Ramsey clenched his jaw until he was in the office and then he all but slammed the door shut before facing Callum. The other man had the nerve, the very audacity, the damn gall, to smile. "What the hell was that about?" he asked through gritted teeth.

Callum gave him an innocent look, one Ramsey wasn't buying or selling. "I don't know what you mean, Ram."

Ramsey leaned back against his desk and frowned. "You were flirting with her."

Callum shrugged as another smile formed at the corners of his lips. "What if I was?"

Ramsey crossed his arms over his chest. "If you did it to get a rise out of me, then—"

"It worked," Callum taunted as he eased his muscular frame into a chair across from the desk. "Come on, Ram. Go ahead and admit you want the woman, which is why you're trying to get rid of her. When you know for yourself, even after eating just one meal, that she's a lot better cook than Nellie and her temperament is a vast improvement to what we're used to. I hate to say it but Nellie hasn't been missed around here and you know why."

Ramsey drew in a deep breath. Yes, he did know why. Nellie's disposition had begun deteriorating months ago after discovering her husband had been unfaithful to her. It was as if she had taken her hurt and anger out on the entire male population and his men knew it. They had tried being understanding, even sympathetic. But then after a while they'd become annoyed and just plain irritated. There was nothing worse than pissing a man off about his food.

Although Nellie's unexpected trip had placed him in a bind, he thought she needed the distance from his men for a while and vice versa. She still had a job when she returned, but the two of them would have a long talk first.

"Okay, so Nellie hasn't been missed, but when she comes back, she still has a job," he decided to speak up.

"Fine. Great. But in the meantime I think your men deserve a nice smile and friendly words every now and then, not to mention food they can eat without worrying about it being burned or overly seasoned."

Ramsey was silent.

"Look, I understand your problem with Chloe, Ram. Welcome to the club. I know how it is to want a woman so bad you ache," Callum said.

Ram frowned. He then narrowed his eyes on his friend. "You're referring to my sister," he said in a warning tone.

Callum snorted. "I'm referring to the woman I intend to marry who refuses to give me the time of day and it's getting damn near frustrating. Don't be surprised one day if you wake up and find us both gone." A smile touched Callum's lips. "I might resort to kidnapping."

Ram's frown deepened. "You'd better be joking." He then shook his head at Callum's outrageous threat. And then he couldn't help but chuckle. "Go ahead and kidnap her. I'll give you less than a week and you'll be bringing her back. Gemma will make your life a living hell if you did such a thing and I wouldn't be one to close my eyes on her if I were you. She likes getting even."

Ram smiled. Although he'd gone a little overboard he knew Callum got the picture. Of his three sisters,

Gemma was the one who had a knack for not only speaking her mind but for backing up her thoughts. Callum knew this and was still in love with her. Go figure.

"Are you really thinking about letting Chloe go?" Callum asked and Ramsey figured he was now desperate to change the subject from Gemma back to Chloe. "I think it's a sin and a shame that your men will have to suffer just because you can't control your urges," Callum said.

Ramsey knew there was really no reason to deny what Callum had just said. It was true. He was finding it hard to control his urges around Chloe. And they were urges he'd been controlling just fine before she'd shown up.

"The men are taking a bet as to how long we'll keep her." Callum grinned and said, "I bet some will be surprised to find her still here this morning."

Ramsey didn't see anything amusing. He didn't like being reminded that others had noticed his interest in her yesterday. "She's not the only good cook around these parts."

"I'm sure she isn't, but not many would want to have to live on the ranch. Most would probably have homes of their own; families they had to take care of when they left here like Nellie." Callum rubbed his chin thoughtfully. "Um, that makes me wonder."

Ramsey lifted a brow. "About what?"

"Why would a woman with her looks take a job where she'll have to live here in the middle of nowhere for two solid weeks. Doesn't she have any family?"

Ramsey considered Callum's question. To be honest

Chloe's personal life hadn't crossed his mind, mainly because he hadn't intended for her to stay. In fact, he had planned to call the employment agency when it opened this morning to see how soon they could send a replacement. But Callum had posed a good question. Evidently she did have a place in town because she had returned last night with her luggage in tow.

"What if she's on the run and took the job to hide out here?"

Ramsey looked over at Callum. "On the run from what?"

"An abusive husband. A psycho fiancé. A possessive boyfriend. Hell, I don't know, Ram. But if I were you I would find out."

Ramsey's frown hardened at the thought that Chloe might be running from a demented stalker. But then when he'd mentioned to her yesterday that she was hired as a live-in cook she'd seemed surprised. And last night she claimed that she'd only returned after deciding she didn't want to risk being late this morning. What if there was more than that?

"I don't think she's married or engaged because she's not wearing a ring and there's no indentation around her finger to indicate that she's worn one in the past," he said.

Callum chuckled. "You're as bad as Eric and Thel if you noticed all of that about a woman's finger."

Ramsey shrugged his shoulders, refusing to let Callum bait him. "Whatever."

"Well, it might be *whatever* if you don't find out. If you make her leave, then you could very well be sending her to her death."

Ramsey rolled his eyes. "Spare me the dramatics."

Callum stood. "Don't say I didn't warn you if something were to happen to her." He headed for the door.

Ramsey watched him about to leave. "Hey, where are you going? We haven't had our meeting yet."

Callum smiled over at him. "And we won't. At least not this morning. I smell homemade biscuits and *both* bacon and sausage. If you're still thinking about getting rid of her, then I need to make sure I eat well this morning. No telling what we might end up with for lunch."

Ramsey had always been a man who'd prided himself on two things: strength of mind and self-control. He felt both take a flying leap when he walked into the dining area an hour later. His men were gone and Chloe was clearing off the table. She glanced over in his direction and the moment he looked into her eyes, he wanted to cross the room and pull her to him and kiss her until she was nothing more than a limp body in his arms.

"You missed breakfast, but I kept you something warming in the oven. The eggs will be made to order," she said.

He nodded, surprised she had thought of him. "Thanks." He had deliberately remained in his office, trying to concentrate on finishing reports he had failed to do last night. His men's voices had carried to his office and he could tell from their conversations that they had enjoyed breakfast and were looking forward to lunch.

"Your men were wondering why you didn't eat breakfast with them."

He glanced over at her as he poured a cup of coffee, wondering if his men had been the ones speculating or if it had been her. "Were they?"

"Yes."

When he didn't say anything but sipped his coffee while watching her, she said. "If you're ready to eat I'll get your plate out of the oven."

"Thanks. I'd appreciate it."

He moved toward the table and after sitting down he watched her and wondered if Callum's speculations were true. Was she living here at the ranch as his cook because she was on the run from someone? He sipped his coffee thinking that he was not one to overreact, but what if some of what Callum assumed was true?

"How do you want your eggs, Ramsey?"

He blinked, realizing she had asked him a question. "Excuse me? What did you say?"

"Your eggs. Do you prefer scrambled, sunny-side up or over easy?"

It was on the tip of his tongue to say he preferred them *over her* so he could lick them off, but thought better of it. She was wearing another short dress and like last night she had spoiled the effect by a pair of leggings. What was with those things? Why the hell were women wearing them under their dresses? He enjoyed seeing bare skin. Nothing was wrong with seeing a nice piece of feminine flesh on occasion. And although he'd never seen her legs, he had no reason to believe they weren't gorgeous, a real arousal-getter just like the rest of her.

The lower part of his body was already throbbing with the way her outfit fit over her bottom, showing a perfect shape. He could just imagine lying in bed with that backside curved against his front in spoon fashion, dipping his head to nibble on her neck and to place marks of passion there before moving toward...

"Ramsey?"

He blinked again. "Yes?"

"How do you want your eggs?"

"Sunny-side up will be fine."

He watched how she handled the frying pan. There was no doubt in his mind she knew what she was doing. And the way she cracked the egg was sure and precise. He couldn't help wondering about her cooking skills. Had she gone to culinary school? If so, why wasn't she working at a first-class restaurant somewhere? Why was she here on a sheep ranch on the outskirts of Denver? There was only one way to find out. He'd discovered that with some women if you got them talking they would tell you just about anything you wanted to know. It worked with Bailey, although it hadn't been a proven trick with Megan or Gemma.

As she cooked his eggs he studied her. She didn't look like a woman under any sort of duress. She seemed calm and looked cool. And she appeared to enjoy what she was doing.

His gaze moved to her face. She didn't have normal features. She was beautiful. Soft-looking brown skin, a sensual pair of eyes, a cute nose and a pair of lips he longed to taste. Her dark brown hair was shoulder length, lustrous curly strands. It didn't take much to imagine that hair spread across a pillow. His pillow. And those sensual dark eyes shimmering with arousal right as she shifted her body to spread her thighs, open her legs to fill the air with her scent while he stared down at her feminine mound, moist, ready, waiting for him to sample.

The surge of desire that swept through him at that moment was so fierce it almost took his breath away. He needed something stronger than a cup of coffee and was tempted to pull a beer out of the refrigerator. Instead he drew in a long, deep breath, shifted his gaze to look out the window. Think about something else. The bill that was soon to come due on his new tractor. The fact that Gemma was bugging him about decorating the rest of his house. Anything except making hot, carnal love to Chloe.

Trying to regain control of his libido and senses, he looked over toward her. She might know how to wield a frying pan and all that, but there was a refined air about her that disconnected her ability in the kitchen with the way she carried herself. It was as if she should be getting served instead of being the one doing the serving. "Are you married?"

She glanced over at him but only for a second. She went back to concentrating on cooking his eggs. "No."

"You sure?"

Her head lifted and she stared at him, gave him a look like he'd suddenly grown two heads or something. "Of course I'm sure." She held up her left hand. "See, no ring."

He shrugged. "That doesn't mean anything these days."

She frowned as she slid his egg from the frying pan onto the plate. "It would mean something to me."

"Okay, so you're not married. Are you involved in a serious relationship?"

She set the plate in front of him and gave him a pointed look. "Is there a reason for these questions?"

He smiled. Because she asked he might as well go ahead and tell her. She was mature enough to handle it. "Yes, there's a reason. When I get around to kissing you I'll feel better knowing your mouth doesn't belong to any other man. Legally or otherwise."

She didn't say anything for a moment. Then she opened her mouth, probably to tell him just where he could take his own mouth—legally or otherwise—but instead of saying anything right then, she just tightened her lips together.

He chuckled. "Tightening those lips shut won't keep me from prying them apart for a kiss if that's what I want to do, Chloe."

Chloe folded her arms across her chest. "Is there a reason for this madness?"

"Is that what this is? Madness?" he asked as he began eating.

She lifted her chin and glared at him. "You got another name for it?"

"What about hunger?"

She frowned. "Hunger?"

"Yes, hunger of a sexual nature. I need to get you out of my system and I figured I'll start by kissing you to see if that will work."

Chloe dropped her hands by her side. Not believing he'd said such a thing. And not believing her heart was thumping rapidly in her chest at the thought of him making good on his threat. "You're nothing like Daren."

He raised a dark brow. "Who's Daren?"

"The last guy I was involved with."

Ramsey ignored the twinge of jealousy that invaded his gut. "Is not being like Daren good or bad?"

She shrugged. "Not sure. Although, I think it would have been nice if he would have had even a fraction of that *hunger* thing."

He immediately caught on to what she'd insinuated. "I can't imagine any man hanging around you for long without wanting to gobble you alive. He must have been a real idiot."

Chloe kept herself from smiling and refused to admit she'd thought the same thing. "He had his own ideas about what down to earth lovemaking was about. He suggested that we participate in a threesome."

Ramsey frowned. He could handle the fact that her ex-boyfriend hadn't had a passionate bone in his body, but the thought that the man had actually wanted to share her with someone else was as demented as it could get. No man in his right mind would share her.

"Then he wasn't just an idiot," Ramsey spoke up to say. "He was a crazy idiot. Any man who could get it into his mind to share you evidently doesn't have the brain he was born with. There's no way I would consider doing such a thing. I would want you all to myself."

His gaze roamed over her. "It would be me and me alone who would leave a satisfied smile on your lips, Chloe."

Chloe felt a tightening in her stomach as his gaze

slowly swept over her, lingering in certain places and
bestowing a visual caress in others. And his deep seductive voice was stirring all kinds of sensations to
life inside her.

"How long were you with this guy?"

She wondered why he wanted to know. "A year."

"And how long have the two of you been apart?"

Chloe wasn't sure why he wanted to know that, either. Why she'd even shared anything with him about
Daren in the first place was a mystery to her. But she
had and evidently he was curious. "Two years. Now
if you will excuse me I'm about to tackle the dishes."

Ramsey watched her walk off over to the sink and,
since she was doing her best to ignore him, he dug into
his meal. Not surprisingly, everything was delicious
and for the first time in a long while, he was enjoying
his food. He was also enjoying watching Chloe while
he ate. If she only knew all the things that were running through his mind while chewing on a piece of
bacon and swallowing his toast.

She refused to look over at him which was probably
a good thing. Instead she was trying to keep busy and
continued to ignore him in the process. By the time
he had finished breakfast and drained the last of his
coffee, she had stacked all the dishes on the counter
to load into the huge dishwasher. She wiped down the
countertops until they gleamed.

Getting up from the table he crossed the kitchen to
the sink to place his plate and cup in the sudsy water.
And when he turned toward her she made a quick move
to get out of his way. She wasn't fast enough and he
reached out and took hold of her hand.

A shiver immediately rushed down Chloe's spine and she sucked in a sharp breath the instant Ramsey touched her. She tilted her head and looked up at him. He was standing in front of her and his gaze, she noticed, was intense as ever and centered directly on her lips. Then his eyes moved slowly up her face to her eyes. He smiled and then slid his gaze back down to her lips again.

She knew at that moment he was about to make good on his threat to kiss her. Heat began formulating at the center of her thighs, and the way he was staring at her lips made her hot. Wet. Then something within her began to ache. It was a hollowed emptiness she just realized was there. He moved a step closer and his scent inflamed everything within her, pulling her into the depths of his masculinity, swirling her about and drawing her under into his sensual spell.

She studied him, became enmeshed in the starkly strong features of his face. He was a very handsome man, so much so that her senses were betraying her, refusing to let her do the right thing and demand he remove his hand from hers. Instead she felt herself easing toward him at the same time he shifted his body even closer to hers.

Chloe found herself pinned between him and the counter, felt the hardness of his erection come to rest between her thighs like it had every right to be there. For the first time in her life she felt totally in sync with a man, fully aware of who he was and what he could do. And the thought of what he could do, what he *would* do sent an intense shiver up her spine. It made her anxious to the point where she felt her nerves beginning to quiver. She swallowed deeply and when that didn't help her she took her tongue and swiped it across her lower lip.

*Not a good move.*

She looked into his face and saw the effect doing such a thing had on him. By no means was she trying to encourage him and when she saw heat flare in his eyes, she knew something elementally male was taking place and he had no intention of fighting it.

He leaned forward and before she could catch her next breath, he bent his head and captured her lips.

## Chapter 5

Ramsey had told Chloe this wasn't madness, but at
that moment he knew that quite possibly it was worse.
There was no way to explain why the moment his lips
touched hers he'd felt something he couldn't name or
define slid up his spine. And her taste—rich, honeyed
and sweet—drove him to stroke his tongue all over her
mouth, sample her everywhere, taste her, and with a
greed that made him groan. And when he released his
hold on her wrist to place his hands at the center of her
back, he shifted positions as fire spread through him.

Energy he didn't think he had, especially after a
sleepless night, raced through him, gripped him hard,
made his erection swell that much more. He wanted to
think this was ludicrous, but he knew this was as sexual
as it could get, as he took her mouth in a hot and urgent
kind of way. He was determined to make her feel all

the things he was feeling at that moment. And when she took hold of his tongue, he knew he'd succeeded.

The hands at her back became possessive, they lowered to cup her backside and she moaned at the same time she moved against him. They were chest to breast, hip to thigh, with mouths locked tight and tongues mingling wildly. He'd said he was sexually hungry and he was proving just how famished he was.

And the way his hands were now moving over her, as if outlining the shape of her bottom, was driving him insane. He was becoming acquainted with her curves and all her soft yielding flesh. There was no doubt in his mind that while he took her mouth with a passion, she could feel his aroused body part pressing deeply into the juncture of her legs as if that was where it belonged.

He heard the moans coming from her throat and every time one escaped he deepened the kiss that much more. He was tempted to spread her out on the kitchen table at that very moment and have his way with her. Take her with a passion until he was too weak to stand.

"We could always leave and come back later."

The heavy voice made them jump apart like kids who'd gotten caught with their hands in the cookie jar. Filled with both anger and protectiveness Ramsey moved in front of Chloe while glaring at his brothers, Zane and Derringer, and his cousin Jason.

"What the hell are the three of you doing here?"

Derringer smiled. "We had a meeting. You told us to be here at seven. Sharp. Threatened us with dire straits if we were late. Did you forget?"

He had.

"We can understand if you did forget," Zane said. He was two years younger than Ramsey and known as a smart-mouth.

"It's no big deal, Ram," Jason said. Jason was the easygoing cousin and his trademark smile was genuine. "It would be nice if you introduced us," Jason added.

"Yeah," Zane said grinning. "Any reason you're hiding her behind your back?"

Cursing quietly, Ramsey realized he was doing that very thing. He stepped aside and the moment his brothers' eyes lit on Chloe, all three gave her an appreciative male perusal. He loved every member of his family, but at that moment thoughts of doing these three in actually made him want to smile.

"Chloe, I want you to meet my brothers, Zane and Derringer, and my cousin Jason." And then to his brothers and cousin, he said. "Guys, this is Chloe Burton, my new cook."

Chloe had never been so embarrassed in her entire life and actually felt the color stain her already-dark skin. From the way the three were staring at her she could only assume that they'd never walked in on Ramsey kissing a woman before.

She extended her hand to them. "How do you do?"

Their handshakes were firm and as she locked eyes with each of them she saw a friendliness in their dark depths. And there was no doubt in her mind that when placed in the same room with a crowd anyone could easily guess they were related. They all had the same chiseled jaw, dark brown eyes, dimpled smile and creamy brown skin. They were extremely handsome men. Her gaze was momentarily drawn back to Derringer, the man who had her best friend's heart and he didn't even know it.

"Okay, so much for introductions," Ramsey broke into her thoughts and said aloud. "Let's have that meeting."

Zane, she noticed, was still holding on to her hand. He smiled, glanced over at Ramsey and said, "The three of you can have a meeting. I prefer staying here with Chloe. I hear she can whip up the best scrambled eggs this side of the Rockies."

She watched Ramsey tip his head back and sigh. He then fixed his brother a leveled stare. "Don't push things with me, Zane."

Zane drew his gaze from Ramsey and glanced down at Chloe. She thought the smile that tugged at his lips was devilish. "What about a rain check, Chloe? Tomorrow perhaps?"

She could only nod and then watched the three men follow Ramsey from the room.


"That pretty much sums things up," Jason was saying. "I talked to Durango and McKinnon yesterday and they are excited at the prospect of expanding their operation to Colorado."

Ramsey nodded. Durango Westmoreland and McKinnon Quinn were cousins of theirs, Durango by blood and McKinnon by marriage. The two lived in Montana and owned M&D, a very successful horse breeding and training operation. A few years ago they had invited another cousin, Clint Westmoreland, who lived in Texas, to join their million-dollar business.

And now they were making the same offer to Zane, Derringer and Jason. The three had traveled to Bozeman and spent three weeks with Durango and McKinnon and their families, learning more about the operation and to determine if it was a business venture they wanted to become a part of. As all three were fine horsemen, Ramsey couldn't imagine their turning down the offer.

"So the three of you are really thinking about doing it?" he asked as he looked over the report. Everything was in order and M&D was doing extremely well; especially after Prince Charming, a horse they had trained for Sheikh Jamal Yasir—another cousin by marriage— had placed in the Kentucky Derby.

"Yes, and we figured since our three properties are adjacent to each other," Jason was saying, "we can share acreage for grazing land and for future expansions. But what we don't want to do is to reduce the land you need for your sheep."

Ramsey nodded, appreciating their concern. Sheep required a lot of land and his siblings and cousins had been very generous in letting him use some of theirs for grazing purposes. At present he was satisfied with the number of sheep he owned, and other than the lambs due to be born at the end of the month, he didn't intend to increase his herd anytime soon.

"With what Dillon and I own together, there will be plenty enough," he said to the three. "And before Bane took off for the Navy he gave Dillon permission for me to use his land if there was a need. A few days ago I received a letter notifying me that the federal government has approved my use of land at Diamond

Ridge, so I'll start taking part of the herd there later this year for grazing."

Ramsey glanced back down at the report. "Although I have my hands full here with the sheep, I'll be interested in becoming a silent partner with the M&D Colorado-based operation once it gets started. I think it's time that I consider diversifying. It's not good to have all your eggs in one basket."

"True," Zane nodded, casting his brother a smile. "We would love to have you on board. And speaking of eggs, you kind of got uptight when I invited myself to breakfast."

Ramsey snorted as he leaned back in his chair. "What is it with you and Callum with your crazy games? Chloe is off limits."

Derringer, who was slouched down on the love seat, glanced over at Ramsey and asked in a belligerent tone. "Says who?"

Ramsey frowned. Derringer was younger than him by three years and enjoyed being argumentative. "Says me, Derringer. Evidently you either didn't get it or you didn't understand the message I gave Zane in the kitchen."

"So, you're saying Chloe is more than just your cook?" Jason asked, as if for clarification.

Ramsey hauled in a deep breath, irritated at the thought of having to explain anything to his relatives. But knowing them the way he did, he knew he'd better do so. There was no doubt in his mind that there would be more explaining to do to the others when word got around that these three had walked in on him kissing Chloe. Zane was probably just itching to tell everyone, especially because it had been eons since Ramsey had been involved with a woman.

"Chloe is nothing more than my cook," he said.

Now it was Zane who snorted. "I don't recall you ever kissing Nellie."

Ramsey rolled his eyes. "Nellie is a married woman."

Derringer straightened in his seat and lifted a brow. "Are you saying if she wasn't married you'd be kissing her?"

Before he could respond Zane burst out laughing while slapping his thigh. "Damn, Ramsey, we didn't know you had it in you. And all this time we figured you were living a dull and sexually inactive life."

Ramsey took a deep, calming breath. His brothers were trying to get a rise out of him and he refused to fall prey to their tactics any more than he had to Callum's earlier. He tossed the document he was holding on his desk. "Let me get something straight. The kiss the three of you walked in on was something that just happened. Chloe is my cook and nothing more. She'll be living here for two weeks until Nellie returns."

He then leaned forward to make sure they heard his next words clearly. "However, since I know how two of the three of you operate, I want to make it clear here and now that she is *not* open game. You're all welcome to breakfast, lunch or dinner at any time, as always. But that's all you're welcome to."

"Um, that sounds kind of territorial, Ram," Zane said, eyeing his brother.

Ramsey shrugged. "Think whatever you like, just make sure you heed my warning."

* * *

Later that evening Chloe went into Ramsey's living room and sat on the sofa with a glass of wine in her hand. She curled her feet beneath her as she took a sip. It felt good to relax after a tiring day.

Although she enjoyed being in the kitchen, spending her time cooking for a group of men was not how she had envisioned her month-long vacation. Especially one that had started off in the Bahamas.

But she would have to admit that just seeing the satisfied grins on Ramsey's men's faces when they had eaten breakfast that morning and lunch at noon had been worth all the time she had spent over a stove.

The men asked her to make more homemade biscuits in the morning, and they liked having a choice of bacon and sausage. She would surprise them tomorrow by going a step further and making omelets.

She had checked with her office in Florida and had spoken briefly to her editor-in-chief. Everything was going fine, which Chloe wasn't surprised about. She had an efficient team who ran things whether she was in the office, and that's the way she wanted it. Her father had told her time and time again that to be successful as CEO of your own company, you needed a good team working for you who could handle just about anything in your absence. She had built *Simply Irresistible* to the magazine it was and was using her time expanding the market area.

Her thoughts shifted from the magazine to Ramsey and the kiss they had shared earlier that day. It was the kiss that three members of his family had witnessed. She could just imagine how Ramsey felt about it, which was probably the reason he had avoided her most of the day. He hadn't dined with his men at lunch and he hadn't returned to the ranch since she had noticed his leaving early that afternoon.

She couldn't help wondering if the kiss had worked and she was out of his system. She might be out of his, but now he was deeply embedded into hers. Never had she been kissed so thoroughly before. Never had a man explored her mouth the way he had, in such a blatantly carnal way. There had not been anything traditional about his kiss. He had delivered it with an expertise that had left her panting for hours. She had been both affected and infected by his kiss. Even now her lips were still tingling.

She would be the first to admit things were not going as she planned with him. She had been attracted to him from the first, so there was no surprise at that. But what had been a surprise, totally unexpected, was the degree of hot tension that surrounded them whenever they were in the same room. Or her to be thinking about jumping his bones whenever she saw him. In her line of business, she met plenty of good-looking men. But none had ever sparked her interest, or stimulated a deep attraction the way Ramsey had.

How was she supposed to live under his roof, breathe the same air, when sexual thoughts constantly flowed through her mind? And unfortunately that kiss had been the icing on the cake. There was no doubt in her mind that she was now addicted to his taste as well as to his masculine scent.

Chloe's thoughts shifted back to what Ramsey had said about never sharing her with anyone. There had been something about it that had touched her. She drew in a deep breath at the realization that something about Ramsey was getting to her. And she knew at that moment that he was a man in a way that Daren could never be. Ramsey was someone who could and would take care of his own. That was evident by the way he had taken on the responsibility of raising his siblings. Although he could be brusque at times, she believed he didn't have a selfish bone in his body.

And knowing that was what was endearing him to her.

She felt panic in her chest at the thought that anything about Ramsey was endearing to her, but as much as she wanted to deny it she knew it was true. There were so many things about him that reminded him of her father—especially his sense of what was right. She'd seen it in the way he treated his men and his family.

She took another sip of wine. Later she would call Lucia to let her know she'd met Derringer and thought he was definitely a cutie. Although Ramsey had given his brothers and cousin a hard time, she could easily pick up on the love and mutual respect between the four men. And all four were extremely handsome.

But still in her book, Ramsey was her choice. There was something about him that made her heart pound in her chest each and every time she saw him. Maybe the best thing would be to abandon the idea of his posing for the cover of her magazine. She should go ahead and tell him the truth tonight and be packed and ready to leave. But if she did that, it would leave him in a bind. His men were counting on her to provide them with a delicious breakfast in the morning and a tasty meal at lunch. Besides, she was not a quitter, so no matter how tough things got she would not throw in the towel.

She leaned over and placed her glass of wine on the coffee table when she heard her cell phone go off. She pulled it out of her skirt pocket and smiled when she saw the call was from her father.

"Dad, how are you?"

"I'm doing fine. Just where the heck are you, Chloe Lynn?"

She chuckled. Nobody but her father called her by her first and middle names. Only after she'd finished college and started her business did she appreciate what an outstanding man and wonderful person her father was. He had entered politics when she had been in her last year of high school and now he was in his third term as Senator and swore it was the last, but she knew better.

He had always encouraged her to do whatever it was in life that she wanted to do and not live under his shadow as the "senator's daughter." She had gone to the college she had wanted to attend and had gotten the degree in just what she'd wanted. The only thing he flexed his muscles about was his belief in helping others during her summers. In the end she'd never regretted doing so.

"I'm in Denver for now."

"And when will you be coming home?"

She raised a brow. Home for her had always been Tampa, but for her father since becoming Senator Jamison Burton, he'd stayed in D.C. most of the time.

"Not sure when I'll be back in Tampa. Why? What's going on?"

He paused and then said, "I intend to ask Stephanie to marry me tonight, and was hoping you would be here in case she said yes, so we can all celebrate."

Chloe's smile widened. Her father had been dating Circuit Court of Appeals judge Stephanie Wilcox. A fifty-something divorced mother of a son and a daughter in their twenties, her father and Stephanie had been dating for a few years and Chloe had wondered when he would consider asking the woman to share his life.

"That's wonderful, Dad. Congratulations. I'm sorry I won't be there to celebrate, but please make sure you let Stephanie know how happy I am for both of you."

Ten minutes later she was still smiling when she slipped her phone back into her skirt pocket. Finally, her father was about to commit his life to something other than politics and she was happy about it. He had remained a widower and she had often wondered why, when he would be such a good catch for someone. But she'd heard over the years from both sets of grandparents how much he'd loved her mother and he hadn't wanted to give his heart to another woman. It had taken Stephanie three years, but she had done what some would have thought as impossible.

"After all the work that went into feeding my men breakfast and lunch you have a reason to smile?"

Startled, Chloe inclined her head to glance across the room. She hadn't heard the door open and now Ramsey was standing in the doorway and looking at her.

Refusing to be rattled, she reached for her glass of

wine and took a sip, not sure how she would answer his question. There was no way she could share her father's good news on the risk that he might ask questions she didn't want to answer. All he would have to do is to go on the internet and do a search on her father to discover she was his daughter and exactly what she did for a living.

"That's not what the smile is for," she decided to say. "I just received a call from a friend to say he was asking his girl to marry him tonight. And I'm happy for both of them."

She watched as he crossed the room to sit in the chair across from the sofa. She tried not to stare and was surprised he was giving her the time of day when it was obvious he'd been avoiding her earlier, especially after their kiss.

"I guess getting married would make some folks happy," he said.

She took another sip of her wine while holding his gaze, trying not to dwell on just how good he looked while he leaned back in the chair with muscled shoulders, hard jeans-clad thighs and long legs stretched to where his booted feet touched a portion of the coffee table. She wondered if he realized he was still wearing his Stetson. "Um. But I take it that you're not one of them," she replied.

"Nope, I wouldn't be one of them. I intend to be a single man for the rest of my days."

She considered his words. "So, you're one of those men who have a problem with matrimony? Who thinks marriage isn't a big deal?"

He lifted a brow. "And you're one of those women who thinks that it is?"

"I asked you first."

Yes, she had, Ramsey thought. His first inclination was to ignore the question. Move on to something else. And a part of him wondered what the hell he was doing here, sitting across from her at all. Especially because he'd taken great pains to make sure their paths didn't cross after his brothers and cousin had left. He hadn't liked the way Zane, Derringer and Jason's thoughts had been going. He would like to think he had put their false assumptions to rest, but he knew them well enough to know that was too much to hope for.

"Take your time if you need to gather your thoughts," Chloe said.

Ramsey kept his gaze trained on her. Unwavering. He couldn't give her a forced smile even if he'd wanted to because staying single was a serious topic with him. And it wasn't that he had a problem with matrimony per se, after the last fiasco of a wedding, he figured there was not a woman alive who would be able to get him back in a church for the sole purpose of getting hitched. No, he liked his single life just fine. He would think after dealing with the likes of an ex-boyfriend like Daren, so would she.

He continued to look at her, recalled her statement about gathering his thoughts and figured she would get along with his sisters easily because she seemed to have a smart mouth like them. That thought made his gaze shift to her lips.

He then swallowed, wishing he hadn't gone there with her mouth, especially because he knew how it tasted. And then there had been her response to him. He could do bodily harm to his kinfolk for their untimely interruption.

"I don't need to gather my thoughts," he finally said. Otherwise he would be tempted to cross the room and taste her again. "Raphel Westmoreland married enough for all of us."

She lifted a brow. "Raphel Westmoreland?"

"Yes, my great-grandfather. Rather recently we discovered he had a slew of wives. We also discovered he had a twin."

Evidently that sparked her interest, and her movement on the sofa sparked his. She slid closer to the edge and when she leaned forward her blouse gaped open a little, but enough to see some cleavage, as well as the thin pink fabric of her bra. Her skin looked velvety smooth, soft and a beautiful brown. He could imagine removing her bra and then lavishing her breasts with hot kisses, then taking his tongue and—

"Well?"

He blinked, reluctantly shifted his gaze from her chest to her eyes. They were bright. Inquiring. Intrigued. Apparently stuff about long-lost relatives interested her like it did the others in his family. Once they had become acquainted with the Atlanta Westmorelands, who were descendants of his great-grandfather's twin brother Reginald, Dillon had been eager to find out all that he could. His search to uncover the truth had led him to his wife Pamela. So in a way something good had come of it.

"Well, what?" he asked, deciding to play along just for the hell of it. Irritate her a bit. He liked the way her lips curved in a frown when she was aggravated about something. In addition to that, he liked her sexy pose on the sofa and the eager look on her face to find out more. Now if he could only get her out of wearing those damn leggings.

The glare she gave him denoted she was getting impatient, downright annoyed, at the length of time it was taking for him to tell her what she wanted to know. "Tell me some more about your great-grandfather's twin," she said with barely restrained impatience.

He could and would do so if it meant keeping her mind occupied while he continued to check her out. "We discovered over a year ago that our great-grandfather Raphel had a twin by the name of Reginald."

"And none of you had any idea?"

"No. Great-Grampa Raphel led everyone to believe he'd been born the only child. One of the Atlanta Westmorelands' genealogy search provided proof that Raphel and Reginald were twins and that Raphel had been considered the black sheep of the family after running off with a married woman. He finally settled here in Denver five wives later."

Ramsey paused when he felt a rush of sensations hammer his veins when Chloe shifted her body on the sofa once again and his gaze moved to her feet. They were bare and her toes were painted a prissy pink. When had seeing painted toes on a woman become so erotic?

He found it an effort to move his gaze from her feet back to her face, especially when his eyes had to pass over her chest. Of course it lingered awhile before moving on. When he finally settled on her eyes he saw hers were narrowed. "I'm sure there is more to this story," she said.

He nodded. "Of course and maybe one day I'll tell you the rest."

He had no idea why he'd said that. There wouldn't be a "one day" where they were concerned. Although he had changed his mind about calling the agency for another cook, he needed to keep his guard up around her. Yet here he was, misleading her into thinking he would share anything else about his family with her.

He eased out of his chair, deciding he'd said enough and had stayed in here with her longer than he'd needed to. Definitely longer than he should have. It then occurred to him he was still wearing his hat. Damn.

He took it off his head thinking the woman had a way of making him not think straight and that wasn't a good thing. "I'm taking a shower and going out to grab something for dinner," he said, and then wondered why on earth was he telling her his plans. His comings and goings were really none of her business.

He moved to leave the room and head upstairs, but her words stopped him. "I prepared dinner for you, Ramsey."

He stopped, turned and looked over at her. She was only getting paid to fix breakfast and lunch because his men usually ate dinner at their own homes with their families. Usually he dined at Penney's Diner a few miles down the road or with one of his family members.

"You didn't have to do that, Chloe."

"I know, but I wanted to because I need to eat, too," she replied, as if that explained things.

"Suit yourself," he said, knowing he sounded totally nonchalant and ungrateful when he was anything but. After spending practically her entire day in the kitchen preparing breakfast and lunch for his men, she had gone out of her way to prepare him dinner when she really didn't have to do it.

He turned in the direction of the kitchen and when he got to the edge of the room, he paused and then turned back around. She was staring into space as if she was trying to figure out in her own mind what had happened next with Raphel Westmoreland. She had moved from her earlier pose and was now curled up in the corner of his sofa, and every so often after taking a sip of wine her tongue would dart out to lick her top lip as if savoring the taste. Ramsey felt his body tighten with desire as he watched her.

"Chloe?"

She looked over at him and he could tell from her expression she was surprised to see him still standing there. "Yes?"

"Thanks for dinner." He then turned and kept walking toward the kitchen.

Hours later with his jaw clamped together tight, Ramsey walked the floor in his bedroom. This would be another night where he would not be getting any sleep and there was no excuse for it, and he needed his rest. The next two weeks of shearing would be both mind- and body-consuming if today was an example of what was to come.

At least his men had been excited about breakfast and lunch and had kept a steady conversation about both most of the day. Chloe's choice of food was a big hit and at quitting time today the men had been speculating on what they would be getting tomorrow for breakfast. Chloe was a definite asset to his ranch.

Ramsey moved over to the window to look out, not liking what he was thinking. She had done it again, he thought in disgust. The dinner she'd prepared for him had been the best he'd ever eaten, so much in fact that he'd been tempted to lick the plate. He had sat in the kitchen alone, not bothering to eat at the table, but had taken a stool at the breakfast bar instead.

Consuming his meal in silence he had been well aware of the moment she had come into the kitchen to wash out her wineglass. Mumbling a good-night, she had quickly left to head up the stairs. He had watched her go. Neither of them had mentioned anything about the kiss they'd shared earlier that day, and that was fine with him because his brothers and cousin had said enough. Not surprisingly, word of the kiss had reached Dillon and Callum. At least none of his sisters knew about it. Had they been privy to such information, they would have called by now, or even worse, just showed up to introduce themselves.

*Hold up. Time-out.* He wasn't ready for something like that to happen, especially if his sisters assumed the wrong thing like Zane, Derringer and Jason had. But knowing Megan, Gemma and Bailey like he did, there was no doubt in his mind that they would have taken things further by trying to intentionally stir interest even if there wasn't any there.

At least he could safely say from his conversation with Chloe earlier that she was not a woman on the run as Callum had speculated. Other than what she'd told him about her ex-boyfriend, he still hadn't gotten her to talk a lot about herself, although she was trying to get all in his business about good old Raphel.

He shook his head. Other than knowing she was a damn good cook, she'd had an idiot of an ex-boyfriend, and that she had a friend who was getting married, he didn't know a lot about her. But then maybe the less he knew the better. She was doing a good job at what she had been hired to do.

*Although he was losing sleep in the process.*

But then, his inability to sleep and walking the floors at night was not her problem. He had to be the one who garnered more control. He had to stop the flow of sexual tension between them. But how? Imagining her with a sack over her head whenever he saw her wouldn't work because he would still be able to see her body. And there was no way he could look at all those curves without a degree of lust filling his head.

Sighing deeply, he made his way back to the bed. It was close to one in the morning and if he had to lie in bed, stare at the ceiling and count sheep to get to sleep, then so be it. Hell, sheep were his life anyway.

Chloe sat up in bed and clicked on her cell phone to answer it. She smiled when she saw the call was from her dad. "Okay, Pop, it's close to one in the morning here, which means it's later than that on the east coast, so this better be good."

Senator Burton's hearty laugh came in through the phone. "It is. I have Stephanie here with me. I asked her to marry me and she accepted and we just wanted our kids to know."

Tears she couldn't hold back came into Chloe's eyes. Her father sounded happy and if anyone deserved happiness it was him. She swiped at her tears and said, "I'm happy for you and Stephanie, Dad. Congratulations. Have the two of you told Brian and Danita yet?"

Brian and Danita were Stephanie's son and daughter. Brian was twenty-six and in his last year of medical school at the University of Florida. Danita was twenty-one and attending Xavier University of Louisiana. She, Brian and Danita got along marvelously and had been more than ready for their parents to take things to the next level. There was no doubt in Chloe's mind they would be as happy for their mother as she was for her dad.

"Not yet," her father said, interrupting her thoughts. "We thought we would call our oldest child first."

She smiled. Already he was thinking of them in terms of a family. "Okay, and I hate that I'm not there to celebrate, but when I return to Florida we're going to all get together."

"And when will you be returning to Florida?"

Chloe nibbled her bottom lip. That was a good question. "Not for at least another two weeks," she said with certainty. Ramsey's regular cook should have returned by then, and hopefully she would have come clean and told him the truth. She was hoping that once she made it clear he owed her, that he would do the cover and the article, grudgingly or otherwise.

"Okay, sweetheart. Stephanie wants to talk to you."

It was at least twenty minutes later before Chloe

ended the call with the woman who would become her stepmother. They talked about plans for the wedding but only briefly because Danita's input would be needed on any major decisions.

She cuddled in bed wishing her own personal life could be as happy and exciting as her dad's. She took a long breath wondering where that yearning had come from. Probably with her dad's calling and then recalling her earlier conversation this evening with Ramsey about matrimony had stirred something within her, and it was something she hadn't thought about in a long time. It was her own desire to one day settle down, marry and have children. When things had ended with her and Daren, she hadn't given up on that dream. And although such a thing was not in her immediate plans, she still had that desire tucked away somewhere. What woman didn't? Even with her determination to be successful with her magazine company, she believed once that was achieved, she would find her Mr. Right. And one thing was for certain he definitely wouldn't be some surly sheep rancher.

But then if that was the case…and she was most certain that it was, why did she go to bed thinking about him every night? And why was the last thing she saw before closing her eyes his intense, penetrating dark eyes staring at her like they could see right through to her soul.

She closed her eyes. *Like now.* There he was, in vivid color, as he had been that evening, sitting across from her on the sofa with his legs stretched out in front of him, with his Stetson still on his head and looking sexier than any man had a right to look. So much in fact that more than once she had been tempted to get up off the sofa and go to him and curl up in his lap and purr.

She slowly opened her eyes, grateful she hadn't done such a thing. She really should thank him for keeping her agitated during most of the conversation, which stopped her from making a complete fool of herself. But if the truth be told, telling her about his great-grandfather had helped to refocus her attention. She knew there was more to the story and wondered why this was her first time hearing it. If such a thing hadn't come up on one of her computer's search engines that meant it hadn't made the news. Hmm. It was definitely something she would like to share with her readers, which might prompt them to want to start looking into their own family tree.

She shifted in bed thinking she was determined to get the whole story from Ramsey. If not Ramsey, then one of his brothers or cousins would do. Before leaving today Zane Westmoreland had tipped his hat at her, given her a flirty smile and a promise that he would be showing up for breakfast in the morning.

She shook her head. The only Westmoreland she wanted to concentrate on at the moment was the one who was probably sleeping peacefully in the bed only a few doors down the hall.

## Chapter 6

"Good morning."

Ramsey glanced up from reading the morning's newspaper to stare into Chloe's face and immediately wished he hadn't. Her dark eyes looked slumberous and sensuously drowsy. A part of him was tempted to suggest that she forget about preparing breakfast for his men and go back to bed...but only if she would take him with her.

The muscles in his neck tightened at the very thought and he forced out his response. "Morning."

She sniffed the air. "Great, you've made coffee!"

He watched as she quickly headed toward the coffeepot. Today she was wearing another cute short dress with a pair of leggings underneath. He frowned. Did she have a pair of those things for every day of the week? And a different color for every day?

He took a sip of his coffee and watched as she poured hers, adding cream and sugar into the mix before leaning against the counter and taking what looked like a much-needed sip.

"Excellent," she said.

"Thanks." Was she smiling? And if she was, then what the heck for? Could a cup of coffee first thing in the morning do that to her? As far as he could recall she'd been barely speaking to him when they'd parted yesterday afternoon. And why did knowing he'd contributed to putting that smile on her face send a good feeling vibrating through him? Damn.

He gazed back down at his newspaper. To be honest, he was hoping that he would have been in and out of the kitchen this morning before she'd gotten up. He was determined more so than ever to put distance between them. Maybe then he'd be able to get a good night's sleep.

"I'm doing omelets this morning. Would you like to go ahead and place your order?"

He glanced over at her. She was opening cabinets pulling out bowls, pots and pans. Had she said omelets? The last time he'd eaten an omelet was when he'd gone on a business trip and stayed at a hotel. It had been delicious.

"Yes, please," he said, trying to keep the excitement out of his voice. "I'd like that."

"How would you like it?"

He fought back the urge not to say the first thing that came into his mind, which would have given away his lusty thoughts. Hell, it was too early to think about that kind of stuff. But then, early morning sex wasn't so bad. And he had a feeling she would be able to cook in the bedroom with just as much heat as she used in the kitchen.

It took him only a few minutes to fill her in on the ingredients he wanted in his omelet. She nodded and went right to work. He watched her as she added the onions, green peppers, tomatoes…

Ramsey's mouth began watering. For both the omelet and for her. Moving around the kitchen, she was a sight to see. And he felt the lower part of his body getting there. The huge bulge behind his zipper wasn't a joke.

"What about a glass of orange juice?"

He blinked, realized he'd been staring. "Thanks. That will work."

At the moment he couldn't think of many things that wouldn't work, especially if she were to place her hands on it. Shivers went through him when he thought of places she could place her hands…on him.

She crossed the room and placed the plate on the table, right in front of him, and a glass of OJ beside his plate. "Thanks."

She smiled. "No problem."

He began eating while thinking it might not be a problem for her, but it was definitely becoming one for him. He didn't look up when she refilled his cup of coffee. "Thanks."

"Sure."

He took his time to savor the meal which deserved all the savoring it could get. The omelet was simply delicious. He liked glancing up every once in a while to watch as she fried bacon and cooked sausage. In no time at all the smell of breakfast was all over his kitchen.

And he noted she had come out of her shoes. She had kicked them in a corner and was gliding around the kitchen in her bare feet. He smiled as he glanced down at her toes again and felt his breathing come out slow and easy.

They hadn't said a word over the past thirty minutes. He was satisfied in letting her do her thing, and evidently she had no problem in letting him eat in peace while he finished reading the newspaper.

With the newspaper read and his plate clean, he decided to strike up a conversation. There were some things about her that he needed to know. "Do you have any family around these parts, Chloe?"

Chloe kept her attention trained on what she was doing, refusing to let the sound of Ramsey's deep, throaty voice wreak havoc on her mind. It was bad enough she could inhale his masculine scent over that of the bacon frying. That might sound like a lot of bull to some, but she was convinced it was true, which was the reason her nipples felt so sensitive. Bacon would not have caused that effect.

"No. I don't have family around these parts," she said, wondering why he'd asked.

"So you relocated here?"

"Yes."

"Without knowing anyone?"

She wondered how she could answer that without telling an outright lie. "Not exactly. I have a girlfriend from college who lives here and decided to give this area a try."

He nodded. "So you're living with your girlfriend?"

Her answer to that would not be a lie. "Yes, when I'm not staying here as your cook."

He pushed his plate aside and leaned back in his chair. "So where are you from?"

She forced a smile as she glanced over at him. "Where do you think I'm from?"

"Somewhere in the South."

"Yes, I'm from Florida, more specifically Tampa."

Deciding she had answered enough questions, Chloe resolved it was her turn to ask a few. "So, what happened with Raphel and his five wives? I didn't think a divorce was that easy back in the day."

Ramsey shrugged. "During our research we discovered the first woman he ran off with was a preacher's wife. He couldn't marry her because she was already married."

Chloe lifted a brow. "Then why did he run off with her?"

"To save her from an abusive marriage. And before you ask, the second wife he took off her husband's hands, with her husband's blessing, to save a possible scandal."

Ramsey decided that was all he would tell her for now. It was just enough to keep her curious. Why he was baiting her he really wasn't sure. Maybe the reason was that he liked seeing the look of interest in her eyes.

He stood and carried his plate, coffee cup and glass over to the sink.

"You don't have to do that," she said.

"Yes, I do. I was raised to clean up after myself."

And just like yesterday, when he reached the sink

she deliberately moved out of his way. Knowing she was trying to avoid his touch bothered him. He reached out and grabbed hold of her hand. She glanced over at him, startled.

"Why are you afraid of me, Chloe?" It was then that he realized he was running his fingers up and down her arm.

She lifted her chin, but did not try pulling her hand away. "What makes you think I'm afraid of you?"

"You're trying to avoid me."

She lifted a haughty brow. "I could very well say the same thing about you, Ramsey."

That was true, he thought to himself. Instead of denying it, he was silent for a moment. And when he felt a shudder pass through her from the way he was running his fingers up her arms he locked his gaze to hers.

"Why the hell do we let this keep happening to us?" he asked in a low, throaty tone.

Surprisingly, she gave him a faint smile. "Hey, you're the one who was trying to work me out of your system."

He nodded. "With yesterday's kiss," he replied.

"Yes."

Now it was his time to smile. "It didn't work."

She shrugged. "Maybe your heart just wasn't in it."

His smile quickly transformed to a frown. "Like hell. Everything I had was in it."

She seemed to consider his words for half a second. "I know," she said, and sighed in dismay.

With his free hand he took his finger and tilted her chin. "But just to be sure, I think I should at least try it again. Yesterday didn't seem to work."

He then lowered his head and caught her lips in a drugging kiss, deliberately making it hot from the start. His tongue slid into her mouth on a breathless sigh and from there it was on. He deepened the kiss, devouring her mouth with a hunger that made yesterday's kiss seem tame.

He heard her moan. He felt the way the pebbled tips of her breasts were rubbing against his chest as if he wasn't even wearing a shirt. And once again, her stance was perfect to cradle his erection, which was hard as a rock, engorged, as aroused as a male shaft could get.

And just like yesterday, she was returning his kiss, lick for lick. Feasting on his mouth with just as much greed as he was feasting on hers. What was it about her taste, her flavor, the way their mouths fit together? His tongue seemed at home wrapped around hers.

He tried doing a mental calculation in his head, trying to figure out just how many steps it would take to reach the table. There he would strip her naked and…

The clearing of multiple throats had him reluctantly breaking contact with Chloe's mouth, but not before getting one final lick of his tongue across her lips. He lifted his head to glare over at the four men standing in his kitchen doorway with smirks on their faces.

It was Callum, Zane, Derringer and Jason. Of course it was Zane who had the damn nerve to ask, "Could you explain to us why you keep kissing your cook?"

Chloe eased her body into the sudsy water. Now it was late afternoon and everyone, including Ramsey, was gone and she intended to take time for herself. And she intended to get in bed early so she could be well-rested in the morning, now that she knew the routine.

She closed her eyes and thought about the events of the day, beginning that morning when the four men had walked in on her and Ramsey. This time instead of being embarrassed by the intrusion, she had been downright annoyed. And of course Ramsey had done just what she'd expected. He had begun avoiding her again.

He hadn't shown up for lunch. Instead he had locked himself in his office. Then around two o'clock, he left and he had yet to return and it was close to six. She had prepared dinner for him again and had left it warming in the oven. She had even sat on the sofa like yesterday, anticipating his return. But when it became evident he was staying away, she decided to take a bath, make a few calls and then get into bed early.

Thinking she had remained in the bathtub long enough, she stood to dry off with the huge towel. Everything for tomorrow was taken care of, so there was no reason for her to leave her bedroom tonight. She could use her PDA to check for any messages and to call and chat with her dad.

She paused when she thought she heard a car door slam, which meant Ramsey had returned home. Slipping into her robe and tying the sash tightly around her waist, she strolled over to the window and looked out. Ramsey was getting out of his truck.

She felt her body's reaction at seeing him. And as if he felt her presence, he tipped his head back and glanced up and saw her standing at the window.

Chloe sucked in a steadying breath the moment their

eyes met. For a long time they just stood there, seemingly transfixed while staring at each other. And the heat of his gaze, the intensity of his stare touched her in areas that hadn't been touched in a long time.

She actually felt her body tremble at the desire building inside her and the feelings that clawed in her stomach from his unwavering gaze. No height or distance could stop the flow of sensations that were seeping into her every pore. And as she stood there all she could do was remember how he had taken her mouth for two days straight in hard, hungry and demanding kisses.

Unable to handle the intensity of his gaze or the passion he was stirring within her any longer, she drew in a deep breath before stepping away from the window.

Chloe fought the urge to rush downstairs and meet him at the door, to throw her arms around him and lift her mouth up to him, to be bold enough to take his mouth with the same intensity that he'd taken hers with earlier that day. She shook her head knowing there was no way she could or would do such a thing.

Removing her robe, she slipped into her pj's, deciding to stick with her original plan to remain in her room for the rest of the evening. She and Ramsey might be under the same roof, but the less time they spent together, the better. And she had a good reason for feeling that way. She was getting drawn to him in a way that was more emotional than physical. She wished she could blame what she was feeling on irrational hormones but she knew that wasn't the case. Something else was taking place and she didn't want to think what that something could possibly be.

She felt vulnerable around him, like he could be the one man who could pull her into him so much that she would forget about herself. Daren had tried and failed. But a part of her knew if Ramsey took a mind to doing so that he would be successful. He had the ability to break through all the emotional walls she'd erected since her breakup with Daren.

With Ramsey she could feel herself losing her sense of will, her sense of logic and her common sense. There was something about him that was making her think things that she shouldn't. Like a little girl with those same set of dark eyes or a son with Ramsey's smile. She would admit right then and there if she was interested in a serious involvement with a man, he would head the list. And that worried her.

Ramsey opened the door to his home and leaned against it for a moment. He was fully aroused. The last thing he had expected when he'd pulled into his yard was to get out of his truck and participate in mind sex. He had stood there staring at Chloe while his entire mind had partaken in the most erotic fantasy possible. There was no part of him that had not been stimulated.

Through the window he could tell she was wearing a robe and he figured she was naked underneath. The thought of a naked Chloe had made him hard. Desire had surged through him in a way that it had never done before. While standing there staring at her he'd actually felt every muscle in his body tighten.

He glanced up at the stairs knowing the object of his desire, his red-hot passion and his erotic fantasies was up there behind closed doors. He was tempted, boy was he tempted, to go right up those stairs, knock on her door and kiss her in a way that would make the kiss they'd shared that morning seem like child's play. And now that her taste was embedded onto his tongue, he wanted more of it, doubted he would be able to get enough.

He rubbed his hand down his face wondering what in the hell was wrong with him. He had been around beautiful women before. For a while his sisters, who felt he'd still been hurting over Danielle's betrayal, had tried their hands at matchmaking. But no woman had held his interest until now. He was finding it hard to resist her. She was temptation at its very best. And on top of everything else, he was feeling emotions that he couldn't quite identify. The woman was bewitching him.

He had remained in his office the majority of the day, but all it took was to hear the laughter and the excitement in the voices of his men when they'd arrived at lunch to know that once again Chloe had made their day. That point was proven when he'd checked the shearing records for today. More sheep than normal had been sheared. Hell, they had basically set a record. That meant there was a connection between their cheerful attitudes and the work they did. A happy employee produced more and for the past two days his men had produced. And when he had dropped by the shearing plant this evening, right before closing time, he could hear the excitement in their voices when they talked about breakfast in the morning. After the omelets their anticipation as to what tomorrow morning would bring was evident.

He drew in a deep breath and it was at that moment he picked up the smell of something delicious. Pushing away from the door, he crossed the room to the kitchen and saw that Chloe had prepared his dinner again. He lifted the pots and checked the oven. She had made baked chicken, field peas, rice and gravy, and macaroni and cheese. A real Southern meal, something a Westerner like him could appreciate. He had acquired a taste for Southern cuisine after meeting the Atlanta Westmorelands.

Deciding he would wash up for dinner, he moved toward the bathroom thinking he had deliberately stayed away today. That kiss he and Chloe had shared had shredded his senses, making resisting her nearly impossible. It was already rumored by his men that he had the hots for her and he didn't want to give them any more to talk about or speculate on. So leaving here for a while had been the decision that he'd made.

And then he'd had to deal with the ribbing from his brothers, Jason and Callum. Trying to convince them that Chloe was nothing more than his cook was beginning to sound lame even to his ears. He had walked away from them when he saw they were intent on drawing their own conclusions about his and Chloe's relationship, and he'd made a point not to accept their invitation for a game of poker over at Jason's place.

Luckily for him Dillon and Pamela had returned to town for a few days for Dillon to attend a business meeting, so he'd had the chance to visit with them. The newly married couple divided their time between here and Pamela's home in Gamble, Wyoming, because one of Pamela's sisters was in her last year of high school.

Dillon seemed extremely happy as a married man and Ramsey was happy for him. From the time he could remember, he and Dillon had been closer than just cousins. In essence, they were best friends and when their parents had perished in that plane crash, he had more than supported Dillon's desire to keep the family together.

Because Dillon was the oldest by some months, he had become head of the family and guardian for everyone. But the two of them had worked hard. It hadn't been easy raising their siblings and cousins, nine of whom had been under the age of sixteen.

Now all of them were over twenty-one, either in college or working alongside Dillon at Blue Ridge Land Development, the company that the two Westmoreland brothers—his father and Dillon's—had formed many years ago. Under Dillon's guidance, Blue Ridge was now a multimillion dollar company well known in the Mountain States. It employed over a thousand people. Every family member had worked there at some point in their lives before pursuing their dreams and other ambitions.

An hour later Ramsey had finished eating and was still licking his lips. The meal had been delicious. Chloe hadn't come downstairs and in a way he hadn't expected her to. She was well aware, just like he was, that something was taking place between them and it was something neither of them wanted. So it would be best to avoid the situation by avoiding each other. The attraction between them was too strong, the passion was too thick. And she was becoming his weakness. If he didn't get things in check, the desire he felt for her would consume him and that was something he simply refused to let happen.

He shook his head as he moved toward the stairs and the moment he lifted his leg to take a step he inhaled her scent. It was the scent of a woman he wanted. Her fragrance was emitting from behind closed doors, drenching the air, teasing his nostrils and making him even more aroused. He hadn't gotten much sleep last night and he doubted things would be any better tonight.

When he reached the landing, he worked his shoulders to relieve the tension that had built there. Drawing in a heated breath he made it down the hall, forcing one foot in front of the other, intent on passing Chloe's door without stopping.

Easier said than done. When he reached her door he couldn't help but pause. He even raised his hand to knock before snatching it back to his side.

*What the hell was happening to him?*

He forced himself away from her door and quickly moved down the hall toward his own. He had to formulate a plan, at least until the weekend. Hopefully, she would leave those two days to go back to her own place, get her mail, water her plants, check in with her neighbors or whatever else she needed to do. By then they would need the distance. They would need the space. The weekend was three days away and he hoped like hell that he could hold out until then.

## Chapter 7

"So what do you think of Derringer?"

Chloe couldn't stop the smile from touching her lips. This was the third time this weekend that Lucia had asked that same question. "I told you twice already, but I'll tell you again," she teased, as she pulled off her jacket. "He is a very handsome man. I like him. He, Zane and Jason come by for breakfast and lunch quite a bit. They're nice guys. Big teasers."

She saw the wistful look in Lucia's eyes. They had just returned from having dinner together after going to a movie. "You know how you can make yourself known, don't you?"

Lucia rolled her eyes. "I know how *you* would make yourself known to him, Clo. You go after whatever it is that you want. You're daring. I'm not."

Chloe placed her hands on her hips. "So what are

you going to do, Lou? Wait another year or so for him to need more paint thinner and hope you're in your father's store when he does?"

Lucia dropped down on her sofa with a downhearted look on her face. "Of course not." She then looked up at Chloe. "Enough about me since I refuse to have a pity party. How close are you to getting Ramsey to do the magazine cover and interview?"

Chloe shook her head and dropped down beside Lucia, looking just as downhearted. "It's not going well. Ramsey is avoiding me like the plague."

"Why?"

Chloe smiled over at her friend. "Too much sexual chemistry in the air when we're within ten feet of each other."

"Must be nice."

Chloe leaned back against the sofa and closed her eyes thinking that in essence it *should* be nice, but it wasn't. Ramsey made an appearance only when he had to. He got up each morning for his cup of coffee while she prepared breakfast and instead of hanging around, he took his breakfast and coffee into his office, claiming he had a lot of work to do. He came out for lunch to eat with his men, said very little and only stayed long enough to eat and leave. In the evenings, although she prepared dinner for him each evening, he usually stayed away until he was sure she was in bed.

He hadn't been home when she'd left to come here for the weekend. She had left a note on the kitchen table letting him know she would be returning Sunday evening. She had left her cell number in case something came up and she needed to be reached.

A smile touched her lips. Who was she kidding? She was hoping he would contact her for any reason and that wasn't good.

"Okay, Clo, you've gotten quiet on me. Open those eyes and tell me what's going on."

Chloe slowly opened her eyes to gaze over into Lucia's curious ones. She had an idea what was going on, but to say it out loud would be speaking it into existence and she wasn't ready to do that yet. There was no way she could tell Lucia that she might not be the only woman who'd fallen for a Westmoreland man.

"Stop being a worry wart. Nothing is going on." Chloe drew in a breath thinking that Lucia had no idea just how true that was. Nothing was really going on. She was no closer to getting Ramsey to agree to that cover or an interview than before she'd shown up. Somehow, she had to get him to stop avoiding her, sexual chemistry or no sexual chemistry. And if she were to come clean now and tell him the truth, he would probably kick her off his land so fast it would make her head spin.

She stood, not ready for Lucia to question her further about anything. "It's late and I think I'll turn in early."

"I think I'll turn in as well. Mom and Dad invited us to dinner after church tomorrow and then later Aunt Pauline wants us to drop by her place."

"All right and then after that I need to return to the Westmoreland place." This would be her last week and she needed to make some kind of headway.

Later that night as Chloe lay in bed, images of Ramsey flowed through her mind. Two days ago while preparing lunch she had glanced out the window in time to see a shirtless Ramsey carrying a lamb in his arms across the yard to the barn. With jeans riding low on his hips she had stared at his physique, taking in every inch of his tight abs, strong arms and tight buns. He was the only man alive who could literally make her drool.

And if that wasn't bad enough, the following morning at breakfast when he'd sat with his men, she saw again how well he got along with them as well as his brothers and cousin.

She shifted in bed admitting she missed him. She missed the ranch. And as crazy as it sounded, she even missed preparing food for the men. They were so appreciative and complimentary.

She closed her eyes thinking of Ramsey and knowing she would be glad to see him tomorrow when she returned to the ranch.

Ramsey pushed back the curtain and looked out, something he'd done too many times over the past hour. Where was she? The note she'd left on the kitchen table said she would return Sunday evening. In his part of the world the evening time came well before ten at night. The last time he had glanced at the clock it was heading toward the eleventh hour.

She had left her phone number, but he had thrown it away, refusing to be tempted to call her and now he was worried. What if something had happened. He had no way of reaching her and had no idea just where she lived in the city.

It had rained earlier and the road off the main highway leading to Westmoreland Country was known to be slippery after a storm. He let the curtain slip back in place and began pacing the floor again. At that moment he realized just how little he knew about Chloe, other than she was the woman who aroused him to no end.

This was crazy. He'd let a woman in his house to cook for his men, sleep in his guest room, use his washer and dryer to wash her bed linens before she'd taken off for the weekend, and all he knew about her was her name.

Okay, he knew a little bit more about her than that. He knew she was a hell of a cook and beautiful as beautiful could get. He knew she had a hell of a body, although he was yet to see her bare legs. He knew she got along with his men and had cooked a huge chocolate cake last week when Colin Lawrence had turned fifty.

He also knew what she did to him whenever she looked at him for any length of time. Truth was, although he wished like hell he didn't have to admit it, in one short week he'd discovered a taste unlike any he'd ever sampled before, and her scent was one hell of a fragrance, an aroma he could breathe into his nostrils for days. But she had managed to do something no other woman had been capable of doing in ten years.

She had ignited his passion.

He wanted to know how it felt to lose himself inside her, to feel her heat, have her body, legs and all, wrapped all around him, feel his erection swell to the fullest size possible inside her, and be as greedy for her breasts as he was for her mouth.

His hands clenched into fists at his side. He was the Westmoreland, so he'd been told, who had the least amount of charm. The one who didn't need sex as often as the rest to maintain a normal life. Yet here he was with his heart thumping like crazy in his chest as he imagined doing all kinds of naughty things to Chloe. For the first time in hell knows when, he was thinking about getting laid. Bottom line, he was horny as hell.

The unwanted direction of his thoughts no longer shocked him. Instead what it did was propel him to want to do more than think about it. He wanted to act on it and let the chips fall where they may. He wanted...

His thoughts were suddenly interrupted by the sound of a vehicle pulling up. Quickly crossing the room he glanced out the window and saw it was Chloe returning. He frowned as he dropped the curtain back in place. She was late.

He dismissed the feeling of relief knowing she was all right and was filled with anger. The least she could have done was call to let him know she would be late. Standing across the room he faced the door with his arms over his chest. She had a lot of explaining to do. The nerve of her to make him worry for nothing.

Her scent filled the air the moment the door opened, but in anger he chose to ignore it. But when she walked over his threshold wearing a white blouse and a short denim skirt—with no leggings underneath—that showed the most beautiful pair of legs he had ever seen, he gritted his teeth knowing there was no way he could ignore them.

Chloe closed the door behind her, saw Ramsey standing across the room glaring and quickly knew she was so not ready for this. In fact, she had decided to wait before returning in hopes that he would be in bed already. She tried to ignore how good he looked. The man wore a pair of jeans like they'd been made just for his body. They fit snug, showing impressive hard thighs and tight abs. Another thing she noticed was that it looked as if he hadn't shaved since she'd left. The stubble look suited him. It made him look even sexier in a sinful sort of way.

Trying to take her mind off his ultra-fine body, she stared back at him, wondering what his problem was. She had left everything in perfect order before she'd headed into town for the weekend. She had even washed and dried her bed linens, although he'd mentioned he had a housekeeper who came every Saturday morning to clean and do laundry. And why was he staring at her legs like he'd never seen a pair of legs before? Her skirt was short, but it wasn't that short. She'd worn some shorter. If he was about to tell her there was something wrong with her outfit, that it wasn't appropriate to wear on his ranch, then she would let him have it.

Deciding to just get this over with and give just as good as she got, she lifted her chin, glared back at him and asked, "Ramsey, is there a problem?"

Ramsey's gut clenched and his jaw tightened. Her legs were long and shapely. They were the kind that looked perfect in a short dress from the top of her thighs all the way down to her ankles.

"Ramsey, I asked was there a problem?" she asked testily.

His gaze moved from her legs to her face. "You're late."

What on earth did he mean by that? Chloe wondered as a confused frown covered her face. She must have heard him wrong. "Excuse me?"

"I said you're late. Your note said you would be returning Sunday evening and it's almost eleven."

She dropped her overnight bag by her feet. "And what of it? I'm not on a time clock. In fact, I am not even working for you today. As long as I'm here to prepare breakfast in the morning what business is it of yours?"

Ramsey stiffened. She had asked a good question. What business was it of his? He then said the first thing that came to his mind. "This is my house."

She seemed taken aback by that response. "Are you standing here telling me that I have a curfew?"

*Was that what he was saying?* He shook his head. "No, you don't have a curfew, but since you left a note saying you would be returning in the evening, at least you could have had the decency to call."

Her gaze locked on his face. *Decency?* Blood rushed through her veins as anger consumed her. He had the gall to utter such a word? She crossed the room to him. "Let's talk about decency, Ramsey. If you would have had the *decency* to be here when I left instead of avoiding me like I have the pox, I would not have had to leave that note."

Ramsey was taken aback by Chloe's anger. As far as he was concerned she didn't have a damn thing to be angry about. She hadn't been the one who'd endured sleepless nights knowing she was just down the hall from him when the need to bury himself deep inside her had nearly driven him insane. Hell, if only she knew that the reason he'd deliberately made himself scarce most of last week was because anytime he saw her he got an automatic erection that wouldn't go down.

Furthermore, he was sick and tired of finding places to go in the afternoons just so he wouldn't be tempted to make one of those erotic dreams he'd had over the past week come true. Tired of unexplainable emotions, escalated hormones and a frantic urge to make love to her until neither of them had an ounce of energy left.

He took a step closer as his anger level moved up another notch. "You don't get it do you?" he asked in a voice that was rough, close to the edge. "I stayed away to do us both a favor, Chloe. Had I been here you would never have walked out that door."

The hard, cold reality was that he was a lit piece of dynamite ready to explode, preferably inside her. Point-blank, he wanted her in a way he'd never wanted any woman and with a need that was pushing him over the edge and he was determined to take her right with him.

He could tell by her expression she hadn't liked what he'd said. She took a step closer, got in his face, put her mouth just inches from his, their noses almost touched. "Ha! And just what were you going to do? Tie me up?"

A slow smile slid over his lips. If only she knew how many times such a thought had crossed his mind. He'd never been into that bondage stuff, but he could just imagine such a thing with her. "Considering the state I've been in all week, the state I happen to be in right now, tying you up would have definitely been an option."

Chloe stared at him, stunned at his admission, and at that moment she realized not only what he'd said but what he'd meant. Somewhere along the line their conversation had become sexual. Maybe for him it had always been that way, but due to her raging anger she had failed to see it. However, she was seeing it now. She could feel his heat and that heat was being passed on to her. Even the distended nipples pressing against her blouse felt like they were ready to detonate. And the area between her legs, more specifically the depths of her womb, felt hot.

"And do you know what I would have done after tying you up, Chloe?"

Nibbling on her bottom lip she held his gaze while her entire body felt like a bonfire. She'd never considered herself a fiercely passionate woman, but at that moment the raw images going through her mind, of her bound to his bed, legs spread, with him naked and crawling over her, to mate with her, had her speechless.

He didn't wait for her to respond to his question. "I would have stripped you naked and then licked you all over from head to toe."

Added to the very image flowing in her mind, she could definitely see him doing that. A heated ache settled between her thighs and when she felt her panties get wet she tightened her legs together. Hot passion, deep desire was taking over her entire body with his words and every part of her was responding, without any restraints.

"But do you know where my mouth would have lingered, Chloe? Where it would have devoured you to the fullest, given you the most sensual pleasure?"

When she didn't say anything, he leaned in, whispered close to her ear and what he said, as well as the erotic picture his words made, had her weak in the knees. And it didn't help matters that she could feel the warmth of his breath against her neck.

"And trust me, you aren't out of the woods yet," he said in a deep, husky and sexually-laden voice. "So if you don't want me with the same intensity that I want you, with the same intensity that I plan on taking you, then I suggest you walk out that door right now, because I refuse to avoid you any longer."

Chloe swallowed tightly while admitting inwardly that she wanted him, wanted him to take her and with the same intensity he was alluding to. There was no way she could or would deny that. And she knew that standing before her was a fiercely passionate man. She had known it from the first time she had seen him that day crossing the street. There had been something about him that had sent a sensual thrill through her, had made her entirely aware of him as a woman. It had made her fantasize about him every night since then. So what he was threatening to do stimulated her more than he would ever know.

But then at the same time, he was giving her an out without having to feel guilty about leaving him in a tough spot in regard to losing a cook. She should take it. But the bottom line was that she didn't want to take it. She wanted to take him instead.

"Chloe?"

Her name flowed from his lips in a deeply throaty tone. She met his gaze. "Yes?"

"I'm waiting."

She inhaled deeply, took a couple of steps to him,

flattened her hands against his chest, looked up into his eyes and then told him calmly, "So am I."

Ramsey's self-control snapped and the speed in which his mouth swept down on Chloe's had his head spinning. But the twirling stopped and was replaced by an explosion going off in his skull the moment his tongue was planted firmly in her mouth.

She tasted like the strawberry cake she had baked on Thursday and he was tempted to eat her mouth with the same greediness with which he'd consumed that slice of cake. And when his tongue began lapping her up, savoring every inch of her mouth, exploring every nook and cranny, he heard the moan that escaped from her throat. Her delicious taste consumed him, went to his head, speared every part of his body and enflamed his senses.

And he still wanted to draw her deeper into himself.

The hard throbbing of his erection was letting him know that kissing her would not be enough. His control was eroding and taking his sanity right along with it, while at the same time his hunger was being escalated. And his body, every nerve ending, every cell, was demanding to be fed. He suddenly pulled his mouth away, needing more. And needing it now.

"Ramsey?"

Her voice was soft, her breath hot, and the sound of his name from her lips was as sweet as her taste. He knew at that moment he had to remove her clothes and the thought of taking off that skirt and getting between those legs sent a shudder through every part of him.

He knew there was no way he could make it up the stairs to his bedroom. The sofa would have to do. It was sturdy and strong which was a good thing because she was in for a hard ride. He had given her fair warning, but she hadn't taken it. Soon enough she would discover just what she had unleashed.

The air surrounding them was thick with sexual tension. The rush of sensations that were pounding through his veins and making his insides quiver, drove him to reach out and draw her back close to him. His hands began moving, roaming all over her and lifting her short skirt to touch the backside he enjoyed looking at so much.

He felt her shiver in his arms, heard her say his name again and with the sound of the hunger he heard in her voice, more than ever before, consumed him. He needed to kiss her again, let his tongue stroke inside her mouth while his hands stroked her flesh.

That wasn't enough.

Suddenly, his hands went to her blouse, his fingers gripped the fabric and with one hard tug ripped it from her body.

Chloe gasped and when she saw the intensity of desire that burned in Ramsey's eyes she knew her blouse was just the beginning. He proved her right when his hands reached for her bra. Blood surged through her veins when he opened the front clasp, freeing her breasts, but not for long.

After pulling the bra off her shoulders and tossing it aside, he took the twin mounds in his hands as if testing their softness and shaping their fullness. And then he lowered his mouth to capture a puckered nipple into his hot mouth. The moment his tongue touched the tip, sucked it deep, she dug her nails into his shoulders as sensations ripped through her. Intense pleasure trailed not far behind and caused her nipples to harden even more.

"Ramsey..." She whispered his name, barely able to stand on her feet any longer as he attacked her breasts with his mouth like a starving man.

Instead of answering, with his mouth still on her breasts, he moved his hands downward to raise her skirt. His fingers found the crotch of her panties. The moment he touched the drenched spot she moaned, but not before she heard his rough growl. He pulled back, released her breasts and gripped her skirt to pull it down her hips.

Within seconds she was standing in front of him wearing nothing more than wet panties. He took a step back to remove his shirt, popping buttons in his haste, before stripping it from his shoulders. His naked chest was perfect and she couldn't help moving, closing the distance and reaching out to rake her nails across the hard, muscled hairy chest, liking the feel beneath her fingertips.

He captured her hand and holding her gaze he began licking her fingers, one by one. His tongue felt hot against her sensitive flesh and she shuddered when sensations tore through her.

"You like that?" His voice was heavy, deep, sexy.

She could only nod.

"You enjoy my tongue on you?"

"Yes," she whispered, barely able to get out the single word.

"Good, now let's see how you enjoy my tongue *in* you."

He eased down in front of her and holding her hips he leaned forward, pressed his nose against the crotch of her panties, as if to inhale her scent. And then he flicked out his tongue and it felt blazing hot against the silky material. Pleasure eased over her and she felt on the verge of exploding.

Ramsey leaned back and looked up to hold her gaze as he began easing her panties down her legs. When she stepped out of them he could only lean farther back on his haunches and look at her up and down, fighting hard to breathe while doing so.

He was mesmerized. Her legs seemed endless. They were beautiful, shapely, alluring. They were silky smooth and should never be covered with a pair of leggings again. Unable to hold out any longer, he reached out and touched her legs, stroked them up and down, front and back, the pad of his fingers reveling in the feel of her skin. These were legs that were making him harder just looking at them. Legs he wanted wrapped around him tight, holding him inside her body while he thrust in and out of her.

But first, he had to taste her.

Leaning in closer his hands slid to her hips as he angled his mouth to her center. Instinctively, she parted her thighs and when he gently opened her up and his tongue delved inside her, she clung to him to hold on, which to him was a good thing.

His tongue swiped at her a couple of times before going for the gusto, stroking her, licking her and sucking with an intensity he felt all the way to the exquisitely painful tip of his erection. She began moving against his mouth and he gripped her hips tighter to hold her steady and then his hands shifted and went to her rump, gripping it and pushing her closer to his mouth, while at the same time he lifted her legs off the floor to wrap around his shoulders, cupping her backside in the palms of his hands for support. Keeping his mouth locked to her his tongue was having a field day, licking her into pleasure, deliberately searing her senses. She clenched her hands to the side of his head, moaned his name over and over. And then she began to shudder. He felt it. He tasted it. And he didn't intend to remove his mouth from her until he'd gotten his fill.

Moments later he pulled his mouth away, untangled her legs from around his shoulders and eased her down with him to the floor. He glanced over at her and licked his lips. "Delicious," he whispered in a throaty voice.

She had been more than delicious. She was incredible. The taste and heat of her was still on his tongue. At that moment, something inside him snapped. The need to join his body with hers was monumental.

He released a growl before he shifted his body, capturing her mouth the moment he could do so. He was going to take her, give them both pleasure, have them exploding all over the place, and his erection throbbed violently in anticipation.

He couldn't get out of his jeans quickly enough and she didn't help matters when she began nipping on his shoulders, as if branding him hers. *Hers.* A groan left his chest when she bit down and he stared at her. She gave him one hell of a naughty smile not the least regretful. "I'm going to make you pay for that," he promised in a deep voice. With that said, he kicked his jeans away and pulled her to him.

"Condom?"

"Damn." Her mention of protection made him realize just how over the edge he was and the risk he had been about to take. Looking around for his jeans he quickly found them and fumbled through the pockets until he located his wallet. He found a condom packet, not wanting to think just how long it had been in there and hoping like hell it would still be effective.

Ripping open the packet he quickly sheathed himself knowing her eyes were glued to him and watching every move he made. When he was finished, he went back to her, pulled her into his arms and kissed her deeply, hungrily and wildly.

He hadn't expected this. He hadn't expected a need erupting inside him so intense that he felt driven to make love to her in a way he hadn't ever made love to a woman before. She was demanding something from him, pulling it out effortlessly and he knew the only way he would be totally satisfied was when he was embedded deeply inside of her.

He pulled his mouth from hers, reveling in a need so intense he was goaded into immediate action. She was so responsive, filled with as much passion as he was feeling and he wanted her now. He shifted their bodies to place her beneath him, pressing her back on the rug. Ramsey spread her legs with his knee. Gripping her hips tight in his hands, he surged inside of her, going deep, all the way to the hilt.

He watched her eyes widen at the intrusion and when he began moving, thrusting inside of her, her gaze became filled with a pleasure that touched his soul and made his erection throb even more inside of her.

Her heat surrounded him. Her muscles clenched him, pulled everything out of him; made pleasure build inside of him, gather in his shaft, and he felt snug inside of her, like it was where he belonged.

He began moving harder. Going faster. Thrusting deeper. And when he called out her name the sound detonated like a bomb. He exploded at the same moment she did. Pleasure ripped through them both and he gripped her hips tighter as he drove even deeper inside of her.

"Chloe."

Her name was a guttural sound off his lips and he moved his hands from her hips to her hair as he filled her with his release. Shivers ran down his spine and he could only sigh as sensations filled him to capacity.

And when he eased up to take her mouth in his, he promised himself that sometime tonight, they would make it to the bedroom.

# Chapter 8

Sometime hours later, they made it to the bedroom. Barely. The most difficult part in getting there had been the stairs. Ramsey couldn't recall ever making love to anybody on stairs. He was a more traditional guy. But there had been nothing traditional about anything he and Chloe had done tonight, and even now as he lay flat on his back while she slept literally on top of him, he couldn't help but think about everything that had happened from the time Chloe had returned.

He'd been keyed up, part angry and part fighting an intense desire that had been eating away at him since the moment he first laid eyes on her. And when she had walked through the door tonight, and he'd seen her... and her bare legs, he had tried smothering his desire with anger by lashing out at her in a subject matter that really hadn't made any sense. That hadn't worked. And he was glad it hadn't. If she had taken the option to walk out that door, he probably would have died then and there. His need for her was so strong, so intense that even now he was getting hard all over again.

He was tempted to wake her but he would let her rest. She deserved every second that she slept. The woman was amazing and had more passion than he could ever imagine any woman having. She had met his every thrust and fueled his passion in a way that even now made him breathless. She had ridden him to the point of madness and it was only after their passion had exploded in a gigantic maelstrom that she had slumped down on top of him. She hadn't moved since.

He could only marvel at the soft body on top of him and even now their bodies were still intimately connected. He inhaled, taking in her scent. Her bare breasts pressing deep into his chest and her legs, those legs that had been his downfall earlier, were entwined in his. He closed his eyes to sleep awhile.

Ramsey wasn't sure just how long he'd slept, but when he lifted his lids it was to stare into a gorgeous pair of dark eyes. At the realization that she was awake, his body immediately became aroused. His erection jerked to life inside of her and from her expression he knew she felt it the moment he had.

He saw the rush of heat that inflamed her features and that same heat was there in the depths of the eyes staring down at him. Together they felt his shaft continue to expand inside of her, stretching her fully to accommodate him totally.

And when her muscles began clenching him, he knew it was time to start moving. But not until he was on top. She was the one who'd ridden the last go around and now it was his turn. He gritted his teeth as she continued to clench his hardness and to get control of his mind and senses. He began sliding his hand up and down her back, loving the feel of the soft texture of her skin. And then when he knew he had her absolute attention, he flipped her onto her back.

Surprise lit her eyes. "Hey! That's not fair."

Ramsey smiled, deciding he wouldn't waste time arguing with her, not when he wanted to make love to her, ride her, pump inside of her over and over again.

Automatically, she wrapped her legs around his waist and when she smiled up at him, he knew before it was all said and done, she was going to drain everything out of him. It was hard to believe they had already made love several times that night. In fact, except for the time he'd allowed her to sleep, they had made love nonstop.

When he pushed himself deeper inside of her, the groan that curled in her throat triggered something within him and he began moving, lifting up her hips to receive his strong strokes. His thrusts were fine-tuned, primitively precise and painstakingly deliberate.

"Ramsey." She moaned out his name over and over while thrashing her head back and forth against the bedcovers.

"Look at me, Chloe," he said in a guttural groan and when she did, and her eyes clashed with his, his grip tightened on her hips and what he saw in her gaze ignited something within him to the point where he felt consumed in fire, torched by desire. But he didn't stop. He continued going, moving in and out of her, needing her, wanting her and determined to consume her the way she was totally consuming him.

Chloe actually felt every muscle in her body, every single vein that ran through her, become electrified, gush with a need so extreme that she could only shiver, shudder in pleasure as Ramsey continued to drive deep and hard inside of her.

And when he leaned forward to capture her lips, she felt the sensations that started at her center, tear straight up her legs and went all the way to her toes. And like all the other times when they kissed, he took her mouth with a mastery that had her as responsive to a man as any woman could be. She wrapped her legs around him even tighter, locking him into her body.

She held tight to his shoulders, clung to him as he wrapped his tongue around hers while imitating the same rhythm of his thrusts below. She had never experienced passion this hot, this torrid, this out-of-body uncivilized. It was as if she was being sucked into a raging sea of unrestrained fervor, a heated craze that had her body literally begging for more, and she was showing him just how much more by the way she was lifting herself off the mattress to meet his every turbulent thrust.

She wanted this. She needed this. And the necessity of her desire had become essential, a crucial desperation. There was nothing trivial about the way she was feeling and when she suddenly felt herself tumbling headlong into an abyss of sensations that had her screaming his name, she shuddered straight into a climax that rocked her world. And when he finally let go of her mouth to throw his head back and let out a guttural growl, she was thrown off the edge all over again and together they went skyrocketing into another mind-blowing orgasm.

He tightened his hold on her, gripped more securely to her hips and locked their bodies into a bond of sensual fulfillment. She felt him totally and completely, and there was no part of her left untouched. Unconsumed. Not taken.

And when he leaned up to take her mouth again, she was very much aware of one major thing. He was breaking through her barriers and making her feel things that were emotional as well as physical. She had never intended for such a thing to happen. But it had, and as he continued to kiss her in a way that she felt all the way to her toes, he had proven that he *could* put a smile of satisfaction on her face all by himself.

Although he didn't plan for it to happen, Ramsey slept later than usual the next morning. It was only when he heard the sound of a man's laughter, namely his brother Zane's, that Ramsey realized he was in bed alone. He didn't recall Chloe getting out of it. Had exhaustion knocked him into a dead sleep? He'd never been a sound sleeper before and was known to be an early riser. But then he'd never had sex all night with a woman before either.

He slid out of bed. It was not his intent for Chloe to prepare breakfast alone and he had meant to help. It was the least he could do when his voracious sexual hunger had kept her up most of the night. Granted he wasn't an ace in the kitchen like she was, but he could at least follow directions.

Before heading for the bathroom for a quick shower he glanced over at the clock on the nightstand and frowned. It was just a little past four, so what the hell was Zane doing here already? And if Zane was here that meant so was Derringer and Jason because the three were thick as thieves. And he wouldn't be surprised if Callum wasn't downstairs, too. The four had shown up early one day last week. The day they had walked in on his kissing Chloe. It had been a second occurrence for his brothers and is what had prompted him to start putting distance between him and Chloe. A lot of good that did.

And as he stepped in the shower he did know one thing for certain: He wouldn't be putting distance between them any longer.

"Come on, Chloe, there's no way that brother of mine is still asleep. Ramsey wouldn't know how to sleep late even if it killed him," Zane was saying. He held his coffee cup midway to his lips, looked over at Chloe a little too long to suit her, before a smile touched his lips. "Unless…"

Instead of finishing what he was about to say, his smile widened as he took a sip of his coffee and then continued eating. Chloe was grateful for that although she wasn't sure what Zane Westmoreland was thinking at that moment. And she was grateful for the conversation going on between Jason, Derringer and Callum and the fact they hadn't heard Zane's comment. But because they knew Ramsey just as well as Zane, they had to be wondering the same thing. Why was he still in bed asleep?

She was beginning to feel uneasy. Had Zane or any of the others seen passion marks on her neck? Were they wondering why she was wearing a scarf of all things this morning? When she had eased out of bed careful to not wake Ramsey, and had gone back to her bedroom to take a shower, she had been appalled at all the marks Ramsey's stubble had made all over her body. And then there were some he had intentionally made. Specifically, the ones on her neck. It was as if he had been determined to mark her as his and the very thought of that sent shivers down her spine.

"About time you got out of bed, Ram. What are you? Sick or something?"

Chloe heard the smirk in Derringer's voice and turned to see that Ramsey had walked into the kitchen. He was wearing nothing but his jeans that hung low on his hips, and her breath stopped and her pulse leaped at the sight of his broad shoulders and bare chest. His feet were also bare and the thatch of dark hairs on his chest was damp, which indicated he'd just gotten out of the shower.

Ignoring his brothers, cousin and friend, his gaze was on her and without acknowledging their presence he made his way to where she stood. Before she could finally release her breath, he leaned over and kissed her in front of them.

There was what seemed to be shocked silence in the room. At least she thought there was, but the only sure thing she knew at that moment was that he was kissing her in front an audience. It wasn't a long kiss, but if he'd intended to make a point, he most certainly had. And when he finally pulled his mouth away, she stared up into a face that was smiling in a way that showed both dimples.

"Good morning, Chloe."

If the kiss hadn't done her in, then his throaty and husky voice definitely would have. She forced herself to begin breathing normally and said, "Good morning, Ramsey."

With his arms still locked around her waist, he turned toward the four men sitting at his breakfast table. "Is there a reason the four of you feel you should be getting preferential treatment for breakfast? Especially when three of you aren't employed by me."

Zane smiled. "But we're family."

Ramsey nodded slowly. "Just make sure you remember that when dealing with Chloe in the future."

Derringer lifted a brow. "So that's how things are going to be from now on?"

"Yes," Ramsey said without a smile on his face. "That's how things are going to be from now on."

Chloe's eyes were glued to Ramsey as her gaze ran over him. Her attention was directed to him so much that she missed part of what he'd said to the others. All she knew was that when she glanced at the men, they were staring at her as if with new insight. Subconsciously, she reached for her scarf to adjust it around her neck, wondering if they were seeing far more than she wanted them to see.

Deciding the mood around her had turned much too serious, she pulled out of Ramsey's arms and said, "I suggest you go put on a shirt. I'm about to fry some more bacon and I'd hate for popping grease to hit you."

She saw the grin on his face and was almost taken back at how different his attitude was from last week. It was a vast improvement. Would one night of mind-blowing lovemaking do that to you? She would be one of the first to admit that whereas she should feel tired because of the brevity of sleep the night before, she felt renewed energy running through her body. Although she had to force herself out of bed, after having slept wrapped in Ramsey's arms, once she had begun moving around the kitchen she had actually felt rejuvenated.

"Thanks for the warning," he said, and leaning closer he placed a sensuous peck on her lips before strolling out of the kitchen. The swagger on his walk was enough to give any woman heart failure, while making her wonder just what he could do with that swaggering body beneath the sheets. She knew the answer to that firsthand and remnants of pleasure flowed through her body from the memory.

Pulling in a deep breath she glanced at the four men who were staring at her. They had become a bunch of regulars during breakfast and lunch, always arriving earlier than everyone to chat with her and with each other.

From their conversations she knew about the horse breeding and training business Zane, Derringer and Jason were about to embark on, as well as the fact that Callum was in no hurry to return to Australia, although she hadn't figured out why.

Clearing her throat, she asked, "Would any of you like anything else? More coffee?"

Before they could respond, she could hear vehicles pulling up in the yard. She was grateful her day was about to begin and welcomed the opportunity to stay busy.

"And you're sure without Zane, Derringer and Jason's spread that you'll still have enough land for your sheep to graze?" Dillon Westmoreland leaned back in the chair behind his desk to ask his cousin.

Ramsey didn't respond but looked as if he was lost in other thoughts. "Are you okay, Ram?"

Dillon's concerned question snapped Ramsey's attention back and he couldn't help but smile. "Yes, I'm okay."

After breakfast Ramsey decided to leave the house for a while, not to avoid Chloe, but to give her the time she needed to prepare for the noon hour. Had he remained he would have done everything he could have to get her back upstairs or better yet, he would have played his hand at enticing her into participating in a number of quickies. So trying to behave he had driven over to Shady Tree Ranch to spend time with Dillon and Pamela.

He could feel Dillon staring at him and looked up and met his gaze. "I understand things have turned somewhat serious between you and your cook, Ram."

Ramsey didn't have to wonder where Dillon had gotten that information. And today, Ramsey had no problem acknowledging that was true. Even when he had dated he'd never been into sex just for the sake of sex, which is why a casual relationship with a woman never appealed to him. And because he hadn't been in the market for a serious relationship either, he'd been satisfied to remain a loner. It was only when things with him got so bad and sexual needs got the best of him, that he would seek out female companionship for a night. But those times had been few and far between. Now he couldn't imagine not making love to Chloe on a regular basis, not waking up during the night with her beside him, their legs locked together, her delectable bottom curled up against him. His...

"Ram?"

He glanced up, realizing Dillon had caught him daydreaming again. "Yes?"

"You sure you're okay?"

Ram leaned back in his chair, deciding to be completely honest. "No, I don't know if I'm okay," he finally said. He studied Dillon thoughtfully. "I can recall the first time you mentioned to me about meeting Pamela. I could hear something in your voice."

Dillon chuckled. "Yes, and it was probably the same thing I could hear in yours that day you came over here and mentioned Chloe Burton was your temporary cook."

Ramsey was taken aback by Dillon's claim. "No way. I had just met the woman that day."

Dillon nodded. "And remember, I had just met Pam that day when I spoke to you on the phone as well."

Ramsey frowned, not sure he liked what Dillon was hinting at. He quickly stood up. "Trust me, Dillon, it's not that kind of party."

A smile curved the corners of Dillon's lips when he said, "I didn't think it was that kind of party for me either, so I can understand you wanting to be in denial.

When you figure out it *is* that kind of party, make sure I'm one of the first to get an invitation."

Chloe slipped off her shoes before easing onto the sofa. Breakfast had been crazy and she needed to grab a private and quiet moment before preparing lunch. At times she wondered if she was growing men. There seemed to be more of them showing up for meals every day.

She smiled and inwardly admitted that she was becoming attached to each of them. They were good men, hardworking men, family men who often would talk about their wives and children and their love for them. Working for Ramsey was more than a way to keep food on the table. From the bits of conversations she'd been able to pick up, she knew they considered Ramsey a good employer, the best. He was fair and provided them with a means to provide for their families. She looked forward to seeing them every morning and didn't mind taking the time to prepare all the foods they liked.

To her surprise, and she was sure to his men as well, Ramsey had spent time with his men this morning. Of course they had teased him mercilessly before settling down to the huge meal she had prepared. And on the invitation and insistence from Ramsey, after everyone had been served, she had sat down with him at the table and had a cup of coffee when he conversed with his men. During that time she felt like a member of Ramsey's working-crew family. She felt as if she truly belonged. And she was learning more and more about Ramsey from those who knew him the best. It

was great information she could use in the article she
wanted to write on him.

*The article she would not be writing now.*

She breathed in deeply. She had come here with only
one goal in mind and that was to convince Ramsey to
pose on the cover of her magazine and to also obtain
information to share with her readers. Considering everything, there was no way she could go through with
doing that now. She had crossed over the line of what
was professional, of what was right.

She did not want him to think she had gone to the
extreme and shared his bed only as a means to an end.
Therefore, she needed to tell him the truth and would
do so tonight when she had his complete attention,
and somehow she would convince him not to send
her away, but to let her work through the end of the
week because his regular cook would return on Monday.

She didn't want to think about how he would possibly feel once he learned the truth. It hadn't been her
intent for things to work out this way, but they had and
now their time together was about to come to an end
and she could feel her heart breaking. Things were beginning to get complicated. She was not only deceiving
Ramsey, but she was deceiving his family as well, at
least those she'd met. She needed to get out of dodge
before drowning in her sea of lies.

She heard a quick tap and then the front door
opened. She stood when three women walked in and
she found herself under the intense gaze of three pairs
of eyes the exact color of Ramsey's. She knew immediately these were his sisters.

\* \* \*

Ramsey cursed under his breath when he pulled into his yard, recognizing the three vehicles haphazardly parked there. For his sisters to come calling at this time of the day and all at the same time meant curiosity had gotten the best of them and they were here to check things out for themselves.

He glanced in his rearview mirror, surprised Callum wasn't pulling up behind him. The man seemed to have some kind of built-in radar where Gemma was concerned. Whenever she showed up at his place, Callum homed in on her and would find just about any excuse to show up.

As he got out of his truck, the rich scent of something delectable cooking filled the air. This was Chloe's last week and he wondered how his men were going to readjust when Nellie returned. He had called and left a message on her cell phone letting her know they needed to talk before Monday. Chloe had raised the bar of expectations and although he knew Nellie was a darn good cook, she hadn't displayed a lot of that skill lately. And her attitude toward his men definitely needed improving.

But still, just the thought that this Friday would be Chloe's last day did something to him. He refused to believe what Dillon had hinted at earlier that he was developing feelings for her. Yes, he had enjoyed sleeping with her last night and intended to do so again, but he had no intention of progressing to anything remotely serious between them. He was a loner. He preferred things that way.

He heard the sound of feminine voices the moment

he walked into his house. He paused and noted the chatter, the laughter, the downright friendliness in the conversations being shared. It seemed the four women were getting along, and for some reason that pleased him. Why it would, he wasn't sure.

Following the sound of the voices as well as the scent of food cooking, he headed toward the kitchen and then leaned in the doorway at the sight that greeted him. His sisters were sitting down at the table, sampling whatever was smelling so damn good, while Chloe stirred something in a big pot. If he didn't know better, by the way they were carrying on, he would have thought they had known each other for years.

"Forgive me if I'm interrupting anything," he said when it became obvious no one had noticed him.

Four pairs of eyes turned his way, but it was only one pair that he sought out. And the moment Chloe's gaze met his, he felt it, a deep stirring within the pit of his stomach, and it had more depth than just a sensual ache. He was tempted to do what he'd done this morning in front of Zane, Derringer, Jason and Callum, which was to cross the room and take Chloe into his arms and kiss her, ignoring their audience. But there was no way in hell he could ignore the three sitting at the table who had huge smiles on their faces like he'd cut muster about something. And he couldn't help but notice they were watching him closely.

"You're not interrupting anything," Bailey said sweetly, smiling with too much saccharin on her lips to suit him. "We were just sitting here chatting with Chloe, trying to get to know her better."

He lifted a brow and almost asked why they saw fit

to do something like that when Chloe would be leaving this Friday, but he refrained from doing so. "Suit yourself. If you will excuse me I have work to do."

He moved to walk toward his office wondering why he was doing the very thing he said he would no longer do where Chloe was concerned. But then he knew that putting any ideas into his sisters' heads would be dangerous. They wouldn't take it and run, they would take it and rush off in a mad dash. Besides, by retreating he was saving Chloe from being interrogated later, not that his nosy sisters hadn't probably tried pumping her for information already.

When he reached his office he eased down in the chair behind his desk wondering how long his visitors intended to stay. His men would be showing up in a few hours for lunch and he hadn't had any private time with Chloe since they'd last made love this morning. He at least wanted to kiss her the way he had wanted to do without an audience.

He picked up the folder on his desk. He would try to get some work done and hoped like hell his sisters would leave in a timely manner. Otherwise, he would be tempted to ask them to leave.

He smiled thinking doing something like that wouldn't go over well. He'd escorted them to the door before, but always in a teasing manner; however, today he would be dead serious. And he intended to do something about the locks on his back door where anyone thought they could just walk in whenever they wanted. That had never bothered him before but now it did.

He threw down the folder he'd been holding in his hands, not believing the way his thoughts were going.

The only reason he was considering changing the damn lock was because on two different occasions he had been caught kissing Chloe. Because she would be leaving after Friday, did it really matter now?

He slumped back in his chair, finally admitting to himself that yes, it did matter. He didn't want things between them to end yet. He could ask Chloe to go out with him on occasion, he would take her to dinner and pursue some sort of a relationship with her. Nothing real serious, mind you. Was that what he really wanted? With lambing starting next week as well as some of his men returning to sheepherding, would he have the time? He knew at that moment he would do something he hadn't done in well over ten years and that is to make time for a woman.

He glanced up when he heard a knock on his door. His pulse leaped. Had his sisters left and Chloe had come looking for him? He stood and a frown settled on his face when Callum walked in. He dropped back down in the chair disappointed.

Ramsey didn't have to ask his friend why he was there. He knew. And the way Ramsey was feeling about his sisters at that moment, he was tempted to pay Callum a hefty fee to take Gemma off his hands. There was no hope for Megan and Bailey. Megan wasn't dating anyone seriously since she had finally dumped that asshole of a doctor she'd gotten involved with last year. And lucky for him Bailey was more into her books than the opposite sex. She was determined to finish college in three years instead of four and then obtain a law degree. Although she could get on his last nerve at times, he was proud of her and her dedication to her studies.

"What are you doing here, Cal?" Ramsey couldn't resist the opportunity to tease his friend. Callum had given him enough grief over Chloe during the last couple of days to last a lifetime, so to Ramsey's way of thinking the ribbing was justified.

"What do you think?"

Ramsey rolled his eyes. Callum had been hanging around Zane too much lately. He was beginning to sound just like him. "You do know that one day you're going to have to take matters into your own hands, and I don't mean something as extreme as kidnapping," Ramsey said.

Callum didn't say anything, he just smiled. At any other point in time that smile would have made Ramsey uneasy, had him somewhat worried, but not today. He had his own problems to deal with and for once Callum and Gemma were the least of his concern.

His only concern was whether Chloe would be interested in continuing their relationship after Friday. And he intended to do whatever it took to make sure she wanted that as much as he did.

## Chapter 9

As soon as the last vehicle pulled out of Ramsey's yard, Chloe glanced over at him. He was leaning in the kitchen doorway staring at her. The men had arrived on time for lunch and Ramsey's sisters had stuck around to join them for the meal. Zane, Derringer and Jason had also shown up, and Callum had appeared out of the back with Ramsey, which meant he had been there for a while.

After everyone had been fed, Ramsey's sisters had been kind enough to help clear the table and help load the dishwasher. Ramsey had assisted with cleanup duty as well and in no time at all, the kitchen was spotless. If she didn't know any better Chloe would have thought Ramsey had pitched in to hurry off his sisters. Evidently they got the message and had taken Zane, Derringer and Jason right along with them. Callum had returned to the shearing plant with the men.

And now for the first time since waking up that morning, she and Ramsey were alone. She held Ramsey's gaze as memories of last night flooded her mind. She instantly recalled his mouth on her body, how his lips had trailed over every inch of her, his tongue, hot, wet and greedy, had devoured her breasts and the area between her legs. She took a deep breath as she thought about how perfectly their bodies had fit and the sensations she'd felt with him moving inside of her.

He had been the most passionate of lovers, creative and imaginative all rolled into one, and she knew without a doubt that last night each and every one of her fantasies had been fulfilled. Whether he ever appeared on the cover of her magazine no longer mattered because she knew firsthand that Ramsey Westmoreland was indeed the most irresistible man that existed.

"Come here, Chloe."

His words, spoken in what sounded like a heated breath, floated across the room to her, touched her all over and in the very places, his hands, mouth, lips and tongue had traveled the night before.

And without hesitating, she crossed the room and walked straight into his arms. When he gripped her tightly to him, she lifted her face and stared into his eyes.

When he leaned down and captured her mouth in his, every part of her was stirred into action and she returned his kiss as hungrily as he gave it. Her chest settled against his and she knew he could feel the hardened tips of her breasts pressing into him. She could certainly feel his burgeoning erection that was cradled intimately between her thighs.

Moments later, their mouths broke apart and she felt her fingers flexed as they held on to his shoulders, otherwise she would have fallen to her knees. The sensations flowing through her heated her insides.

"I want to make love to you right here. Right now. But I can't risk any unexpected visitors," he murmured hotly against her lips. "It would greatly upset me if we got interrupted."

From the sound of his voice and his aroused expression, she knew he was serious. He wanted her just as much as she wanted him. "Then maybe we should go upstairs," she invited in a husky whisper.

From the darkening of his eyes she knew he'd heard every word she'd said. And before she could let out her next breath, he swept her off her feet and into his arms and headed toward the stairs.


Ramsey placed Chloe on the bed and stood back. He needed to look at her, study her, analyze how this woman had changed his life to the point where he was up here in his bedroom, about to make love to her, when it wasn't even three in the afternoon. There were forty million other things he could be doing around his ranch. Nearly half his herd was pregnant, lambing began next Monday and he needed to make sure all the lambing stalls were ready.

But at that moment nothing was more important to him than getting inside of Chloe, locking his body to hers, feeling her muscles clamp down on him, pulling him in and drawing every single thing out of him. Sensation was building in his erection, arousing him to the point where he wanted to tear off his clothes and hers. He wanted to mate with her. Stay inside her body and never come out.

Ramsey glanced over at her. He wanted her wet all over and easing onto the bed he reached out and pulled her to him, and began stroking his tongue along her lower lip. There was something about her mouth that enthralled him, made him want to keep kissing her, but first he wanted to taste her all over. He remembered all the things he had done to her last night, but was convinced that it had not been enough.

His hands moved to her blouse and within seconds he had pulled it over her head and tossed it aside. Then his gaze lowered to her chest and he saw how the nipples of her breasts had hardened to pebbles and were pressed against the lace material of her bra. And it was a pink bra that matched the color of the blouse he had removed earlier. He wondered if her panties would also be the same color. He'd noticed that about her last night. She had been wearing a light green lace bra and had been wearing matching lace panties. He found her color-coordinated lingerie downright sexy.

With eager fingers he undid the front closure of her bra and watched as it parted, exposing two of the most beautiful globes he'd ever seen. He had thought that very thing last night and it still held true in the bright sunlight. They were perfect for his hands and incredibly delicious to his mouth.

Removing the bra completely he leaned forward and captured a hard nipple between his lips and then his tongue went to work, reacquainting his taste buds with the flavor he had enjoyed last night while holding her breast firmly in his hand.

He heard her soft moans as he feasted on one breast and then another, taking his time while his tongue so effortlessly devoured her. It felt hot, inflamed as it went about licking her hungrily, sucking the tip greedily. Never before had he gotten such pleasure from such an assault on a woman's breasts.

He finally lifted his head and pulled back as a slow smile touched his lips. Without saying anything he gently eased her back while his hands went to her skirt and he gently pulled the denim material down her hips, thighs and legs, leaving her in those leggings. A pretty pink pair.

He studied the footless tights and although he much preferred seeing her legs bare as they had been last night, there was something about all those colorful leggings she wore that definitely made a statement. But at that moment he was going to enjoy peeling the damn things off her.

"You do know I really don't like these things," he said as he reached for the waistband.

She quirked a brow at him. "Why?"

He smiled and said simply. "They hide your legs."

Chloe smiled. "Leggings are part of the latest fashion trend. And they don't hide my legs, Ramsey, they accent them. Usually my dresses or skirts are rather short. Leggings work well with my outfits and with the flat shoes I normally wear it makes the perfect casual outfit."

Ramsey nodded, not believing he was actually discussing a woman's attire.

"Would you prefer I not wear leggings while I'm around your men, Ramsey?"

His answer was quick in coming. "No."

"Okay, then, rancher. You can't have it both ways."

He sort of disagreed with that. "In private I'm taking them off you because I love looking at your legs."

"Suit yourself."

And he intended to, he thought. And then his throat tightened, not allowing another word to slip through when he inched the leggings past her hips to uncover a very skimpy, very sexy pink thong.

Once he had peeled the leggings completely off her, his attention went back to that very hot-looking thong, dying to reveal what it covered and deciding not to wait.

Adjusting his body he slouched down on the bed between her open legs and lifted them on his shoulders. And just like last night, the feel of those bare legs on his shoulders, smooth and silky, rubbing against his skin made the lower part of him throb with an intensity that sent shudders through his body. And it wasn't helping matters that he was drowning in her scent. Being this intimately close to her hot mound made him crave her taste even more.

As soon as he felt he was in the right position, he leaned in and flicked his tongue across her crotch, dampening her thong in the process but getting a taste of what was behind it. She moaned and the sound went straight to his erection and made it surge.

"What are you doing to me?" she asked, in a voice that seemed strained, breathless, panting.

"What does it feel like?" He flicked his tongue across her again, wanting her to feel the strength behind it. "But if what I'm doing is bothering you, I can always stop," he said and grinned at her.

"No," she said quickly. "Please don't stop."

He glanced up at her and his response was just as quick. "I won't." The look he saw in her face, blatant need and transparent pleasure, fueled his hunger and he pulled back slightly, lifted her hips to remove the thong from her body.

He had gotten his first taste of her in this very feminine hot spot last night and had been craving more of her ever since. He hadn't known the extent of his sexual desire until he'd made love to her. When he recalled all the orgasms they had shared last night, his desperation in wanting her again was warranted.

Tossing the skimpy undergarment aside, he eased back in place between her thighs and rubbed his chin against her naked skin, liking the feel of her and the look of her Brazilian wax. Not able to hold back any longer, he began licking at her, taking his tongue and outlining her feminine mound wanting her to feel the urgency of his desire.

"Ramsey," she called out his name in a whispered tone as she tightened the legs around his shoulder.

"Yes, baby?" he asked in a deep tone.

"I—I like that."

A shiver swept through him. "I like it, too." And then he showed her just how much when he parted her feminine folds and let his tongue go to work. Her taste stirred a yearning in him that could only be appeased this particular way and by doing this precise thing. And the sound of her moans, her whimpers, the tightening of her legs around his shoulders, and the sweet liquor her body was producing, sent what seemed like an unquenchable greed through him.

He knew it was only a matter of time before she came and when that thought raced through him the pressure of his tongue inside of her increased, lapping her up like his very life depended on it. And when he felt Chloe's body jerk beneath his mouth he held on tight, knowing her spasms would soon become his.

They did. And with as much pleasure as his mental state could take, he went for the gusto, using his tongue to push her even more so over the edge while keeping his mouth locked tight to her.

Chloe was convinced her mind was splintering under the intensity of the explosion that ripped through her. She breathed in sharply and felt the lower half of her body actually being lifted off the bed, but Ramsey was there, holding on tight to her, gripping her hips, keeping her bolted to his mouth.

His tongue was assaulting her core as he continued to lap her up. She screamed out his name as spasms, as vicious as they could get, tore into her, spinning her senses out of control and into a turmoil or passion.

It was only when the last tremble passed through her that he released her and pulled back. There was nothing she could do but slump back on the bed. She felt weaker than water. She watched through partially closed lashes as he moved from the bed to remove his clothes.

She could only lay there, trying to get her breathing back to normal as she watched him lean over to take off his boots. He then straightened to unbutton his shirt and then eased it off his muscular shoulders and tossed it aside. Sliding the brass buckle belt through the loops, he lowered his zipper before pushing the jeans down his legs.

Even while lying there, with barely enough energy to breathe, Chloe watched as Ramsey removed every stitch of clothing and then he stood, fully naked and all male. Her eyes latched on his erection, big and powerful, and upon seeing it, fiery sensations swept through her, giving her renewed energy while stirring desire within her all over again.

When he reached into the nightstand to retrieve a condom packet and tore it open with his teeth, before proceeding to roll it over his swollen shaft, she felt what amounted to fire raging through her veins. She exhaled a deep breath when he came back to the bed and with gentle hands he reached out and eased her legs apart.

Moments later, in position between them, he leaned down and captured her lips in a kiss so painstakingly tender that it almost brought tears to her eyes and made her fall in love with him that much more. When he tore his lips from her to pull back, he tilted her hips up to him before surging deep within her. The pleasure she felt with his entry sent a moan from deep within her throat. And then the mating of their bodies began as he eased in and out of her, giving her the pleasure her body was aching for.

"Look at me, baby. Feel me," Ramsey said as his fingertips caressed her chin.

She did feel him. He was as deep as he could get and his need was raging just as out of control as hers. Then he picked up the tempo and she clung to him, determined to meet him on every level. Especially this one.

And when he called out her name in a guttural growl she knew that here, in bed, making love, the two of them were in the same sensual vibe. And when she cried out her pleasure, felt her body explode yet again, and knew he was following her over the edge, she could have sworn at that moment she actually felt his hot release shooting inside of her, all the way to the womb. But she knew that wasn't possible. She had watched him put on a condom. It was nothing more than her imagination at work, and when he continued to drive hard within her she knew the night was just beginning.

A long time later Chloe lay in Ramsey's arms in the position she'd discovered he liked the best: spoon style. Her backside was cushioned by his front and his muscular leg was thrown over hers. Her head was resting back on his chest and his arm was thrown over her middle.

She felt satiated, relaxed, secured. After their last lovemaking session, Ramsey had eased out of her and had gone into the bathroom to discard the condom and to put on another. He liked being ready and chances were today would not be any different than last night when they had made love, rested and made love again all through the night. However, at some point they needed to prepare something for dinner to keep up their strength.

They enjoyed each other and she couldn't see them

not making love several more times before they finally drifted off to sleep. The thought that he desired her as much as she desired him made her heart thump rapidly in her chest.

She pulled in a deep breath knowing she had to level with him. No matter how he handled things she needed to tell him the truth. She would let him know she no longer wanted him to pose for the cover, nor did she want to do an article on him.

Knowing it was best to just get it over with, she turned into his arms. She could tell the move surprised him and deciding to just tell him and not waste any time, she took a quick breath and said, "Ramsey, there's something I need to tell you."

Ramsey quickly placed a finger to Chloe's lips. Knowing his sisters and how desperate they were for him to become involved with a woman, they had probably gone overboard, shaken her up by tossing her some ideas she wasn't quite ready to catch. So she was about to bail out. Let him know that for her things weren't quite that serious. He understood, but he wasn't ready to hear her acknowledge that yet.

At the end of the week, right before she left for good, then they would talk. He would tell her of his desire to see her again when her work here ended. He wanted to take her out, make love to her, he wanted for them to continue what they had started here. He recalled what he'd said to Dillon earlier that day and knew that he *did* want it to be that kind of a party.

"Let's not get into a serious discussion about anything. Not now. We can discuss any serious topics on your last day. I need to continue to have the peace I've found with you, Chloe. Could you hold your thoughts for a while and give me that?"

She slowly nodded. "Yes, I can give you that."

"And," he continued by saying, "with shearing wrapping up this week, the sheep that's not pregnant will be taken to pasture and—"

"You have a lot of sheep pregnant?"

He smiled. "Yes, almost half my herd."

He saw the look of surprise on her face. "How did that many sheep get pregnant at the same time?"

"It's timed that way. The female sheep, the ewes, are put out with the rams during mating season and five months later they deliver during what is call lambing. That's when the lamb is born. Luckily ewes won't deliver the same day, but typically they will all deliver within a two-week period of each other."

"Wow!"

He chuckled. In a way he was pleased with Chloe's interest in his ranch. "The rams and the wethers are—"

"Wethers?"

"Yes, castrated male sheep," he explained. "While the pregnant ewes are lambing, the rams and wethers and the ewes that aren't pregnant are taken to pasture by the sheepherders. And that is where most of them will be for the next few months out on the pasture grazing."

An idea popped into his head. "One of my men, Pete Overton, won't be able to begin sheepherding until Sunday morning, so I'm going to drive his herd out to pasture early Saturday morning and get things all set up for him. Will you come with me? We'll be back here before noon Sunday."

Chloe smiled up at Ramsey. She had wanted to come clean and tell him the truth, but he preferred they hold off and not discuss anything serious until her last day. That was fine with her because she knew that once she told him the truth he would probably be upset with her.

She leaned up and wrapped her arms around his neck. "Yes, I'd love to go with you."

# Chapter 10

Over the next few days Chloe accepted the realization that she was falling in love with Ramsey. They would share a bed each night and get up before daybreak every morning and together they would prepare breakfast for the men.

It was during those times that he would share more information about his life as a sheepherder and had begun telling her about members of his family. Five of his siblings had been under sixteen when his parents had gotten killed—Megan, Gemma, the twins by the name of Adrian and Aiden, and his sister Bailey. Zane had been a senior in high school, ready to go off to college and Derringer had been about to enter his senior year of high school. His cousin Dillon had been placed in a similar situation with four siblings under sixteen.

From what Ramsey told her, Adrian and Aiden were

now in their last year of college at Harvard, as was their cousin Stern. Another cousin by the name of Canyon was in medical school at Howard University in D.C. Brisbane was in the Navy. Micah, who was Zane's counterpart in age, was a graduate from Harvard Medical School and was an epidemiologist with the federal government.

Just listening to Ramsey share information with her about his family's turbulent years and the struggle that he and Dillon had had to endure to keep their families together, she had to admire the two men. Although she had yet to meet Dillon, she had met another one of his brothers, Riley, and found him to be just as handsome as the others.

And Ramsey had shared more information about sheepherding with her. One afternoon they had walked around his ranch. He had taken her to where the lambing stalls were and explained how next week more than a thousand of his ewes would be delivering. She had found the whole process fascinating. He had also given her a tour of the shearing plant and she was able to watch the men at work. She'd seen the dogs at work, too, and Ramsey had explained how important the sheepdogs were in managing and protecting the herds. You could definitely see that running a sheep ranch required maintaining a tight schedule and sticking to it.

Hanging the last pot back on the rack, she turned when she heard the back door open and smiled when Ramsey walked in. Closing the door behind him, and without missing a step, he crossed the kitchen floor and pulled her into his arms and kissed her.

Chloe returned the kiss, for the moment refusing to

acknowledge that she was making it harder and harder to leave after this weekend, to walk away and not to look back. The thought of doing so caused her heart to ache, but that's what she would be doing. She decided she didn't want to think beyond it, so she tightened her arms around him as he deepened his kiss. His mouth slanted against hers and she could feel her knees weaken.

Moments later he broke off the kiss and pulled back slightly and whispered against her moist lips. "Why do you always taste so sweet?"

His words further eroded her sensibility. He sounded so serious like there was truly an answer for his question. There wasn't one, so she shook her head, tilted it up and smiled at him. "For the same reason you always taste so delicious."

And to show him just what she meant, she took the tip of her tongue and licked a corner of his mouth. The instant she did, his long eyelashes swept upward to reveal the depths of his darkened gaze, and she could just imagine what he was thinking now.

"Doing something like that can get you into trouble," he warned, as his arms tightened around her waist, drawing her even closer into the fit of his muscular form.

She smiled. "So you say."

"So I can prove." He took a step away from her. "But not now. First, I need to let you know that we've been invited to dinner."

She lifted a brow. "Dinner?"

"Yes, my cousin Dillon and his wife Pamela want to meet you."

Panic settled into Chloe's bones. She didn't want to pull any more of Ramsey's family members into her web of deceit. She liked all of the ones she'd met so far and from what she'd heard about the oldest Denver Westmoreland, Dillon, there was no doubt in her mind that she would like him as well.

"Why do they want to meet me?" she asked, not sure she was ready to meet the man Ramsey was so close to.

"They've heard a lot of nice things about you and want to meet you for themselves."

She didn't know what to say to that. She had heard a lot of nice things about them as well. "I bet it was Jason who told them how I could fix his eggs just the way he likes them," she said in a teasing voice, trying to make light of what Ramsey had said.

Ramsey chuckled. "Might be. Or it could have been one of my brothers or sisters. You've made quite an impression on them."

Chloe glanced down to study the floor. At any other time knowing she had impressed the family of the man she loved would have been a feather in her cap. But not now. When they found out the truth it won't just be Ramsey who'd think she'd deceived them. Lucia had been right. Chloe had been around them long enough to know the Westmorelands stuck together and if you were to hurt one, then you hurt them all.

"So, will you go to dinner with me at Dillon and Pamela's?"

A part of her wanted to come up with an excuse not to go. She should claim a headache or something, but she could not do that. Although she deserved nothing, she wanted it all. She wanted to get to know more about the man she had fallen in love with. As well as to get to know those he loved and those who loved him.

She pulled in a deep breath and then said, "Yes, I'll go to dinner with you."

Ramsey could not remember the last time he'd brought a woman to a family function. Even with the annual charity ball they sponsored each year for the Westmoreland Foundation that had been established to aid various community causes, he usually went solo. For him it had been better that way and because there had been enough eager-beaver Westmorelands who enjoyed being the center of attention with beautiful women on their arms, he was left alone.

He couldn't even recall bringing Danielle to dinner when they'd dated. He never had to bother because his mother had liked Danielle enough to invite her to dinner whenever she saw her at church most Sundays. He knew the main reason he had dated Danielle as long as he had was because his family had liked her. And then because she'd hung around waiting for him to finish college, he had felt marrying her was the least he could do.

The truth of the matter was that she hadn't been idle while she'd waited. At some point she had met someone, slept with the person and had gotten pregnant. The sad thing about it was that the man never married her and she ended up being a single mom.

He glanced around the room thinking that this was not supposed to be a family function. Dillon and Pamela had invited him and Chloe to dinner and they had accepted. He had expected to see Pamela's three younger sisters because this was spring break back in Gamble. But he hadn't expected to see his three sisters who were smiling sweetly at him at every turn. Nor had he expected to see Zane, Derringer and Jason. He saw them enough around his place for breakfast and lunch. Callum was not a surprise because the man took advantage of every opportunity to hang around Gemma. Riley wasn't a surprise either because he was known to drop in whenever and wherever there was a free meal.

"You might have disappointed me for not doing that magazine cover, but you've more than made up for it with Chloe, Ram. I like her," Bailey said.

Ramsey turned and met his baby sister's gaze. "And just what do you like about her?" he asked, curious to hear what she had to say.

"She fits you."

Because he'd been expecting a long, drawn out discourse, he was surprised by those three words. This was definitely a night for surprises, but then he thought he would not let Bailey get off that easily. "She fits me in what way?"

Bailey shrugged. "She's pretty. You're handsome. She can cook. You can't. She's an extrovert. You're an introvert." She lifted her brow. "Need I go on?"

"No."

"Because we all know you have a tendency to stretch things out, Ram. If you are interested in her, you probably want to step up your game a notch."

Now it was his time to raise a brow. "What makes you think I'm interested in her?" he asked, glancing across the room to where Chloe sat talking to Pamela.

The two women were getting along like they were old friends.

"She's here isn't she? That in itself says a lot." And without saying anything else, Bailey strolled off.

He was tempted to follow Bailey and tell her that no, nothing said it all. They were seeing things that weren't there. Seeing what they wanted to see. But when he glanced back over at Chloe, he was beginning to wonder if perhaps everything that Bailey had said just now made sense. If so, that was real scary only because it was Bailey and she never thought logically.

Not for the first time tonight Chloe quickly glanced over at Ramsey before turning her full attention back to the conversation going on around her. The topic of conversation had shifted from just how good the First Lady had looked at a nationally televised event last evening to what was happening overseas.

More than once he had caught her gaze and the smile he'd sent her way was enough to send heat escalating through every part of her body. And memories of his touch would wash over her, make her wish they were someplace else. Someplace private.

"So you're an only child, Chloe?"

Chloe glanced up at Gemma and smiled. The Westmorelands had been asking her questions about herself. Getting to know her. She had been wording her answers so they wouldn't be outright lies. "Yes, I'm an only child but not for long. My father is getting married in a few months and the person he's marrying has a son and daughter."

"And you don't have a problem with that?" Bailey asked.

Chloe chuckled. "Not at all. Dad's been single long enough. My mother died when I was two, so it's about time he tied the knot again."

The conversation shifted to Megan as she told them how her day went as an anesthesiologist. Chloe glanced back across the room at Ramsey. He was talking to Dillon. There was no mistaking the two men were related. Dillon Westmoreland was also a good-looking man.

Ramsey caught her eye and like before, the look he gave her made her heart thump erratically in her chest. And as she continued to look at him she could actually feel his heat, reaching out across the perimeters of the room and actually touch her. And then he whispered something to Dillon before walking across the room toward her.

When he reached her side he tucked her hand in his, something that wasn't missed by his sisters. "Thanks, Pamela, for a lovely dinner. It's time Chloe and I left."

Chloe glanced up at him, not surprised by what he said. It was either leave so they could go somewhere private or put on a real show for his family.

Pamela glanced at her watch. "It's early yet. Are you sure you have to go?"

Ramsey smiled. "Yes, trust us, we do."

Later that night Ramsey was wide-awake as he watched Chloe sleep. They had barely made it through the front door before they began stripping out of their clothes. They hadn't thought about making it up the stairs to the bedroom; instead they had been satisfied just to get to the sofa. By the time he had slid his body into hers, all the restraints he'd held in place over the past twelve hours came crashing down.

He had made love to her with an intensity that had even overwhelmed him. She had writhed beneath him, filled with the same turbulent need as she strained against him, meeting his strokes, his single-minded thrusts as if her very life depended on it.

She had dug her nails into his shoulders and on one or two occasions, had actually bit him. He had growled and then had increased the pace as his control and hers had continued to get shot to hell. He gave it to her hard, and at her encouragement, even harder. She had transformed into a wildcat, a woman who knew the degree of pleasure she'd wanted to experience. A woman who intended for him to give her just what she needed.

And he had. The more she'd wanted, the more he'd given. And by the time their world exploded into one hell of a combined orgasm, he was barely holding on the edge of sanity. He had known the moment pleasure had ripped his soul apart that this was not just a normal lovemaking session between two consenting adults. It was a hell of a lot more than that. The word *normal* didn't even come close. There had been nothing ordinary about their joining. It had been the most atypical thing he'd ever experienced.

*And now he knew why.*

For the first time in his life he wanted to have a serious relationship with a woman. And he now knew more than ever that what he felt for Chloe wasn't just a sexual thing. Tomorrow was officially her last day at the ranch, although she had agreed to spend Friday and Saturday night with him on the range sheepherding.

He could tell from the murmurs he'd been hearing over the past couple of days from his men that she would be missed, and it wasn't just about the meals she had prepared for them. It was about the woman they had come to know. A woman who took joy in making their nourishment.

Yet she had remained professional while developing friendships with them. They looked forward to seeing her in the morning and again at noon. She not only talked to them, but she also listened. On occasion, he knew she also offered advice to a couple of the men when they'd inquired as to what to purchase their wives for birthday and anniversary gifts.

They would miss her, but none of them would miss her more than he would. In just two short weeks she had touched him, given him a bone-deep feeling of total and complete satisfaction, one he could not have explained until now.

He leaned over and brushed a kiss across her brow. Last week he could barely make sense of what was happening to him, but now he knew and accepted his fate. He loved this woman. He really loved her.

And he wanted to keep her.

He knew that might be easier said than done. She might not want to have a relationship with him, one with the potential of going somewhere. She might like her life like it was now—not seriously involved with anyone. That Daren guy had probably left a bad taste in her mouth. In that case, he would do whatever he needed to do to make her change her attitude about a serious affair.

Unfortunately he did not have Callum's patience. Starting now he would rev up his campaign to win her over, prevail in getting her love. At least his situation didn't appear to be as hopeless as Dillon's had been when he'd met Pamela. At the time she was engaged to marry someone else. But with his encouragement Dillon hadn't let that stop him.

Now was time to take some of the same advice he'd dished out to Dillon. He knew what he wanted and there was no excuse in his not getting it. He had a goal. By this time next year Chloe Burton would have a permanent place in his bed as his wife.

"Are you okay, Chloe?"

Chloe glanced over at Ramsey. No, she wasn't okay. Saying goodbye to his men had been the hardest thing she'd ever had to do. And she had fought back tears when they'd given her a going-away gift.

"Yes, I'm okay," she said, knowing she really wasn't. Ramsey had helped her to clean up the kitchen after lunch and then she had thrown a couple of items into an overnight bag. When she had stepped outside it was to find a huge RV parked in his yard. He had explained that the modern-day sheepherder believed in living out on the range with all the conveniences of home. Granted most didn't have anything this large and extravagant. The majority of them did have campers that they pulled behind their trucks and would set up residence without having to sacrifice doing without satellite television, indoor bathroom and kitchen and dining facilities.

The luxury coach Ramsey was driving was his own personal beauty and as Chloe glanced around she was impressed with just how nice it was, and how much an expert driver he was behind the wheel. This was definitely a luxury coach worth owning. It was a home away from home on wheels. His men had already taken the sheep up in the high country, a portion of Ramsey's land that connected to Dillon's. Chloe hadn't been aware of how much property the Westmorelands owned until now.

"The men are going to miss you."

She smiled. "And I'm going to miss them."

"And I'm going to miss you as well, Chloe."

Chloe thought about the words Ramsey had just spoken as she watched him kill the engine of the RV. He glanced over at her and the pull that was always there between them was tugging at her today in the worst possible way. "And I'm going to miss you, too, Ramsey."

He leaned over and she was there, meeting him halfway over the vehicle's console. And when their mouths connected she thought that nothing could get any better than this.

He pulled back, but not before taking his tongue to swipe across her lower lip. "Come on, let's get out so I can show you the rest of the property while there's still daylight."

Moments later, holding hands they walked near the area where the sheep were grazing. One of Ramsey's men, Pete Overton, smiled when they approached.

"Now that you're here boss, I'll just skedaddle so I'll be on time for the party." Pete's oldest son would be graduating from the university tomorrow and his wife had planned a party in his honor. Ramsey had volunteered to tend to the sheep until Pete came back to relieve him Sunday morning.

"Sure, Pete, and give Pete Jr. my congratulations and best wishes. I know that you and Jayne are proud of him."

Pete beamed proudly. "Thanks, Ram." He then glanced at Chloe and his smile got even wider. "The guys and I meant what we said earlier today, Miss Chloe. You're going to be missed. Nobody makes homemade biscuits quite like you do."

Chloe returned his smile. "Thanks, Pete." They then turned and watched Pete get in his truck and leave.

"Pete is a person who doesn't take to people easily, but it's plain to see that he likes you," Ramsey said, wrapping his arms tightly around Chloe's waist.

She leaned into him. "I know," she murmured, resting her head back against Ramsey's chest. "I like him, too. I like all the men who work for you."

Ramsey introduced her to the four dogs that would be manning the herd and told her the animals made a sheepherder's job relatively simple. The dogs were the ones who looked after the flock, making sure none of the sheep wandered off and alerted the sheepherder to any mishaps.

After Ramsey gave her a tour of the area where the sheep would be grazing for the next few months, they returned to the travel coach and ate the sandwiches Ramsey had purchased from a deli in town.

Then when it got dark he took out folding chairs so they could sit outside under the stars. They ended up doing a lot more than just sitting under the stars. Ramsey selected a nice spot to spread a huge blanket on the ground where they made love, under the beauty of a Colorado sky. Later when the night turned chilly, they went inside the coach and after taking a shower they tumbled in bed to make love all over again.

The next morning after a breakfast they had prepared together, they walked the area checking on the sheep. After lunch they curled up in each other's arms on the sofa and watched several video movies. Chloe could tell that neither she nor Ramsey wanted anything to intrude on their idyllic weekend.

Ramsey told her about how he'd grieved after the deaths of his parents and his beloved aunt and uncle. He explained how he'd had to put aside his grief to care for his siblings.

She was touched that he'd shared details about that heartbreaking moment in his life. She was tempted to share things with him as well. She wanted to tell him that although she was too young to remember much about her mother, what she had recalled while growing up was the sadness that always appeared in her father's eyes on her mother's birthday, their anniversary day and during the holidays. That was one of the reasons she was glad for the happiness in her father's life now. But there was no way she could tell Ramsey that without telling him everything and he'd made it known he wasn't ready for any hard-and-heavy discussions between them.

Later that night they showered again together. The

moment he pulled her inside the shower with him and water began spraying down on their naked bodies, Ramsey turned her into his arms and kissed her, while pinning her back against the wall.

He reached up and turned off the water and then getting down on his knees, he spread open her thighs to get the taste he always seemed to want and was intent on getting whenever he could.

The sensations he could evoke with his tongue inside of her had Chloe moaning and it took all she could not to scream out loud. Ramsey had introduced her to lovemaking in its richest form; positions that were so erotic her knees weakened at the thought of some of them.

She did scream when his tongue delved deeper into her and she gripped tight to his shoulder. And just when she thought she couldn't take any more, he eased up, lifted her to wrap her legs around his waist and then he plunged into her.

With whipcord speed he began thrusting inside of her as another scream from her filled the shower stall. She then heard herself begging and pleading for more, for him not to stop and to do it harder. Those were words she never thought she would utter, which proved just how over the edge she was. Just how Ramsey's lovemaking had torn up her mind.

Her legs tightened around his waist even more, locked him inside of her as much as possible. He threw his head back and let out a curling snarl that sounded like pain, but the look of his face showed it was definitely one of pleasure.

His features distorted in sexual gratification were

a mirror of what she was feeling. And when she felt him explode inside of her, she felt her world get rocked as he continued to pump inside of her as impassioned heat rushed all through her body. And then he leaned closer to her and captured her mouth in his.

His kiss snatched her breath and, combined with the shudders ripping through her, was almost too much. His kiss was hungrier than before, just as intense. And when he finally released her mouth, she slumped against his wet chest. Regaining strength to lift her head, she met his intense gaze and it took everything within her to hold back from telling him that she had fallen in love with him.

Pete returned to relieve Ramsey early Sunday morning. Ramsey couldn't wait to get back to the ranch so that he and Chloe could have a serious talk. If he had any doubts in his mind that he loved her, then this weekend only confirmed it. He hoped he would be able to put into words how he felt and why he wanted them to continue what they'd started.

He glanced over at her. She'd gotten quiet on him and he would allow her this private time. He'd come close twice this weekend of telling her how much he loved her. But he'd held back, not wanting to screw things up.

He drew in a deep breath when they pulled into his yard. Butterflies were going off in his stomach. He'd never been nervous around a woman before. Hell, he'd practically raised three of them. But this was different. It wasn't every day that a man poured out his heart the way he planned to do. But he had to be careful how he did it. He didn't want to run the risk of scaring her off.

"Will you be talking to Nellie before she returns tomorrow, Ramsey?"

Her question broke the silence that surrounded them in the RV. He turned off the engine and leaned back in his seat. "Yes. She's supposed to call today."

"Good."

Ramsey couldn't help but smile. He found it amusing how loyal she was to his men. He parked the RV on the side of the barn and when they got out they walked to the house holding hands. For him it seemed such a natural thing to do.

Ramsey opened the door and once inside Chloe said, "How would you like a cup of coffee?"

"I'd love one. Thanks."

At that moment the phone rang. "That's probably Nellie calling. I told her I'd return this morning around eleven."

Chloe nodded as she headed for the kitchen.

"Hello?"

"Mr. Westmoreland?"

Ramsey didn't recognize the feminine voice. "Yes?"

"This is Marie Dodson of the CDS Employment Agency and I regret we were unable to serve your needs before. However, if you're still in need of a ranch cook, I have someone who might work out for you, and she's—"

"Whoa," Ramsey said, cutting in, confused by what the woman was saying. "You did serve my needs. The woman you sent to us two weeks ago worked out perfectly and—"

"There must be some mistake. We didn't send a woman to work for you."

Now Ramsey was *really* confused. "Sure you did. Chloe Burton."

There was a slight pause and then, "There's no Chloe Burton working for us. The woman we had planned to send you was Constance Kennard. Because of a mix-up, she was sent to another job by mistake. I called myself that Monday morning around nine-thirty to inform you of what happened but was told you weren't available. The woman who answered your phone said she would make sure that you got the message about what happened."

A knot tightened in Ramsey's stomach and a frown settled between his brows. What Marie Dodson was saying didn't make sense. Chloe had shown up that morning. She'd been late but she had shown up. And there was no doubt in his mind that Chloe could cook. Every single man in his employ could attest to that. But if what Ms. Dodson was saying was true then…"

"Mr. Westmoreland?"

Ramsey pulled in a deep breath. "I'm going to have to call you back Ms. Dodson."

"Oh? Well, okay."

No sooner had Ramsey hung up the phone, Chloe walked in with two coffee cups in her hands. Ramsey stopped her in her tracks when he asked in a fierce and angry voice. "Who the hell are you?"

# Chapter 11

Chloe was knocked speechless by Ramsey's question. Pulling in a deep breath she thought it best to place the cups of coffee on the table before spilling them all over herself. Her hands were shaking because she had an idea why he'd asked what he had.

She exhaled a nervous breath before she spoke. "That's a crazy question, Ramsey. You know who I am. I'm Chloe Burton."

"Are you?"

"Yes."

He crossed his arms over his chest. "And you work for CDS Employment Agency?"

"No."

He lifted a brow. "No?"

She nodded. "No. I don't work for CDS."

He frowned. "Well, who do you work for then?

I didn't contact any other employment agency for a cook."

"I work for myself."

She could tell her answer surprised him. "Yourself?"

"Yes, and while I'm at it, I might as well tell you that I'm not really a cook. I enjoy cooking but normally do so for pleasure."

Ramsey didn't say anything for a long time, he just stared at her with an intense look in his eyes. He was angry to a degree that she had never seen before in him. Even when they'd been at odds with each other during that first week, he hadn't been this angry.

"I'm going to ask you one more time," he said through gritted teeth. "Who are you? If the employment agency didn't send you and you're not a bona fide ranch cook, then who are you and why did you pretend to be Nellie's replacement?"

Her hands nervously clenched into fists at her side. Now she wished that she had been more insistent when she'd wanted to tell him the truth a week ago. There was no doubt in her mind that now he would think the worst of her.

She stared at him, saw the hard, cold look in his eyes and knew it was too late. She cleared her throat. "I saw you last month in downtown Denver, going into a feed store. I thought then that you would be perfect."

"Perfect for what?" he almost asked in a snarl.

She swallowed deeply. "To be on the cover of *Simply Irresistible* magazine."

She watched the expression on his face as the implications of what she'd said became clear. "Do you mean to tell me that you work for that magazine?"

She shook her head. "Not exactly."

His eyes narrowed. "Then what exactly?"

She nibbled on her bottom lip. "I don't work there exactly. I own the magazine."

The next thing Chloe thought was that if looks could kill, she would definitely be dead…but not before getting sheared first. She watched Ramsey's lips tighten, his jaw clench and the eyes that glared at her appeared to be dark orbs. "And just what were you doing here that morning?"

"I had come to talk to you about being featured in my magazine," she answered.

"Why?" he said in a tone so sharp it almost made her flinch. "I'd told the person who called I wasn't interested."

"I know, but I wanted to meet with you personally. Try to persuade you to change your mind."

He shook his head. "So instead you decided to pretend to be my cook and sleep with me?"

She did flinch at that. "No. That's not true. I tried to tell you the reason I was here, but you were in a hurry to leave that morning and you left me here with your front door wide open."

"Because I assumed you were the cook," he snapped.

"I never told you I was the cook, Ramsey. And you assumed wrong. Once I walked inside your house, the phone rang. It was the lady from the employment agency who said that the cook you were expecting wouldn't be coming. I could have left you in a hot mess, especially after you indicated you would have twenty hungry men to feed come lunchtime. But I decided to help you out."

"Why? So I could feel I owed you something and do that damn cover?"

"Initially, yes. I'd even planned to squeeze an interview out of you as well."

She could tell her answer, as honest as it could get, only made him angrier. She saw it in his features to such a point where she actually felt her heart in her throat. "But like I said, that was at first, Ramsey. Once I got to know you—"

"Spare me. Lady, you have some nerve. Pretending to be someone else and—"

"And what? Helped you out for two weeks? I tried to tell you the truth a few days ago, but you wouldn't listen. You said we would put off any serious talk until today. So you can't hold that against me."

Ramsey snorted at that and the scowl on his face deepened. "I can hold it against you and I do. You should never have been here under false pretenses in the first place. As far as having a cook, I would have worked something out. You didn't need to do me any favors. And regardless of what you did for me, I still would not have posed on the cover of that magazine, so your plan wouldn't work."

"Once I got to know you, Ramsey, the cover didn't matter anymore," she implored, thinking she had never met a more bull-headed man.

"And you expect me to believe that?" he asked in an angry tone.

"Yes."

"Is there anything else you've failed to tell me?"

She shrugged. "My father is a senator from Florida. Senator Jamison Burton. My mother died when I was two and my father raised me by himself. My home is in Florida."

Ramsey stared at her, not believing what little he'd known about her.

"And the reason I could not deceive you any longer, the reason I wanted to tell you the truth that day after we'd made love was because I knew I was falling in love with you."

He stared at her for a long moment. "If being dishonest is your idea of falling in love, Chloe, then you need to keep your love to yourself because I don't want any part of it."

He breathed in deeply and grabbed his Stetson off the rack. "I'm leaving and I want you packed up and out of here by the time I get back."

And then he walked out the door, slamming it shut behind him.

Ramsey's hands tightened on the steering wheel of his truck as he drew in a deep breath, not believing what had just taken place. What he had just walked away from. And just to think he'd intended to pour his heart out to Chloe, tell her how much he loved her, and all it had been for her was nothing more than a sinister plan to get him to pose on the cover of that damn magazine.

A part of him felt torn up inside, absolutely wrecked. Anger, the likes he'd never known before, was consuming him. He was driving with no particular destination in mind. It was Sunday, and most of his family had gone to church. Dillon and Pamela had left for the airport that morning to return to Gamble, and Callum and Zane had driven to see a rodeo in Oklahoma. Maybe it was for the best because he sure as hell didn't feel like socializing with anyone right now.

He pulled over to the side of the road and hit his fist against the steering wheel. How could he have been so stupid to let his guard down? Why was he always the last to know anything about a woman's trickery? It hadn't been any different with Danielle. Although he'd been relieved she'd ended the wedding, the fact still remained that she had made a fool of him.

He pulled back into the road. He'd meant what he said. Chloe had better be gone by the time he got back. And he hoped like hell that he never saw her again.

"Here, drink this," Lucia said, handing Chloe a cup of herbal tea. "It will help your headache."

Chloe glanced up at her friend, not wanting to tell her it wasn't her head that was hurting as much as her heart. "Thanks," she said, accepting the cup of hot tea.

"And now you need to go take a shower and get into bed."

Chloe rolled her eyes. "Lou, it's the middle of the day."

"Yes, but a nap might make you feel better."

Chloe shrugged. "I doubt it." She knew nothing would make her feel better unless Ramsey was to walk through that door and tell her that he believed her, that he knew she truly did love him, and that even though she had planned on making him indebted to her initially, she had discarded that plan once she'd fallen in love with him.

An hour later Chloe still sat curled up on Lucia's sofa. Lucia had finally left to go have Sunday dinner with her parents. Chloe felt she needed this time alone to go back over and over in her mind what happened earlier that day at Ramsey's house, and everything else that had transpired from the moment she'd driven onto his property over two weeks ago.

She thought of the angry words he had spoken to her before he'd left his home, ordering her to pack up and leave before he got back. A part of her had wanted to rebel and be there when he returned to have it out with him. But then there was nothing she could say that she hadn't already said.

And he hadn't believed her.

It had been a teary ride from Ramsey's ranch all the way to Lucia's home, and now she knew she couldn't remain in Denver. It was clear as the nose on her face that there was nothing here for her anymore. But a part of her refused to run.

Chances were her and Ramsey's paths would not cross anytime soon, so that would give her the time she needed to recover from a broken heart.

His men were watching him and Ramsey was well aware that they'd been watching him off and on for the past couple of weeks. Today he would do something he usually didn't do. Ignore them.

And for good reason. They wanted something he could not deliver. They wanted Chloe back. Nellie had returned and although he'd had a talk with her before allowing her back in his kitchen, after one good week she was sliding back into her old ways. The men, like him, were comparing what they had now with what they'd had for two weeks.

A part of Ramsey wanted to shout at them, to tell them that although Chloe's cooking skills were superb, she was not a cook. She had done it for fun. It had been all a part of her deliberate scheme to get him indebted to her.

His cell phone rang and he welcomed the excuse to leave the table and answer it in private. He had stepped into the living room when he spoke into his cell after checking the Caller ID. "Yes, Dillon?"

"I was asked to call and talk to you. To try and convince you to get that chip off your shoulder you've been carrying around for almost ten years but has gotten most noticeable the last two weeks."

Ramsey rubbed his hands down his face. He could imagine which one of his relatives had called Dillon. It could have been any one of them. He hadn't been in the best of moods and they all knew it. And they had no idea as to why.

"I don't need this, Dillon."

"Okay, but can I ask you one thing?"

"Yes."

"Do you love her?"

The question, to Ramsey's way of thinking, came out of the blue. It was one he definitely hadn't expected. But with Dillon he would be honest because even now, his very heart, every part of his body, knew the true answer.

"Yes, I love her."

Dillon was silent for a moment and then he said, "She might have set out to deceive you. However, you did admit that she wanted to confess all, but you talked her out of saying anything."

"Yes, but only because I assumed she wanted to talk about something else."

"Does it matter? I can't help but remember the woman who for two solid weeks got up before five o'clock every morning and cooked two meals a day for your men. She befriended them. And when you think about it, she really could have left you in a bind. Even you admitted the guys worked harder while she was there and that they broke all kinds of shearing records."

Ramsey threw his head back. "Is there a point you're trying to make, Dillon?"

"Just a suggestion."

"Which is?" Ramsey said in a hard tone.

"Basically the same one you gave me a few months back. You were the one who told me that in some things you need to know when and how to adjust your thinking, to be flexible. Especially if it's a woman you want."

"I don't want, Chloe. At least not in my life."

"You're absolutely sure about that?"

Ramsey knew that, but now, he wasn't sure. When it came to Chloe, the woman still had him tied in knots. And he wasn't sure about anything, other than the fact that he still loved her.

He pulled in a deep breath. The truth of the matter was that he hadn't been able to adjust his thinking when it came to Chloe. It had been a while since he'd had a woman in his life and over the years he'd gotten pretty set in his ways. But what Dillon said was right.

She hadn't had to hang around preparing those meals for his men for two weeks. She could have bailed after the first day. But she hadn't.

She had told him that she loved him, but he'd never told her that he loved her as well. Instead he had asked her to leave. What if she'd left town? Suddenly he didn't want to think about that possibility.

But he did. He thought about it a lot. He was still thinking about it later that evening when he and Callum got together to shoot a game of pool over at one of the local pool halls they frequented. The thought that if she were to leave Denver he would not be able to find her grated on his mind. As well as the thought that he needed to let her know that he had appreciated what she'd done for two weeks, feeding his men good food, letting them know they were appreciated. She had gone out of her way to put a little sunshine in their days.

All right, he would be the first to admit he probably did still carry around that chip on his shoulder that might have caused him to overreact. After all, she had tried telling him something that day, but he hadn't wanted to hear anything she'd had to say, fearing the worst and not wanting to deal with it. And although her original intentions might not have been honorable, she had stayed around, hung in and made a difference.

His thoughts shifted back to the possibility that she had not remained in Denver. Not being able to take not knowing any longer, he turned and handed his pool cue to Callum. "I'm going after her."

Callum accepted the cue stick and merely rolled his eyes. "About time."

Ramsey raised a brow. "And you think you can talk?"

Callum gave him a sly smile. "Yes, now that I've made up my mind about something."

Ramsey would have taken the time to inquire just what that *something* was had he not been so eager to head out the door.

Chloe pushed away from her desk and glanced out the window. It was hard to believe it had been three weeks since she had left Ramsey's ranch. Three solid weeks and this morning her suspicions had been confirmed. She was pregnant.

If she thought hard enough she figured there were a number of times they had gotten careless, like one of those times in the shower. But it really didn't matter when it happened, the fact remained that it had happened. Now she had to decide whether she would tell him before returning to Florida. He had a right to know, but whether she would tell him now or later, she just wasn't sure.

She had had lunch with Ramsey's sisters last week. Evidently, he was in rare form and they figured his less-than-desirable attitude lately had had something to do with her. Chloe was surprised he hadn't told them the entire story and fighting back tears she'd ended up telling them everything. How she had initially deceived him and then fell in love with him. Instead of taking their brother's side as she had figured they would do, they ended up crying right along with her. They were convinced she loved Ramsey and that it was a shame he couldn't see it for himself. They were convinced once he thought things through he would see the truth for himself. If only she could believe that.

Chloe stood and walked over to the window to continue to look out. Her work here in Denver was finished and Lucia would be handling things from here on out. Her east coast staff was presently looking for a new prospect for the October issue of *Simply Irresistible*, and that was fine with her. She was ready to move on.

Going back to her desk, she picked up her cell phone to call Lucia who had left that morning for Atlanta to sit in on a leadership workshop with a few of Chloe's other employees. She got Lucia's answering machine. "Lou, I'm not feeling well, so I'm going to leave early for your place. That's where I'll be if you need me for anything. Otherwise, I'll see you tomorrow when you return."

Feeling tired and sleepy, Chloe took a long nap as soon as she got home. When she awoke, she saw it had gotten dark outside and she felt hungry. Reminding herself that although her pregnancy was in the very early stages, that whenever she ate she was eating for two, she went into the kitchen and prepared a meal.

Hours later she had showered, changed into her favorite yellow sundress and had grabbed a book to read when the doorbell sounded. Chloe went to the door and glanced through the peephole. Her breath caught in her chest and she pressed a hand to her throat. Standing on Lucia's front porch was the man who'd captured her heart, the father of the baby she carried in her womb. Ramsey Westmoreland.

When Chloe opened the door, Ramsey could only stand there and stare at her. At that moment he thought the same thing he had that first morning he'd seen her: She was beautiful.

He did recall that morning. He remembered how he'd tried getting away from her once he saw how attracted he'd been to her. That was something that had not been her fault. And he had done something that morning so unlike him. He had raced off in his truck, leaving his front door open to a stranger. He had assumed she was the cook and he hadn't given her time to state otherwise.

Once he'd knocked the chip off his shoulder and had taken the time to analyze the situation, sort out the mess, he saw he had contributed to the misunderstanding. She was right in saying that although her original plans may not have been honorable, she had hung around and helped him out. He could just imagine how things would have turned out if she hadn't.

"Ramsey, what are you doing here?"

Her question brought his attention back to the present. "I'd like to talk to you, if at all possible."

He saw the wary look in her eyes before she nodded, opened the door wider and then moved aside.

When he passed her the first thing Chloe thought was that Ramsey certainly smelled good. And he looked good, too. He was wearing a pair of jeans, a Western shirt and boots. He had removed the Stetson from his head once he'd entered the house.

Not asking him to sit, she turned to him. "What do you want to talk about?"

"I owe you an apology. You did try to level with me that day and I stopped you from doing so. Actually, I was afraid to let you."

Chloe lifted a brow. "Why?"

"If you recall, it was the same day my three sisters came to visit and I, of all people, know how overwhelming they can be. I thought that perhaps they may have tried boxing you into a corner about a relationship with me. I haven't been involved with a woman in a while and was afraid you might have begun feeling forced into a situation you weren't quite ready for, and I didn't want to hear you say it. Especially after I'd made plans to ask you to continue a relationship with me once your time was up at the ranch."

Chloe's reaction to his words was a total surprise. "You wanted to continue a relationship with me?"

She saw the intensity in his eyes when he said, "Yes."

Happiness swirled in her veins and the intensity was back in his eyes. But still...

She searched his face. "Why, Ramsey? Why did you want to continue a relationship with me?"

He didn't say anything for a moment, but the look on his features basically said it all. There were emotions there she hadn't seen before, emotions he'd never revealed to her until now. But still, she needed to hear him say the words.

He must have known what she needed. Placing his hat on the rack, he then walked the few feet over to her to stand in front of her. She sucked in a deep breath and lifted her face to meet his gaze when he did so.

"The reason I wanted to continue a relationship with you, Chloe, is because I had fallen in love with you."

He reached out and took her hand in his. "I know for us to be in love is not a cure-all. But at least it's a start and is more than most people have. I do love you, Chloe, and I want for us to be together. I don't want it to sound like I'm rushing things, but I want to marry you. I want to give you my babies one day. Bring you to the ranch to live with me as my wife. But I know those have to be the things you want. I'm not asking you to give up anything for me, for our love. When you have to go away and travel for your magazine company, I'll modify my schedule to travel with you. I—"

Chloe held up her finger and placed it on his lips. "If nothing else, these past two weeks have shown me I have people capable of managing the magazine without me. Besides, I rather like the idea of living on your ranch, being your wife and the mother of your babies."

The brilliance of his smile touched her. "So you will marry me?"

"Yes."

"And if you want, we can have a long engagement," he said pulling her into his arms.

Chloe chuckled, shaking her head. "Now there's the kicker. A long engagement might not work for us, unfortunately."

He lifted a brow. "Not that I'm complaining, but why wouldn't it work?"

She paused and then she reached out and took his hand in hers and carried it to her stomach. "Already, your baby is here," she said in a whisper.

Chloe thought the look on his face at that moment was priceless. His mouth dropped open in shock. "You're pregnant."

She threw her head back and laughed. "No, *we're* pregnant."

Filled with more joy that he could stand, Ramsey didn't care how such a thing could have happened when they had used protection. It didn't matter. He wanted their baby. He pulled her closer into his arms and captured her mouth with his. The kiss was hungry, it was intense and, Chloe thought, it was full of love.

When he released her, he wrapped his arms tightly around her waist. "We're getting married as soon as it can be arranged."

She looked up at him. "We don't really have to, you know. Women have babies out of wedlock all the time and—"

"My child will be born a Westmoreland."

She chuckled. "If that's what you want."

"That's what I want. Will you go back to the ranch with me tonight so we can make plans?"

She lifted her brow. "Is that the only thing we'll make when we get there?"

Now it was Ramsey's turn to smile. He answered honestly, "No."

Chloe wrapped her arms around Ramsey's neck. "Um, I didn't think so."

When Ramsey bent his head to hers, she was ready and knew that this was just the beginning.

# *Epilogue*

No one had asked why Ramsey and Chloe wanted a rather quick wedding. They were just happy to see Ramsey finally tying the knot. It was a beautiful day in May and all the Westmorelands came.

Chloe was overwhelmed at the huge family she'd married into. And there were several celebrities—national motorcycle superstar Thorn Westmoreland, well-known author Stone Westmoreland (a.k.a. Rock Mason), and Princess Delaney Westmoreland Yasir, wife of Sheikh Jamal Ari Yasir. Everyone welcomed her into the family with open arms. She couldn't help but smile, thinking it was a small world in that her father had already met the young, up-and-coming Senator Reginald Westmoreland at a fundraiser for a Georgia congressman last year. And Chloe was practically beaming in delight that Ramsey had also told her a few weeks ago that he would pose for the cover of her magazine.

Deciding they didn't want a huge wedding, Chloe had worn a beautiful tailored white pantsuit and with Ramsey by her side they walked around Shady Tree Ranch, where the beautiful outdoor wedding had taken place, greeting their guests. She got a chance to talk to one of Ramsey's elderly relatives, James Westmoreland. He was the one responsible for bringing the Atlanta and Denver Westmorelands together.

Chloe enjoyed talking to James and after talking with him she knew most of the story about Raphel and the mystery about the man's life that was yet to be solved.

A short while later, Ramsey took Chloe's hand in his and led her away from their guests. Even his men had come to the wedding and had brought their wives. She thought they looked good in their Sunday best.

"So, we don't know if those women were wives of Raphel or not." She noticed Ramsey was leading her farther and farther away from their guests.

Ramsey threw his head back and laughed. "I can only vouch for one of them and that's my great-grand-mother Gemma. I know they got married because we have a copy of their marriage certificate. The others… we shall see."

"Is there anyone else besides Dillon even interested in finding out?"

"Yes, Megan. But she plans to do things differently. Unlike Dillon, she doesn't want to do the research herself but plans to hire a private detective to solve the mystery for her."

Ramsey stopped walking and turned to her. "I didn't bring you out here to talk about Raphel."

Chloe glanced around and saw they were a distance from the house. "And why did you bring me out here?"

He pulled her into his arms. "To say in private what I said in front of everyone today. I love you, sweetheart, and for the rest of my life I promise to show you just how much, and I will love and honor you always."

Tears sprang into Chloe's eyes. "And I love you."

The moment Ramsey had pulled her into his arms, Chloe knew that their lives would be filled with love, passion and plenty of hot Westmoreland nights.

\* \* \* \* \*

# REQUEST YOUR FREE BOOKS!

## 2 FREE NOVELS PLUS 2 *FREE GIFTS!*

KIMANI™
ROMANCE

### Love's ultimate destination!

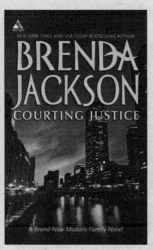